SWORDS

&

SORCERIES

Tales
of
Heroic Fantasy
Volume 9

SWORDS
&
SORCERIES

Tales of Heroic Fantasy
Volume 9
Presented by
David A. Riley
Jim Pitts

PARALLEL UNIVERSE PUBLICATIONS

First Published in the UK in 2024
Copyright © 2024
Cover & interior artwork © 2024 Jim Pitts
The Cold Maiden © 2024 Eli Freysson
Assassin Eternal: The Memory Eaters © 2024 Andrew Darlington
To Raise the Shining Walls of Irem Once More © 2024 Tais Teng
Fulgin the Grim: Retribution © 2024 Ken Lizzi
Snow in Kadhal © 2024 Jaap Boekestein
Voyage to Vancienne © 2024 Gavin Chappell
A Pathway Forward © 2024 Lyndon Perry & David Bakke
The Left Eye of Phun Margat © 2024 Scott McCloskey
Sorcery in Nekharet © 2024 Steve Dilks

ISBN: 978-1-7393674-8-0

Parallel Universe Publications, 130 Union Road, Oswaldtwistle, Lancashire, BB5 3DR, UK

Dedicated as always to the memory
of writer, editor,
and publisher,
Charles Black
who inspired this anthology series
Plus also
Clark Ashton Smith, H. P. Lovecraft
and Robert E. Howard scholar
Scott Connors
who died at the end of October

CONTENTS

 # INTRODUCTION

Welcome to our ninth volume of swords and sorcery stories. As usual there is a wide selection of contributions, showcasing some of the best talents in the sword and sorcery genre today with a mixture of names that will be familiar to our regular readers plus some new to our anthology series. As usual we have also stretched the boundaries of the genre with some of the entries – though I sincerely hope not too far!

This time we open with a newcomer to our series, Eli Freysson, who had this to say about himself: "I was born in northern Iceland in 1982, and I'm still not sure how to feel about the choice of location. I'm on the autistic spectrum, so I'm exactly weird enough to spend my days alone at a computer, thinking up stories. I've spent years writing fantasy and science fiction tales, bouncing  between subgenres as my whims dictate. After hitting a slump early in 2024, I decided to ease back into writing with short stories, which let me finally get around to trying my hand at Sword and Sorcery. I started off with my personal homage to Robert E. Howard's classic muscle-monster barbarian before branching out into different ideas. And… here we are."

To read more about Eli Freysson and his books use any of these links:

https://www.royalroad.com/profile/341990/fictions
https://www.amazon.com/stores/author/B00TRW7CZ8/allbooks
https://www.elifreysson.com/

Meanwhile, from Andrew Darlington: "While interviewing Fairground Attraction for their recent second album, Andrew Darlington found himself discussing favourite biscuits and the correct art of dunking with singer Eddi Reader. As part of UV Pop, Andrew's own lyrics can be found on the CD *See You Later, Cowboy*. While a collection of his popular *Eternal Assassin* stories are due shortly from Tule Fog Press, taking the chronology from prehistory all the way into the far future. There is also his track-by-track history of The Yardbirds due for 2025 publication from SonicBond press, following his books on the Hollies, the Human League and the Small Faces. Andrew recently visited Hadrian's Wall, and wonders – if the Romans were so damn smart, why they didn't build their wall closer to the carpark!"

Tais Teng is a Dutch sf writer and illustrator with the quite unpronounceable name of Thijs van Ebbenhorst Tengbergen, which he shortened to a humble Tais Teng to leave room for exploding spaceships.

His drawings range from talking teapots to quite beautiful bat-winged ladies with a naughty character. In his own language, he has written everything from radio plays to hefty fantasy trilogies. One was even a mythos novel with Paul Harland: *Computer-code Cthulhu*.

To date he has sold seventy-five stories in the English language, while Spatterlight recently published his SF novel *Phaedra: Alastor 824*, set in the universe of Jack Vance.

Teng is a great admirer of Clark Ashton Smith and the last years he has been writing stories set in his Zothique, the last continent of Earth, under a dying sun. His Dutch publisher published them as a collection titled *Gekleed in soepel mummieleer (Clad in Supple Mummy Leather)* with 21 interior illustrations.

A second Sword & Sorcery series is set in the alternate Arabian Nights universe of the Inland Sea. You can find samples of both of the series in *Swords & Sorceries*. His most recent S & S sales are to *Cirsova, Carpe Noctem* and *Strange Aeon 2024*.

Ken Lizzi is an attorney and the author of an assortment of published novels and short stories. When not travelling – and he'd rather be travelling – he lives in Texas with his lovely wife Isa and their daughter, Victoria Valentina. He enjoys reading, homebrewing, and visiting new places. He loathes writing about himself in the third person. Find him at *www.kenlizzi.net*.

Ken's most recent work, the four-volume *Semi-Autos and Sorcery* series, is available in print, digital, and audio from Aethon Books.

Jaap Boekestein (1968) writes science fiction, fantasy and horror since the late 1980's in Dutch and English.

Over 500 stories and about a dozen of his novels and novelettes have been published. Although his stories can be pretty wild, he lives a very normal life in the coastal city of The Hague where he works in IT as a civil servant.

Together with Tais Teng he started a few years back the only indigenous Dutch SF genre: ziltpunk, which are stories about positive, grandiose, idea-rich futures of the Netherlands after huge and diverse climate changes.

Futures where tornados are herded for their energy, where the Netherlands are flooded by an ice sea, or the Dutch tame the seas with living dragon-dikes and armies of crabs.

His most recent story 'Vrees de sexy hellefurie!' ('Hail Hell's Whipping Fury!') can be found in the Dutch anthology *Vampieren en Demonen*.

Most of his work in English can be found on Amazon.com

Over the last quarter century Gavin Chappell has been published by *Leidstjarna Magazine*, Penguin Books, *Countyvise*, Horrified Press, *Nightmare Illustrated*, Red Cape Publishing, Innsmouth Gold, and Parallel Universe Publications, among others. He has worked variously as a business analyst, a lecturer, a private tutor, a local historian, a tour guide, an independent film maker, and editor of *Schlock!*

Webzine, Rogue Planet Press, and *Lovecraftiana: the Magazine of Eldritch Horror*. His influences include Tolkien, Robert E. Howard, Michael Moorcock, H. P. Lovecraft, Lin Carter, and Terrance Dicks. He lives in northern England.

Lyndon Perry is a writer, editor, publisher, and coffee drinker. His indie publishing platform is Tule Fog Press *(www.TuleFogPress.com)*. There you can find a wide selection of projects across a variety of genres, including sword and sorcery, science fiction, fantasy, speculative, suspense, crime, mystery, humour, and middle grade adventure. He's edited several anthologies, including *Swords & Heroes* (S&S), *Sherlock & Friends: Eldritch Investigations* (supernatural mystery), and two volumes of weird western

horror, *Monster Fight at the O.K. Corral*. His own heroic fantasy is titled *The Sword of Otrim*.

As a publisher, Perry has released a number of collections and novels of dark fantasy and sword and sorcery adventures by such authors as Gustavo Bondoni, Michael T. Burke, Andrew Darlington, Charles Allen Gramlich, Tim Hanlon, and David A. Riley. He also publishes a quarterly magazine of speculative fiction, *Residential Aliens*; and a bi-weekly ezine via his *Swords & Heroes* newsletter which features an S&S tale 'straight to your inbox every other week'. One can subscribe for free at *tulefogpress.substack.com*.

He and his wife are semi-retired and currently live in Puerto Rico where they explore, walk the beach, and take care of their twenty-one-year-old cat, Charlie.

David Bakke is a married father of two living in the Southeastern United States. After growing up overseas, his family came back to the States where he went to college, graduated, and began a career in IT. His love of books, as with many children, started with *The Hobbit* and *The Lord of the Rings* trilogy. He gravitated towards anthologies later in life both out of enjoyment and a passion for collecting. *Medea: Harlan's World* opened his eyes to the process of world building and collaboration which he hopes to explore further. This is Bakke's first publishing credit in collaboration with Lyndon Perry.

Scott McCloskey counted the dead with Crom across many ragged copies of *The Savage Sword of Conan* throughout much of the 1980s. Though the issues are now but tarnished steel, the influence on his writing is as pure as a platinum blade. Today he stands beside his wife and daughters on the eastern coast of the United States with a gaggle of Russian Wolfhounds to mind, but hooves still beat in time to the endless ride across the scorched sands in his heart.

Scott's work in swords, sorceries, and the supernatural has been featured in publications such as *Negative Space 2: A Return to Survival Horror* by Dark Peninsula Press; the *Cellar Door Series Volumes 3: Dark Highways* and *4: After Tomorrow* by Dark Peninsula Press; and of course, *Swords and Sorceries: Tales of Heroic Fantasy Volumes 6* and *8*, by Parallel Universe Publications. His contribution to volume 9, 'The Left Eye of Phun Margat', is a dingy tale of a hapless peasant waif, torn from her homeland to be thrust into a web of mystical treachery and bloody conquest.

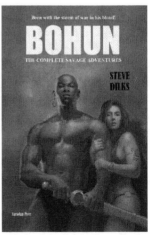

Steve Dilks was last seen in volumes one and two of *Swords & Sorceries: Tales of Heroic Fantasy*. His collection, *Bohun: The Complete Savage Adventures*, was released earlier this year and collects together all the character's pre-viously published appearances, including 'The Horror from the Stars' which originally appeared in volume one. You can't keep a good sword-swinging adventurer down though as Bohun returns here in a brand new short-story, 'Sorcery in Nekharet', which closes out this volume. For those that like to keep track, this story takes place between the events described in 'Intrigue in Aviene' and 'Black Sunset in the Valley of Death.'

And, as usual, this book is favoured with the amazing artwork of Jim Pitts. As well as being busy on the collection of Elak of Atlantis tales by Adrian Cole, Jim is regularly featured these days in the pages of *Phantasmagoria Magazine, Lovecraftiana*, and *Schlock! Webzine*, and elsewhere.

I don't usually mention anything of my own in the Introduction, but I will break with tradition this one time to mention an upcoming collection of my sword and sorcery tales to be published soon by Tule Fog Press in the States. *Welgar the Cursed* chronologically follows this tragically doomed northern barbarian's journey from a carefree mercenary to a demonically cursed anti-hero.

Some of these stories have appeared elsewhere, such as in *Savage Realms Monthly* and *Swords & Heroes*, but some are brand-new to this collection.

These then are the authors and artist whose work appears in the pages of this, our ninth volume of sword and sorcery stories. We hope you enjoy them!

In closing I would like to mention that our dedication this time is not only to the author, editor and publisher who inspired this series, Charles Black, but also to H. P. Lovecraft, Robert E. Howard and Clark Ashton Smith scholar, writer and editor Scott Connors who sadly died in October this year. A veteran of the United States Army (1980-1990) he was prolific in the weird fiction scene and very much admired and liked. He will be missed.

David A. Riley
Oswaldtwistle. 2024

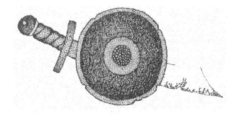

THE COLD MAIDEN

Eli Freysson

War could not be avoided.

It was no rational observation that filled Klakkr with this certainty, as he saw the silhouettes approaching from the south. It was simply a feeling in the air, as intangible as cold fog but every bit as real. He was no völva, no true diviner, but it was said that every person possessed a trace of foresight, if they were alert for it. All men were connected to the strands of fate woven by the Norns, after all.

And now, watching the summer sun gleam on incoming helmets and spear tips, Klakkr somehow just knew that this parley would be a failure. And bloodshed would follow.

Still, he was chief of the settlement, not through lineage, but through the trust of his people and his past efforts. He had said he would attend this meeting and do his best, and so he would. The Norns would decide when his thread was cut.

The incoming group moved at a leisurely pace; twelve men, all on horseback. Klakkr took their measure as they drew ever nearer, noting their arms and armour and making comparisons to his own group.

He gave his companions a look, and kept his face stern and impassive, his movements slow. He had brought the cream of the settlement's warriors. None of them were huskarls, trained as professional warriors all their lives and equipped through the wealth of a king or mighty chief. But five of them had spent time as sea-raiders in their early years, and the rest had trained in combat as all free men did and had since proven themselves in land disputes. All wore a helmet and had a shield, six wore mail shirts, and the rest wore layers of quilted cloth. Between them they had twelve spears, eight axes, and four swords.

"They come to us gleaming with iron, wealthy from their conquests to the south-west," Klakkr said to his men, making the most out of the powerful voice with which he had been gifted. "No doubt their success has made them arrogant, and they may look at us as poor men, farmers and labourers on shores foreign to us. But we have *earned* our place here. Our roots in this land are fresh but fed with blood. We will not be driven from here. We will not be subjugated. Every man here has proven his mettle before. We are more than clan kin and neighbours; we are brothers in battle."

There was a collective grunt of approval, and a few quick words praising his words.

"Stand firm, brothers," Klakkr went on, as their approaching foes got close enough to make out faces. "Show them strength and solidarity that looted gold cannot buy. Let them see what awaits them if they continue with their plans."

"We shall!" declared Ulf, the oldest man present, the most seasoned of the sea-raiders, with grey in his long beard.

"I know you all shall," Klakkr said, and was then silent.

The south-westerners stopped their horses and dismounted, just outside of easy javelin-range. The spot for this parley had been chosen carefully. The land was split by a tributary to the great Guti River, and while the waterway wasn't great it had dug a deep channel into the landscape. It was far thinner than it was deep; there were many spots where a strong man could leap across. But that man would promptly die like a fool upon spears.

Barriers made for the best parleys.

Their leader stood out through his dark-blue cloak with gold-coloured trimmings, and a helmet-plume made of ribbons of the same materials. He took the helmet off, revealing a rather young face beneath dark hair, and handed the covering to a warrior without a word or a look.

"A tall man with a reddish beard, I was told!" he announced as he fixed his eyes on Klakkr. "Are you Klakkr Svendsson?"

"I am."

"Well, then!" the enemy leader went on, still loud, and still with a showy cheer. "Here you are! And no ambush! I am almost disappointed, as alert as I was for it!"

"I suggested this parley in earnest, for earnest reasons," Klakkr replied, and deliberately contrasted the man's ebullience with a stern, stoic front.

"Indeed."

The man stepped closer, near to the edge of the channel, and put a hand on his armoured chest.

"Before you stands Eggert of Baudra, soon to be lord of the lands behind you men."

"For now, you are simply an intruder, Eggert of Baudra."

"But your people are intruders yourselves."

"My people have a long history on these shores," Klakkr said. "Our own shores are only a swift boat ride away, after all."

"You have a long history of being driven away, and returning. Like a seasonal pest. Well, now the seasons have turned, and it is your turn to leave once again."

"Only the fates know what will be. And you are but a mortal man, Eggert of Baudra."

"Oh, indeed!" Eggert said, and put both hands on his chest. "Indeed! It is indeed blood that runs through this body. But I serve a thing greater than myself. The world is changing, Northman. The chaos of dark days is being swept aside in favour of a new order. A new god, above all others."

"Your demon serpent is no god of mine," Klakkr told him. "He has no sway over me."

A chill entered the other man's manner, a stripping away of that mask of friendliness. Though he was clearly still enjoying himself.

"But his servants do," Eggert said. "Aman-Ka's coils reach ever further. His church expands. Lords and kings owe their thrones to it. And now it is *my* turn. For my efforts, for my proven qualities, I have been given the task of taking the Landing. I will control the entrance to the Guti River. None shall use its waterways to raid, nor to smuggle. It shall be *our* tool to wield."

"If you wish to make use of the river mouth, you need only to pay for your passage," Klakkr said.

"No. I do not think I do."

Eggert pointed at Klakkr.

"You wanted this meeting, and it sounds like you have made your offer. Now here is mine: Submit to rule. Give up your armour. Abandon your gods, swear by Aman-Ka, and give up the tithes demanded by his priests. That way, your community may survive. Or you can simply board your ships and be gone from these shores by the time my army arrives.

"When your army arrives," Klakkr told him, "it will find a community built on blood and iron. You will find people who do not yield. You will find our spears and our earthworks and our walls. You will find arrows and slings and javelins and fire. You –"

"I am no stranger to boasts, Northman!" Eggert interrupted. "And I have seen what they amount to. It is iron and the hands that wield it that win battles, and I have more of both than you do! You are not brave for defying me, you are simply fools!"

Klakkr opened his mouth, to continue the battle Eggert was pretending didn't exist. The battle of spirit and morale. But a sudden unpleasant feeling froze his tongue for a moment, which in turn diverted his attention.

Behind Eggert, something moved. It was a man, one who had ridden at the back of the group and stayed there till now. Like a shadow. Now he drifted up to the front.

He was evil. Before Klakkr knew anything else about the man, even his appearance, he knew that. Just as he had known this parley would yield no results, and how he sometimes knew other things without knowing why. Eggert and his men were enemies of Klakkr's people, but for all the normal reasons men fought. This stranger was *evil*, in some way that chilled Klakkr's spine and stirred an instinctive revulsion.

"Sorcerer," Klakkr said, and spoke the word as he would a curse.

The man wore no armour, simply a dark brown hooded travelling cloak, and a sword-belt. Beneath that lay more elaborate clothes, dyed in various expensive hues. Beneath the hood was a face that had the features of the far southerners Klakkr had once seen in a trade port, but was yet somehow paler than all these other men. It was as if he was sick, and yet he stood up straight and still.

"I am Baudilio," the man said in a thick accent. "A servant of Aman-Ka, and guardian of his wisdom."

"I know what you are, southerner," Klakkr told him

stiffly. This development made him far more uneasy than the sight of a bow would have. But he would not show fear. As a leader, he would not show fear.

"I do not think you do, Chief Klakkr."

His voice was slow, and devoid of any cheer, real or false. It was every bit as soulless and empty as his eyes, and carried far more menace than Eggert's playful posturing.

"Not in truth. I see no signs of wisdom or power upon you. No..."

Baudilio shook his head, slowly and only slightly, and his jaundiced eyes never left Klakkr's. Nor did they blink.

"No, you do not know what is coming for you should you stand in my master's way."

Klakkr had an awful feeling that the villain was absolutely right. He forced his gaze away from the man, and focused both it and his voice back on Eggert.

"So, this is the source of your vaunted victories? Black magic? Sorcery? The foul arts? You are no warrior at all, then."

"I *am* a warrior," Eggert insisted, and finally his good humour was pierced. "I merely have... alliances. As I said, the world is changing. You can accept it, or you can be ground down."

"We will not accept it," said a female voice.

Klakkr turned his head, as surprised as anyone. Coming up behind his group was a young woman. She was clad in white trousers and a shirt, as well as a voluminous, bright-red cloak, and had a sword-belt around her waist. Her hair was a shade of blond so pale as to border on white, and her eyes were an even more striking shade of icy blue. She was beautiful, Klakkr supposed, but he took far more notice of the cold danger in her demeanour.

"We will not," she repeated as she came to a stop next to Klakkr, facing the invaders.

"And who is this bearer of otherworldly beauty?" Eggert asked her, and his joviality was back.

"I am Valgerd Hemmingsdottir, of Kvaki. Only just arrived on these shores to stand by my people against your serpent's influence."

"Indeed?" Eggert replied. "Well, I am glad you did. You hardly seem like a mere mortal. Are you one of those northern spirits I hear so much about, who sometimes walk as men and women?"

Klakkr knew who she was, although he'd never met her before. He knew *what* she was, and it made him almost as uneasy as the sorcerer did. And in the face of their enemies, Valgerd Hemmingsdottir simply smiled dangerously.

"What I am is a child of warriors and old forests and the cold wind. Of long winter nights, the time of hungry wolves and wicked ghosts. All this in a land of many gods and spirits and feuding clans. That is who I am, Eggert of the south."

Most shield maidens Klakkr had known made an effort to deepen their voices, and to overall take on the aspect of men in order to be taken seriously. Valgerd did not. And somehow her words seemed to carry all the more weight for it.

She turned those impossibly blue orbs on Baudilio.

"I have come to slay you, sorcerer. Your foul worm has reached quite far enough, and made enemies of those who observe. You will fall here, and Aman-Ka will gnaw on your soul, if even he will have it."

"I shall give my master a rich feast once this land is conquered," Baudilio told her back, with calm malice. "A signal to all others of the price of defiance. And it shall start with your heart. The sight of your own beating organ shall teach you to fear the great serpent."

"I hope not," Eggert interjected, and still had his eyes on Valgerd. "I sense a deeper story behind your introduction, Valgerd, but I suppose now is not the time for telling it. I hope your people change their minds. I hope they see sense, and that you live, so I may hear the rest. But I have seen this brand of proud defiance before."

Eggert mounted his steed and grinned wolfishly.

"It never did any good. I will march on your settlement with forces you cannot hope to stand against. One way or another, your land will be mine to rule, even if I must kill or enslave every single man, woman and child in your village. But I hope you would rather be subjects."

"Before you ride!" Valgerd shouted, as the rest of the group mounted. "Let me repay your compliments with a kindness of my own: Turn and go back home, Eggert of the south. Let this dark-weaver lead the assault and pay the price himself."

The man actually hesitated for a moment. But then smiled at her.

"No. Iron and blood will decide this."

"And worse things," the sorcerer added.

Klakkr watched them go, waited for the hoofbeats to fade from hearing, and then turned to this new arrival.

"I know who you are, daughter of the cold," he said, and could not keep some wariness out of his voice. "I did not know you were coming, or that you concern yourself with such things. None of us here are your kin."

She turned to face him, and he truly could not guess whether the unsettling effects of her gaze were intentional or not.

"Do not take this as disrespect, or ingratitude," he added. "Merely surprise."

"I stand on the boundary between two worlds, Chief Klakkr," Valgerd told him. "I am here more for one, rather than the other."

"But you will lend your strengths to our defences?"

"I will. And you will find, in your village, the warriors who sailed here with me. Your calls for aid did not go entirely unheeded by your cousin-folk."

"Then we are doubly fortunate on this day," Klakkr said, and held his hand out. "Be most welcome. Valgerd. Please ride back with us now, so that I may do a host's duty. And once we have feasted and sung together we shall make plans together."

"Yes, we shall," the woman said as she put a cold hand into his. "Eggert made no empty boasts. The forces arrayed against you will not be defeated with simple combat."

*

Today was the day. A red day. Another battle, another conquest.

This was far from being the largest force Eggert had ever wielded as his blade, but then this was far from being his largest target. Merchants had painted him a picture of the village and its strengths, and so in addition to seasoned men and Baudilio's arts, Eggert came armed with knowledge.

The northmen had earned fame as sailors and sea-raiders, but many of the boats that had delivered that new community to these shores had then returned home. What they were mostly left with were humble fishing boats. And so, ironically, the great raiders of the sea and inland waterways would be destroyed by a river attack.

Even the odd, unseasonal cold could not foul his mood.

Eggert smiled, from his spot in the bow. He looked back at the long serpent of boats that slithered in his wake. Thirty in all, hefty river boats laden with warriors and what little supplies they needed for this journey. Keeping them a secret had taken careful planning, and taking advantage of the attention a marching army drew, while a smaller force delivered the boats.

He faced the front again. He would have preferred being in the lead; it was only proper, and fighting men fought harder for a leader who displayed courage. But there were two other boats before his. Baudilio had insisted, offering him a spearhead to the assault that would shock the northerners like little else. And all it had cost was for Eggert to pick out the men he least cared for.

It had been an easy choice. The fates had granted him two boats' worth of eastern mercenaries, fresh amidst his forces and unpopular with the rest. He did not understand what Baudilio had done to them, nor did he really want to. But he did not doubt they would make an impression on the settlement.

Somehow, Baudilio's sorcery had driven them utterly mad. The effect had become more obvious as their journey had progressed. They had gotten into their boats with wild looks in their eyes, and an unnervingly twitchy, angry demeanour. As they'd traversed downstream, and Baudilio sat in the stern muttering within the confines of his hood, the mercenaries had started to growl, and finally to scream and howl. Men who were not at the oars would stand up and yell nonsense, flail their arms, and stumble about like caged animals. One had spent a while at the stern, staring back at Eggert and sneering like a rabid dog.

How they maintained the ability to row, and not tear each other apart, Eggert did not know. But once all that angry madness was unleashed on the village it would take a fierce toll before the rest of Eggert's men would land.

Eggert didn't like it. It was a useful little trick, and he was glad to have it on his side. But he didn't like it. Nor did the men, he knew. Baudilio had been unwelcome at every campfire and at every table ever since joining. Eggert understood that just fine, and did *not* understand why the man seemed entirely unbothered by months of exclusion.

Ahead loomed an island in the river. It was a sizeable thing; a cliff on the side that faced Eggert, which he'd been told gradually tapered down along the stream. It split the river in two, which of course narrowed it and would require more caution and precision than before. Eggert decided to seize the brief window he had, and walked the length of the boat, towards the sorcerer.

Baudilio did not react to the approach in any way. He just kept on his odd muttering, making the air around him feel strange and slimy.

Eggert tapped him on the shoulder.

"Yes, warchief, what is it?" Baudilio responded, as if to an inferior. It was an irritating habit of his.

"I want to know what you are doing," Eggert whispered.

"I am praying, Eggert. Conversing. Listening. Weaving. What are *you* doing?"

"Well, I am leading a campaign, fought under the banner and blessing of your church. As such, I would like to know *what* exactly you are weaving. I grow tired of you keeping your works to yourself before you unleash them on the battlefield."

"Are you tired of my results, warchief?"

One had to really focus to notice emotion in Baudilio's speech, and experience with the task let Eggert catch the hint of mockery. He put a hand on the side of Baudilio's head and manually turned it to face him. He looked into the priest's eyes, eyes that saw things Eggert could not understand. It was always an unpleasant experience, but damn it all if he would let his unease show.

"I feel something in the air," he said in a sharp whisper. "There is something on the edge of my hearing, and in the corners of my eyes, some subtle scent I cannot identify. You are preparing something you have never done before, and –"

"Ah."

It was not an exclamation. Baudilio didn't seem to do those, not even when an arrow had grazed him some weeks ago. But something had clearly shifted his attention, and the priest stood up with that weird fluidity of his and pointed ahead.

"There."

He was indicating the island, or rather the top of that cliff they were headed towards. As they drew closer, Eggert now saw hints of buildings up there. Ruins, from what he could tell.

"These shores intersect many paths," Baudilio mused, possibly just to himself. "Men have fought here for as long as men have fought. A fortress stood there once, a last refuge. A place of desperate men and desperate times. That is when false values are dropped, and men embrace any hand that reaches out of the darkness. Blunderers, but honest ones, in their final despair. Dark and vicious things took place there. The truth. The truth of this world, and all others."

"Indeed," Eggert replied dryly. "Is there some point to this?"

The priest of Aman-Ka faced him again, and lightly stretched his lips into that reptilian smile of his.

"Have you no desire for wisdom? For things with more depth than conquest and riches and beautiful, dangerous women?"

Eggert's reply was interrupted when the already cool air suddenly got dramatically colder.

"Damn you!" he hissed, low enough hopefully to go unheard by the men, and grabbed Baudilio's shirt with both hands. "What are you doing now?!"

"This is not mine," the priest told him. "This is a problem."

There was a sudden fog, blowing in from the direction of the ocean. Eggert barely had time to wonder why he hadn't seen it sooner before it was all about him. It was shockingly cold for the season.

Eggert stepped away from the priest and looked about. He was already losing sight of the boat behind his, and the ones in the lead. He looked up, just in time to see the high end of the island pass by before it too vanished into the cold white.

"What is th–" he began, but his throat seized up at the sudden intake of bone-freezing air. "Damn it!" he growled.

A spell. This had to be a spell. Or a curse. Or the will of some entity of power. This was no mere sea breeze at work. He hurried back to the bow, into the little chest that held the few possessions he'd brought for this journey. Their campsite was less than a day's travel away, and so they had come with little other than weapons, armour and meagre supplies. They certainly had not brought winter clothes, but he did have his cloak and was glad to sweep it about his shoulders.

This fog. This damned fog. It froze his skin and hurt his throat and eyes. His nostrils stung with each inhale, and he could already feel the strength begin to leave his body. The men were feeling it every bit as much as he, and speaking about it.

"Interesting," Baudilio mused.

"Listen, priest," Eggert forced out. "You need –"

There was a mighty crash, a snapping of wood, and the

screaming of men. It came from the lead boat, invisible in the freezing fog, and oddly muffled.

Eggert ran to the front and began shouting an order, but again his throat rejected the cold air and stopped his voice. Now the second boat of sorcery-maddened mercenaries was smashed on something as well. There was not supposed to be a large rock here. This way around the island was supposed to be clear.

He cupped his hands over his mouth and shouted.

"LAND! LAND THE BOATS!"

He did not know how far his voice actually carried through this unnaturally freezing air, but his own rowers at least reacted and began making for the right-hand bank. But there just wasn't enough time. Almost. But not enough.

Eggert was thrown off his feet, and forward. The boat did not smash as the others had, but instead beached on something. Eggert bounced to his feet and looked over the bow.

Ice. There was a layer of ice over the river, at the height of summer.

"SHI-" Eggert began, but coughed, then tried again. "SHIELDS! ARMS!"

The two broken ships had spilled some of their cargo of enspelled madmen into the water or onto the ice. The latter were already in combat, and for a moment Eggert allowed himself to hope they'd simply turned on each other like mad dogs.

But no. The northerners now came out of the freezing fog like ghosts, clad in thick winter pelts, cloaks, hoods and scarves.

Eggert picked up his own shield and drew his sword, and that was the moment the fourth boat in line hit the stern. His boat was pushed further up onto the ice, while the new arrival cracked and swung about like a door.

Eggert again picked himself up, and so did his

warriors. The northerners let their javelins fly in a slightly uncoordinated volley. Eggert ducked beneath his shield, though the cold slowed his reflexes. A javelin slid off the rim of his shield, then off his helmet, and as he rose he heard more ships crashing, and the sounds of a full-scale battle blooming.

There was only one thing to do: Fight. And so he did. Eggert shouted commands and encouragements, even as his lips threatened to stiffen, and his throat protested at the cold. The men with him on the boat came together into a rough shield wall and held out against another volley of javelins. The northerners could only have so many of the large missiles, and then the boat would become a makeshift fortress.

Another of the javelins brushed the plume of his helmet, and as he looked about for further danger he spotted a figure that stood out among the northerners for wearing no warm layers. Instead she simply wore mail and a helmet, and a red cloak. And somehow, even through the icy fog, he could see a pair of piercing blue eyes.

*

Valgerd had brought no javelins of her own, only her spear, sword, and shield, so she held back for a moment as her allies launched a third volley of missiles. There was already fighting on the ice itself, against those of the howling madmen that had avoided going under it in the crash. But she was here for a purpose, and she focused on it. She could not see Baudilio, but she felt his work. Or rather, his patron's.

Foul coils slithered about, unseen in the mortal world, oozing venom, piercing the barriers and threatening to burst forth. Evil spirits hung in the air, drawn by the sorcerer's words, and while her allies might neither see nor hear them, they would *feel* them very soon.

"Now, Klakkr!" she hissed at the chief, standing next to her. "We must!"

The plan had always been for a quick, overwhelming attack, rather than a protracted bleeding. That fight would actually favour Baudilio. Klakkr, with only his eyes visible through his scarf and helmet, raised his spear and unleashed his powerful voice.

"CHARGE!"

The dozens that formed the semicircle around the beached boat obeyed. They had observed the old war rites, made offerings to gods and spirits, and danced and sung and chanted for courage. Now it was all unleashed in a charge; a screaming mass of humanity, bearing sharp steel and murderous passions.

The boat had come to rest at a slight angle, tilting the starboard side towards the attackers. The men on board braced with interlocked shields, as best they could, and levelled their weapons. Then the blow landed.

The mail shirts of hand-picked warriors withstood the spears of the invaders, and axes struck shields. Wood splintered or broke, iron rims bent or opened, and follow-up blows did even more damage. A few shields were outright destroyed, coming apart in the hands of their wielders. The attackers didn't let up, pressing hard against the invaders in spite of their elevated position, and for a moment victory seemed imminent, as several of the bolder warriors started stepping over the gunwale and into the boat.

Then Baudilio, standing on a chest in the centre of the vessel, swung his arm, and three men fell over dead. The shock of it halted the assault for a moment, which bought

Eggert a moment to draw his men together, and for a few to grab fresh shields.

Valgerd pitted her own power against Baudilio's. It was a soundless, invisible struggle, known only to the two of them. The sorcerer was mighty, but she did not need to match his magic in order to foul it up. And the accumulated fury of her allies was not so easily quelled, and the assault resumed.

Shields broke, and shields held. Spear shafts clashed with one another, as their tips found either iron, wood, or undefended flesh. Axes bit into iron rims, broke shafts and broke through mail. It was a hideous, pushing, screaming, groaning battle of survival as two tightly-packed groups tried to kill each other. Blood flowed, accompanied by puffs of mist as its warmth met deadly cold. The red coloured the ice and the gunwale, and the shields and helmets that got hit with spray.

Valgerd left the breaking of shields to big, loud men with big axes, and sought instead to get precise stabs in with her masterwork spear. It was longer than most, well suited to pushing over the heads of those groaning and straining at the front, and the wicked tip found necks and armpits and unprotected hands.

Eggert's invaders were veterans indeed, and they stood their ground with courage and skill and fury. But the cold... the cold stole their strength, more of it with every moment that passed, weighing down their limbs and slowing their wits. The momentum of this battle had become inevitable, as the northmen stepped over the gunwale to press in tighter around the increasingly diminished invaders. Now the blood spilled on rower's seats, as Valgerd dropped her spear and switched to her sword for tight-quarters fighting. In the air sounded the ongoing crashes of boats, now mostly into previously crashed boats, and the din of every able man and some of the women of the Landing greeting them with sharp iron.

Still, Valgerd's target stubbornly stayed alive, nestled in the middle of the dwindling crew. He had a sword, but struck no blows. No, he fought in a different fashion, and Valgerd did her best to divide her energies between countering his, and making use of her sword arm.

Eggert came within her reach a couple of times. His sword dented her helmet, her own blade struck his armoured gut, he slammed his shield into hers, and she managed to drag her sword edge against his unarmoured thigh.

But a dying man got in between them, in his flailing death agony, and the cramped, shifting groups they were each caught up in kept them apart after that.

Her whole world was blood and screaming, shuddering impacts upon her shield and helmet and mail-covered body, the stench of entrails and sorcery, the crimson of blood and the white of the steam and the fog.

And then, in a single desperate moment, one of those overpowered all others.

"ENOUGH!" Baudilio screamed.

Safe as he was from immediate harm, his own energies were not divided at all. And so his patron's power burst loose the barriers, and infernal spirits spewed forth.

It was a hazy nightmare, an attack on the mind as much as on the body. Valgerd saw faintly avian shapes swoop down from the air, leading with grasping talons. They circled the fight on the boat, fast as arrows in flight, grasping, clawing, biting, whispering evil secrets and dredging up fears and shames.

Valgerd grit her teeth as she felt every hurt she'd

inflicted on others, every failure, every doubt. She also felt talons scraping her helmet, her back, trying to rip the sword from her hand. She fought against both, waving her sword about while averting her vulnerable eyes, and steeling her will.

I am what I am, she thought. *Worse than some, but better than many. Better than HE.*

Her allies were panicking, and her foes were doing little better. She didn't even know if the shove that hit her was deliberate or not, but in the mess of confused and frenzied bodies, it sufficed to trip her over a blood-soaked rower's seat. Her head hit something, but the helmet and the padding beneath it protected her skull from the worst of it.

Now someone stumbled over her, and she spared a quick look to confirm it was an ally. She got up on one knee and held the shield over her head. Talons still tore at it, and still those terrible voices tore into ear and soul alike.

Valgerd summoned her power, her connection to the otherworldly, her status as one who stood on the boundary, and issued her repudiation. They were not allowed here. They did not belong here. And Baudilio was too busy fleeing to counter her.

"Begone!"

The barrier closed again, and in an instant the spirits had vanished.

That still left mortal men, but they were already fleeing, going over the port side. They were clumsy from the cold and rattled from the spirits, and several simply stumbled and fell. Valgerd rose, gave chase, and leapt off the gunwale. She came down with a slash of her sword, and drove it through the back of a man's neck. Then she cut into the skull of a man whose helmet had fallen off, before slashing another man across the throat as he struggled to rise. A fourth man got her boot to the face as he fought to pick his axe up with numb fingers, and he fell backwards up against the boat. He'd left his armour off for the rowing, and now it cost him his life as Valgerd's sword penetrated his heart.

She ripped the blade out, with a red gush and yet another puff of steam.

"Baudilio!" she shouted. "Where is the sorcerer?!"

There was a small-scale rout in progress, but the thick fog made it hard to make out the details of it. Valgerd chose to run in the same general direction as the fleeing warriors, and in moments she came upon the wrecks of the two leading ships. The ice sheet had torn their hulls open, and only their front half still stood out of the water, dangling off the ice like meat on a hook. Dead bodies lay scattered about; men who had been too insane to be stopped by anything but utter maiming, but too outnumbered after the crash to win.

There was still fighting, still stragglers getting picked off, and of course the men fleeing from Eggert's own boat.

"Come, serpent's slave!" she shouted out to the sorcerer. "Show me the strength and courage you brought all this way! Show me why we should abandon our gods!"

Something came at her out of the swirling white, but it wasn't the sorcerer. Rather, it was one of his victims. The foreign mercenary had stripped down to his waist at some point, which put his collection of gruesome injuries on display as he charged at Valgerd with a demon's howl on his lips.

He had a small axe, and her shield stopped it. He struck again, and again, with that mad frenzy. It was like fighting a berserker, but possessed by something far worse than the totemic spirit of the great forest beasts. This was *hate*, and her sword slicing across his calf as he bashed her shield yet again did nothing to quell it. He only barely limped as he threw himself straight at her. Valgerd's blade came down on his bare shoulder, but an instant later they were both carried over the edge of the ice sheet.

Valgerd managed to leave her shield above water, but her armour pulled her down like an anchor. Her free hand narrowly caught the edge of the sheet, but the madman also caught her around the waist. The cold of the water was harmless to her, but she could still drown like any mortal.

Another body floated by and bumped into her a little. As she struggled to fight both the madman and the current, she saw more coming by. None of them swam. Some bled, some not, but all were carried limply by the river. And all went under the ice.

She tried slicing into his throat with the edge of the sword, but he gripped it and squeezed with all of that deranged energy of his. Valgerd resorted to digging even deeper into her connection to the cold, into its deadliest depths, and in a few moments the madman finally went limp. No amount of madness could keep a man going if his blood had essentially stopped flowing.

A shrug got him off her, and he vanished beneath the ice to join the others. More bodies floated by after him; men who had been thrown from the crashing boats, or who had tried to save themselves from the ambush by swimming, only to be caught by her cold.

Well, they should have stayed at home.

Valgerd reached up with her sword arm and was finally able to pull her head up for a welcome gulp of air. The current still pulled on her legs, and a passing dead body gave them an extra yank, but the water on her palms froze to the ice, giving her perfect traction for climbing out. She picked up her shield, let out a breath, and started walking again.

"VALGERD!" Klakkr shouted from somewhere to her left, and she went to him.

She found the man, and several of his closest warriors, bloodied from the fighting but alive.

"I am here," she said, to get their attention.

A couple of them were actually startled at the sight of her, as all the water was already freezing on her armour, her helmet, her sword, the hems of her clothes.

"We –" Klakkr began but lost his voice. He shook himself vigorously in an effort to force some heat into himself. "Look, the battle seems to be near-won. Can you not undo your spell?"

"My mother's element is not an arrow to be loosed and then forgotten," Valgerd replied. "The cold will fade away, but you will have to leave the area to escape it in time. Now, I have done some service to our shared people, but the spirit world still waits. *Where* is the sorcerer?"

"We think he ran towards the island," Klakkr said through clattering teeth, and pointed. "Along… along with a few others."

"Leave him to me," Valgerd said, and started walking.

"We could… we could spare a few men," Klakkr said. "I feel I should –"

"No, Klakkr. You and your men wrap up this half of the battle. I shall take care of the second half. It is… why I exist."

She smothered the sudden stab of melancholy in birth, and strode past the men and across her ice. She soon set foot on the island, where the ice was replaced with frost-tipped grass and stone. She maintained a walking pace, slow enough to be alert for ambush, and to conserve her strength for the final part of all this.

The battle faded away behind her, devoured by the fog,

leaving her alone with her task, and the accompanying danger. It felt almost like she'd stepped into the spirit world itself, as hazy and lifeless as her environment was. She spotted blood on the rocks beneath her feet, reminding her that this was indeed the mortal plane still. The drops guided her on, upwards and inwards, until she came across a dead man who had fled the battle only for his injuries to catch up with him. It looked like someone had tried dragging him along towards the end, before giving the task up as pointless.

And so she kept on, chasing that nagging sense of foulness that hung around the sorcerer and his works. The cold was still with her, unceasing, deadly, inescapable. Her mother's element, what set Valgerd so aside from ordinary folk.

The trees of this island grew surprisingly tall, strong and close together, providing a wealth of good ambush spots, and Valgerd felt compelled to slow her steps even further. She herself was not at her stealthiest, with the ice frozen into the rings of her mail squeaking and grinding. And so she moved with patience and caution, like a hunter.

It all felt very much like the forested hills of home. There were no actual wolves here for her to call upon, but their memory, their essence, could be called upon, and so she did. Ghostly howls sounded through this isolated little forest; a reminder of the cold, hungry winter nights, when men feared to travel. It would be one more thing to ravage the morale of her remaining enemies.

She also just enjoyed the sound. There was a comfort to its eerie menace.

No ambush was sprung. No one moved within this small forest. The climax to all of this was, of course, at that old fortress.

The first she saw of it was a big fire. It was an oddly big and bright thing for her foes to have gotten started so quickly, and without preparation. Baudilio's sorcery probably had something to do with that.

Valgerd didn't bother with stealth. She just strode on, out onto the little landing on which the fortress had been built.

Time had truly worn it down. There was little hint as to what it had actually looked like in its day. All that was left were overgrown piles too regular to be natural, and something of a platform piled up with uncut stones. The fire had been set up at the centre of it all, and three figures huddled as close to it as they could get.

They noticed her arrival, and Valgerd saw Eggert himself, and two of his warriors, whom she recognised from the parley.

"YOU!" one shouted with hatred. "You witch! You unnatural devil!"

He sprang into action, rushing at her with a long-handled axe, and the other warrior followed him an instant later.

They were all battle-weary, but Valgerd remained unbothered by the cold, and these men had not had long to warm up. The axe-strike was strong and skilled and rather quick, but just a bit slower than it should have been. Valgerd sidestepped it and slashed the man in the neck. She transitioned smoothly into letting the other man's sword slide along her shield, before batting him in the face with it. His helmet had been lost at some point, and so the iron rim hit him square between the eyes. Her own sword then opened his head.

Eggert stayed where he was. His sword was within reach, poked into the ground, as he warmed his hands with the fire and kept one eye on her.

"You called yourself a daughter of the winter cold, or some such," he said after a moment of silence. "I took that to be a bit of posturing. All people posture about their home, if they have nothing else to brag about it. But you… you are something different, are you not? No mere spellweaver, I think."

He smiled, though his eyes were angry.

"I would still like to hear the deeper story. Would you whisper it to me as you lie dying?"

"I would consider the telling well earned," Valgerd told him. "But I am here for the sorcerer, not you."

"You have cost me my standing as a warchief, Valgerd Hemmingsdottir. I am not going to let that go unanswered."

A sound drew her attention away from the man, and to the platform of rocks. Baudilio's silhouette now stood there, tucked well inside all those layers he wore. A quick sprint would take her to him, but Eggert would be able to intercept.

"Your half of this conflict has been decided, Eggert," the southerner said dismissively. "You failed. Your grievances do not matter. It is fortunate that I already called upon more reliable agents."

He stomped his foot down, and Valgerd felt something change in the air. She started her charge, Eggert plucked his sword out of the ground, and Baudilio stomped again.

"RISE!" he shouted.

And they rose.

From beneath layers of dirt and leaves and dead branches, the dead men of this ancient fortress rose. Brown teeth grinned permanently in lipless mouths, and rotting shirts of armour hung around emaciated frames. No battle cries issued from those long-dead lungs, but there was a fierce, deadly energy to their movements, as these risen men brandished rusty swords and attacked.

The nearest target was Eggert, and corpses animated by evil were never picky. Eggert had to fend off an attack with his shield, and then another from another direction.

"Damn you, priest!" the man shouted as he struck back at these new foes.

"The matter of my soul is long-settled," Baudilio replied casually.

Valgerd started her charge up again, seeking to go around Eggert and his troubles, but the corpses came at her out of the fog. She had to defend herself, and a bony arm delivered a strangely powerful blow to her shield. Quick footwork saved her from another arriving corpse, and a swing of its rusty, rotting axe, and she landed a blow. But the dead were notoriously hard to kill.

More of them came, and more, from different directions, shedding the dirt that still clung to their bones and half-mummified flesh. She spotted a narrow window, a way through them and to the sorcerer, and she took it. Her armour rattled and the ice in its rings squeaked as she ran. But the dead remembered their days as warriors, and while she shifted to avoid one, another one darted into her new path. That one led with his shield, and rammed her. The shield broke apart, but the impact was still strong enough to throw her back.

Valgerd hit the ground and lost the grip on her own shield. She was up in a moment, but only had another moment to react to an incoming strike. She had to leave the shield where it was and hop back as a rusted sword clove the air. There were eight of them on her now, and more shuffling over, unbothered by her deadly cold.

Eggert had his hands full, fending off attacks from four of the dead men. He had no time at all to strike at her, and so she trusted her back to him. She drew her knife with her left hand and parried and struck out with both weapons as the dead continued to press her. She was faster than they, more agile, smarter. But there were so many of them to contend with.

She cut into dead flesh and exposed bone, clove old helmets and armour shirts, and broke blades. She made the most of her agility, and the warrior's instincts long and hard training had embedded in her. Her body knew this dance, and her opponents still had all the tells of living foes. She let them guide her through a very narrow path of survival, parrying and weaving and moving and striking.

Still, she took hits. Her skull rang with repeated blows on her helmet, and her torso ached even though the mail held. Her left vambrace took a hit, and then another, leaving her arm weak and numb.

Eggert let out a great cry of rage and effort, and it sounded like he threw all his strength into pushing his foes away for a moment.

"Kill that priest!" he shouted at her, as he came past her and threw that same desperate effort into knocking her foes back as well. "Kill him!"

She did not waste this chance, and ran out of the fight, out of the circle of murderous dead men, and struck one in the head in passing. Baudilio had not moved from his spot upon that platform, but now he threw his cloak open and held his sword at the ready. The place gave him an advantageous position, but Valgerd would just have to trust in her armour and her skill.

Baudilio, meanwhile, trusted in his magic. He held his empty hand out, and his patron's power spewed forth. Valgerd staggered, and felt a choked cry come out of her throat as the life very nearly left her body in one agonising instant. She almost fell forward, almost forgot where she was, almost couldn't think to push back against the spell, as a power from beyond the veil struck at her being.

But her being already lived on the border, with one foot on either side of the veil. And she had power of her own. The power was her sword, and her will served as the arm that swung it back against this foulness. And after a couple of moments, of wracking, spasming pain and the din of death itself in her ears, the spell broke.

Valgerd grit her teeth in fury, and now bounced up the side of the platform. Baudilio swung at her, but she parried and drove him back. Now, at last, she had him within reach, and went at him with a furious chain of assaults. But he proved a surprisingly adept swordsman, and stayed alive underneath her barrage as the dead approached their duel.

The need to finish this quickly prompted a reckless attack from Valgerd, which Baudilio evaded and answered with a sharp blow down onto her left arm. Her vambrace saved her again, but her already-battered arm lost hold of the knife, and it clattered to the stones.

He struck again, this time at her head, but his skill finally failed him, as Valgerd pirouetted smoothly and cut a long gash down his arm. Now it was the sorcerer who dropped his weapon. His only one. Save for his spells.

The death magic hit her again, in one massive, desperate burst. She was ready for it, and it only lasted for a moment, but it was a moment when her senses went black and her body weakened, and Baudilio used it to grab the wrist of her right hand. And then one of the dead struck her in the back.

The wind left her in a gasp, and she fell forward, pulled by Baudilio. He wrenched her wrist, costing her the sword, and put his weight on top of her as she came to rest on her back. The dead were coming, with their ancient blades and otherworldly hate for the living, surrounding the platform of stone to aid their master.

But the sorcerer wanted to kill her himself. His left hand closed around her throat in a brutal pinch, and he added his injured arm to the efforts, with all of his weight behind them.

That cruelty, that personal bloodlust, was his undoing. For now all Valgerd had to do was grip his wrists and call on the hungriest depths of the Deep Winter. Through her flowed death in the white wilderness, the time of stillness and hunger and fear and the furthest removal from the light and life of summer.

The southern sorcerer screamed as the flesh of his forearms froze. He tried to pull back and escape, but his strength was already fleeing him, and Valgerd simply used his efforts to help her sit up. Then she bore him down and pulled with all her strength.

His forearms broke apart, frozen solid down to the bone, and she tossed them aside as her maimed foe shrieked and writhed.

The dead man who had already reached them took another swing at her. She put her arm up and took the blow on her vambrace, before snatching up the dropped knife.

"To your serpent," she told Baudilio, and then drove the blade into his eye socket.

He screamed for a moment more. Then, as he fell silent, there were the thumps of the dead men dropping down, inert once more.

Valgerd knelt over the body for a few moments, gathering some of the strength she'd just spent, and simply savouring her life. Then she gathered her sword and started walking.

Eggert was dying. One of those rusted blades had made it through his armour and pierced his gut. He'd managed to crawl over to the fire, but the wound would clearly kill him soon.

"I never did like him," he said to her in a strained voice.

"I did encourage you to simply go back home."

"You did. And… I did not."

Eggert looked at his oozing wound, then back at her.

"I have time… for a quick story, though. I think. Come now. What are you?"

"You were right that spirits sometimes walk among my people, as men and women," she told him. "Primal spirits, of primal forces. My father was lost in a winter storm, at night, facing his death from cold. Then he met my mother, who offered him life in exchange for lying down with her. He did, and afterwards her wolves guided him home. Nine months later, after the first snowfall, my father and his wife found a newborn baby at their doorstep. Left naked in the snow, and yet untroubled by this."

She drew the fingernails of one hand down along her mail, and the ice that clung to it.

"I am not unique. People like me, one-half mortal and one-half spirit, in the north we stand between the two worlds. Agents of our otherworldly parents, their representatives. I already told you: I am a child of long winter nights."

Eggert, growing paler by the moment, managed a weak smile.

"And you are fierce, and brave, and skilled, and a beauty like no other. I find, right now, that I lament many things. One of them is not having met you under other circumstances."

"Hm."

Valgerd took her helmet off.

"Let me, once again, repay your compliments," she said.

She knelt down over him, took his helmet off, and lifted his head up a little. Then she kissed him. For a moment it was simply that, a kiss. A meeting of tongues and a delightful stirring of lust. Then she let the cold into him. She did it slower than she had with Baudilio. It crept up on him, numbing him to the pain. Shortly after, he was dead.

Valgerd separated from his mouth, and a last puff of frozen air escaped his lips.

"I have fed you well today, Mother," she mused to the cold, as she collected her shield. Then she began walking back.

Yes, she had fed the cold. She had played her part in the eternal conflicts of gods and spirits. And now, hopefully, she could enjoy her human half for a while. She could be a hero of her mortal kin, an object of respect and affection, rather than wary fear. Until the Deep Winter called upon her once again.

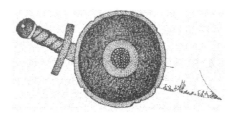

ASSASSIN ETERNAL: THE MEMORY EATERS
Andrew Darlington

The war of attrition had endured twenty years, leaving only desolation.

Adsiduo Sicarius is a lone rider travelling in gathering darkness, hunched in against the fine abrasive dust carried on the wind. It stings his nostrils. It's a dull day, with poor visibility across a land as scarred, dead and lifeless as the face of the moon. Grey-white pinnacles thrust through the shingle like the desiccated bones of the world.

He dismounts and crouches where piled and scattered pebbles rattle as he moves. He hears the song of stones. They whisper intimations of other times, before the long winter, when this was warm rainforest. Where he'd walked, residing in another body, with a woman called Moarne who wore white and whose soft olive skin glistened. Now, there's only stark dark solidity where death hovers ever near.

Looking up now, he sees a vision of towering black ramparts against the yellow sky. Umika of Ruagh had crossed the sea to recruit a name he'd only heard mentioned in mumbled whispers. "To seek the aid of an honest thief."

"To what end?"

"At a single glance we see how our worlds stand in relation to one another," Umika had said. "We need your assassin's intervention."

In a time of despoilers, freebooters, raiders, barbarians and warlords, insanity hangs tangibly in the air. As a grey overcast lowered the sky, crops die and rot in the field. People scavenge or they perish. Hordes of refugees crawl and pullulate like bacteria across the face of the plain. Unlettered, semi-moronic. With desperate hordes migrating in ragged waves, fighting each other for diminishing resources. To Adsiduo Sicarius, such beings must be considered mere mayflies, hatched at morning, dead at sunset. He's separated from them by as great a distance as a journey across the deep night of space between stars.

The young republics on the northern shore of the great inland sea had been put to the sword, looted and burned, although some survive, escaping in ships to build new fortress cities on nearby islands. Only the pearlescent towers of Ruagh remain now, its granite walls besieged by the Black Wolves of Warlord Rurik Varangian. Reavers prepared to take the city by storm until all its spoils are lost. A besieging perimeter cordon stretches around the landward edge, a crescent close on five k in length and irregularly disposed in depth, spaced with tower outposts and war-Mammoth pens. As pirate triremes patrol the waters on the city's seaward side

He stands apart to watch the next ragged assault. A hail of fire-darts ignite the sky, set to the bark of bombards. Waves of savage attackers hurl themselves against the walls using siege towers and ballistae. Followed by the retaliation, troops in bronze armour and metallic kilts pour from the Ruagh garrisons, armed with arbalest crossbows, shooting carefully and with deliberation. Then an impenetrable wall of spears to drive the rabble back towards their cordon.

Adsiduo Sicarius waits. Then he leads his mount. Straight he strides through the besieger's shanty town, his cold eyes never flickering to left or right. He walks as though used to walking alone. Hearing the muted drone of a thousand tongues around him, avoiding stooped dull-eyed men who avoid him, ravaged and dirt-grimed, hungry and drunk on raw napthol. He strides around a huge bonfire of dry brush, catches an unhealthy midden-stench. A fight breaks out between idling hard-faced men, he hears the sound of shuffling feet set to the steely click of sword scabbards. Snarling fury explodes in a primal violence fed on starvation, wine and anger. Firelight splinters from a blade's razor-edge, a sword arcs so fast it blurs into a thin ribbon of light. The victim whimpers and hobbles away clutching his bleeding claw-hand.

Then attention shifts, to refocus on the intruder. A pack of ruffians detach themselves to string across his way, blocking his path.

"I'd have taken you for a ghost." A scrawny and uncommonly ugly man belches. He stares at the pale incomer with open hostility, as the hands of his hunch-shouldered comrades move – as though unconsciously, to heft the hilts of their swords, running fingers down blade-edges in veiled threat.

"This ghost has fangs." Their gestures do not go unnoticed. Sicarius also sees that they're watching his horse with blatant expressions of hunger. "But if we are to fight, should we not fight the towers of Ruagh, not each other?"

Looking into the newcomer's eyes, the ruffian doesn't like what he sees. He spits a discoloured spittle-stream into his beard, and curses to cover his unease.

"We have enough mouths to feed already. We need no more." There's napthol on his breath.

"And you make that decision? Wouldn't it make sense to test my blade first?" The Assassin deliberately makes no move.

The stand-off endures for a long uneasy moment. Then, "Come," the oath tapers away into a monotonous grumble in his throat as the ruffian leads the stranger through the impoverished encampment. Sicarius can see that the besiegers are dangerously hungry, their fragile coalition will not survive much longer without some tangible victory. The stragglers lead him towards a grander marquee in tupik style, extended with canopies and awnings, decorated with shields and spears.

He doesn't enjoy uncertainty. Assassination is a science. Just as it is an art. It requires an experimental process of testing out situations and possibilities. It needs to be dispassionately appraised and assessed in preparation for its successful execution. There must be method and planning. It is the most intriguing kind of puzzle to resolve. Without these challenges there can be no resolution.

Through an arch of light and shadow, an interior lit by torches, jumbled and not too clean, it smells of burning wood and too much sweaty habitation. Warlord Rurik Varangian sprawls on a raised dais, a giant statue of a man, his lazy jet-black eyes fix in a dull glaze on the newcomer. There's a ruffian quality about the Warlord, but something more than brutality evident in his heavy features. He was a fighter, but there was cunning intelligence too. A naked woman sits docile, cross-legged, her bronze collar chains her to the dais. While behind the Warlord, fussily attentive, are three older figures who might have been advisors, but give impressions of the hermetic arts. Adepts at tinctures and potions. The tall Warlock, long hair white and wispy, stand beside the shorter and more stout Theologian and the Chirurgeon with the bald pate. Yet they share an introspective look, faces much lined by the efforts of prolonged contemplation. Yet deviously manipulative.

Adsiduo has seen such wizardry before. They operate on their own agenda. They temporarily align behind this or that warlord for opportunistic advantage.

But his attention is ripped away by a thick-set man in honey-coloured armour, with hands that look capable of ripping stones apart. The Warlord's lieutenant, Magister Militum Ricimus clamps a huge iron fist on Sicarius' shoulder, leaning in, intending his bulk to intimidate. "You consider yourself a fighting man?" As though he's smelling the opportunity for sport. Like something feral that senses blood.

"That is my trade. That is what I've travelled here to barter."

"So, we match skills. We test each other." He draws his broad blade, testing it for balance. An old-civilisation steel blade from before the ice. Blade-shapers have lost the ability to forge such blades. So they are valued.

"To what limit?"

"Until one or the other yields." He makes practice sweeps in the air, as the smirking rabble back away to form a ring about the two potential combatants, and the Warlord leans forward to watch more closely.

Sicarius takes a single backwards step, raises his blade in formal salute to Ricimus, and assumes a readiness stance, blade thrust forward and angled down. Determined to put on a good show. But the Magister was schooled in a rougher streetfighter arena, he lumbers forward wielding his blade in a storm of savage growling strokes. A flurry that Sicarius easily parries, stepping deftly aside. Sicarius strives to contain and channel his anger, to retain control. Until his blade finds its opening. Its razor-tip hacks at Ricimus' cheek, narrowly missing his ear. Blood spills in an animal bellow of rage, and a hungry roar from the jeering observers.

Ricimus knocks the bloodied blade aside with a chiming sound, and circles with fresh respect, watching his opponent with a more cautious eye. Greater cunning is called for. He lunges again, apparently adopting an identical rush of attack, but at the last moment dodges aside, slices low and kicks his antagonist behind the knee, a move he'd learned in a tavern brawl, he never underestimates the gifts of a seedy bar. Sicarius buckles, but Ricimus is not swift enough to use his momentary advantage. Falling is to surrender to gravity, Sicarius has many lifetimes experience to draw upon, and instead takes the momentum of the fall to launch himself into collision with the heavier man's bulk. In a moment the Magister is knocked to the floor, his blade spinning away, his sword arm pinned down by his opponent's knee, and Sicarius, teeth bared, holds his own blade aloft in both hands, directing the point at his exposed throat.

"Yield," he demands coldly.

Warlord Rurik Varangian laughs loudly and claps his hands. "Well done. Well, Magister, how do your rate our new warrior?"

Sicarius eases back. Ricimus stands sullenly, dusting himself down, as Sicarius returns the blade to him, hilt first, with a curt bow. Ruefully, he dabs at the blood that still oozes down his cheek. "I'm certain we can coexist," he concedes. Then grunts, "Come, we share some napthol." As he's led away by his new comrade, Sicarius glances back at the seated Warlord. He's not moved from the dais. As though he's fixed there. The three shadowy alchemists drift around where he sits. Less serving, as controlling? All the while, the Assassin has been memorising the lay-out, the curtained-off living quarters to the rear. The possible access points.

With his blade warily confiscated for 'a trial trust period', he endures a night of drunken carousing with his new comrades. In the early hours, with most of the men and women in intoxicated sleep, Sicarius rises, scratches his groin as if in urgent need of the privy, and lurches unsteadily out into the night. There are hazards. There are always hazards. But there are few alternatives. Only the huge leprous moon sees his posture firm in deliberation, as he retraces his earlier steps back towards the Warlord's marquee, with only the muffled sounds from the Mammoth pens as he draws back into moon-shadows, away from the guard's lazy attentions, and around through the garbage of animal bones and excrement to the rear.

Relying on his memory instinct for surveillance he chooses carefully, draws a concealed poignard, and slits a small aperture through the taut material. Slips through. He's in an alchemist's chamber of retorts, aludel, lutes, pipettes, cucurbits and alembics connected by glass tubes and drips. Bottles of antimony, bismuth, psilocybin, phosphorus, arsenic, opium. Hair prickles along the nape of his neck. It is as he'd thought. There are dark arts at work here. The very air he breathes is tainted, it carries the sharp bite of strange chemistry, making him light-headed. But he's alone here. Only the belching burble of heated liquids.

He hears weeping. He moves aside, past the esoteric conglomeration of dark arts, to peep beyond. There are two huge sleeping dogs.

And there's a pallet where the sleeping Warlord sprawls alongside the tethered naked woman. She stirs. Raises herself slowly to meet his gaze. Her narcotic eyes are drugged into oblivion. She murmurs something that is midway between a deep moan of sensual pleasure, and a desperate cry for help. It slurs into a whimpering trembling appeal, a frightened beseeching terror. All the while, the alien sorcerous odours befuddle his senses. For a confused moment she becomes Moarne, whose soft olive skin glistened.

He should not hesitate. He should accomplish his mission. He should strike. Now. Without distraction. Assassination is a science. Just as it is an art.

Her image shifts and swims. She's not Moarne. And yet she is. How can that even be possible? He has inhaled hallucinogenics in the air. Logically he knows that. But logic is a flimsy defence. He leans over her squirming body to where the shackles secure her. He jams the poignard blade in between the links and twists it, until the link parts and opens. He rips the chain away to release her.

And she screams in terror. She wriggles herself around to shake the somnambulant Warlord awake.

Abruptly, one of the three older 'advisors' is there. He throws a small glittering sphere which detonates into intoxicating powder in mid-air. And Rurik Varangian is roused, fumbling for his blade. This isn't how it was supposed to be. There's no way he can fight back. So Sicarius is to 'die' by the Warlord's blade? So be it. That is simply another way to achieve the same objective. He tenses. Springs towards the raised sword-arm, in a futile attempt to arrest the blow. The arcing blade severs fingers, one, two, three in startling shocks of agony. The blade bites deep, through epidermis, through skull, slicing brain-matter. The detonating shock is numbing. He drops down, plunging into an abyss, hurtling down into a wondrous beautiful death…

The woman cowers away, sobbing uncontrollably, into a foetal curl.

His perspective alters, as Sicarius slips from one host to another. Death bleeds open the floodgates of his mind behind which awareness is stored. Simultaneously, pain grips the Warlord, an inward horror of unbearable anguish. His dark eyes hold the inner suffering of a thousand hells. But this mind is altogether different to those Sicarius had known before. Rurik Varangian is already dead. An animated cadaver. With barely a fleeting hold on life. It had always been so easy to invade another consciousness. But this mind is both dulled and sharper, it offers hindrance, this mind is no stranger to pain. There is a moment of intolerable pressure. His nails bite deep into his palms with a fury he has yet to suppress. Varangian has reserves of resistance. His awareness begins to slip, it's no use fighting.

A long timeless time. His senses reel, his perspective spins in a giddy vortex of nausea, as though in the grip of a neurological seizure. He's hurled deep into a fever of mystic abstraction where only two bodiless consciousnesses clash. This is something from which he can neither hide, nor defeat. He's become the creature of some greater destiny. With all of time compressed down into a single moment.

Through glazed eyes he can see the three dark manipulators kick away the shattered corpse that – moments ago, he'd inhabited. Bodies are tools to be used until they're broken, and are then thrown away. They are expendable. Some might call it magic, others, ensorcellment. Sicarius knows better. Yet the three puppet-masters are there now. They are using the Warlord to their own ends. Rurik Varangian is a man made of untiring muscle. But they are enhancing and amplifying his natural charisma by chemical means. They are pulling the strings. And through him, they are controlling the conquest of the Black Wolves.

Rurik Varangian's body is flooded with dark drugs. That's why his consciousness cannot be penetrated. Sicarius can go so far, but no further. The two are frozen into each other. He's unable to drive down further, to take full residence of the new host body. They are locked in stasis. The impasse does not inhibit the process responsible for heartbeat, breathing, digestion. He can move the fingers. With effort and concentration, he can move the toes. Exertion is possible, but only just.

His coordination slips. He falls free through dark dimensions, into an unfathomable limbo of lost years. Visions adrift in a cascade of curious cities of unearthly architecture, strange landscapes and gargantuan machines, snatches of action and movement. Voices and sounds. A slightly golden elfin figure squats in an emerald glade, it blows through some kind of musical instrument. Curious many-legged entities move in ripples across a mat of black hairy growth against the overhanging ledge of cobalt-blue upthrust rock. A group of tall wispy insectile beings stand before indecipherable machinery. A golden sea draws apart into an endless repetition of droplets, moving together in one great current, but still droplets separate from one another. A scintillating flood of strange landscapes, one after another, with green skies and clouds of flame lit by glowing seas of magma, an ocean of liquid ammonia where breakers dash themselves onto a beach of sharply poisonous green shingle. A linkage of worlds lost in the swirl of nebulae, where silver seeds navigate between the spin of planets, and frog-like beings tilt the controls of their craft down through a scream of atmospheres. Cast into a realm where even the suns and their retinue of worlds are sentient in ways that dwarf the imagination, involved in an eternal dialogue beyond our knowing, in star songs that murmur in darkness.

Are these visions of worlds created and destroyed by his own diseased imaginings? Dreams are seldom exact.

Despite himself, fronds of drowsiness steal over the body they share.

*

It seemed the ultimate flame-lit night.

Dawn is a wan grey luminance creeping in from the east, a vague blur that gradually assumes a pale golden tinge streaked with rapidly moving shafts of light as the pale sun filters down through madly racing cloud-shadows that ripple across a hard-swept plain of deep rills, where only a few scavenger birds fight over rotten entrails, towards the towering black walls of Ruagh.

His eyelids gummed together. Only to be dazzled by the torch-glare when he forces them open. Emerging in a cold sweat of terror. Unsure if the visions roaring through his consciousness are true insight, or just the drugged hallucinations of the vile narcotics being pulsed through his bloodstream. A tongueless mouth howls in silent horror.

The three alchemists preside over his paralysed body. The Warlock, the Theologian and the Chirurgeon. But he's immobile, as if carved from stone, barely breathing. Assassin, and Warlord are still two halves of a single whole. His skin is chill, like worn leather. Needles, fire and acid provoke no response. Even when they sever the forefinger of his right hand, the pain is excruciating, but he's incapable of reacting. He hears their words as if he's hearing their voices through swirling tide.

"He's being eaten alive from inside." There's malevolence in the Theologian's words. "It is a non-physical entity – at least, as we define physical. A mind parasite."

"No, he is bewitched," says the Warlock. "I sense ensorcellment." His chest is sunken and hollow, yet still he carries a vigour and an undeniable force of will. His fierce expression defies them to argue.

There was a silence. Then the more conciliatory Chirurgeon smiles grimly. "I don't know. We are just guessing. We shall see, my forked-tongued sparring partners."

"Those who wish to play with poisons, must learn the rules that poisons play by." The Warlock pulls his gown around him, and stalks from the chamber.

In stasis, what had begun as a mere tingling, trembling sensation had built until the cranial pressure in his head is more than migraine, it's a savage intensity more like the flaying of skin from a body already raw with burning. He fights it. Strives to place a mental barrier, a filter, to become psychically veiled. Repeating his own story in an attempt to reinforce his own identity.

Mine is a story with no real beginning, he tells himself. I watched. I learned. I adapted. Pursued by dark forces intent on hunting me down. Always escaping, but always at great cost. Hated and envied by others. My hunters were relentless, determined to track me down and expunge me, when my only instinct was to survive, just as theirs was survival. I'm both a relic of past time, and the promise of an endless future. I've earned eternal rest... but I'm always denied it. Battling demons, others as well as my own. Forced into actions that appal me, the deathly corpse stench that clogs my nostrils. In a momentary surge of pity, I learn about the fragility of the human form, and the sometime greatness of its spirit.

I wore silver armour. The woman, Moarne, wore white, and her soft olive skin glistened, as though it holds its own inner light. Eyes that trap midnight. Eyes that hide secrets. She is beautiful.

Tasked with rescuing her when she'd been abducted by island pirates, my small boat scuds out to the exchange point. Under the guise of delivering ransom, instead, I use my blade at the moment their attention is most distracted by the promise of booty, and carve my way through the ruffians to release her. Despite her manacles she seizes her opportunity and inflicts her own revenge on her tormentors. They would never have released her anyway, despite whatever ransom was paid, they'd have their evil sport with her before killing her. We make good our escape in my small boat... there are said to be monstrous serpents in these waters, but we cross without further incident to beach among the breakers along these wild shores.

There's a nearby village of crude beehive huts constructed of rough stone, besides echoing sea-caves rich in crabs and shellfish. The people are squat and cowed, as if afraid. A bestial tribe barely evolved beyond the age of stone. A headwoman, who announces herself as Primador, seems nervously hesitant, she offers us a shellfish meal, and as we eat she advises our best route to strike out overland for Moarne's home city. She says there are treacherous marshes to the west and vast red mountains eastwards, but between the two there's a narrow, overgrown valley. We sleep together overnight in one of the huts, and become lovers, our hunger for each other's bodies driven by the sharp knife-edge of danger. We swim together in the sea, and make love on the beach, in a torrid honeymoon of mutual desire. My soul thirsts for her. My body hungers for her touch.

Until we start out at dawn, holding hands as we stroll along the narrow valley corridor. The warmth is comforting. Time seems to slow. We are lost in each other. To our detriment.

There are high fronds way above our heads, and the cliff walls are lined with dense fungus growths. As we saunter, pods on the fronds explode in sharp detonations, scattering a hail of soft seeds in a mauve mist of particles. There's a slight intoxication. We become careless and strange. There's a dance of tiny naked humans swooping and gliding on dragonfly wings, circling and looping around our heads. Moarne is beguiled, she spins and gazes up into the brightness of the sky where daylight shatters into mirages of delight. I'm smiling with joy, wonderfully blurrily drunk on the rage of sensations storming through my body. Humming and screaming, squealing and moaning in the slow turning of air-borne particles. The faerie folk alight on the skin of our arms and forehead, and each contact is a narcotic kiss of ecstasy. Or is it the pods that embed in our skins, spreading an anaesthetising glow?

I suddenly became all attention. Too late.

We were lying on the ground. The harsh sound of my own breathing is loud in my ears. Her face bears a ghastly pallor in the eerie light. It was as though the fungus has slithered in a foul tide to flood over our bodies, absorbing us into the glutinous mass while we were distracted in hallucinogenic wonders. I yell to alert her, and fumble for my blade, but the mass has drunk all the energy from my body, leaving me lethargic. I can no longer recall how we'd got here. I no longer know my name. I no longer know who the woman is who lies by my side. I realise that the mass is eating my memories, my identity, my mind. That I am disintegrating. Chasing darkness.

I look up. Primador is standing there, watching us. Her skin is sheened in a coat of mud. She has filters that fatten her nose like a bruise. She knew this would happen. We were some kind of pagan offering to appease these growths.

I reach out my one free hand to her. "Kill me, please. I can no longer bear this pain of living."

She seems to consider for a long moment. Then she draws a crude flint blade. She stoops over me and cuts my throat in one single slicing arc of her fist.

As I die, I absorb up into her. So that I'm looking down at the half-devoured figure caught up in the fungal mass. I barely recognise him. There's a dead woman, little more than a skeletal frame with parchment-dry tissue stretched across exposed bones, where powerful muscles had rippled beneath smooth skin. I can't recall her name, or why she's there.

With no place else to go I shuffle back to the village of crude beehive huts. I live as Primador until she dies, transferring to her children and children's children for a further century. They are dull, slow-witted inbred creatures, but they provide a kind of stability as I heal, as some memories seep gradually back in taunting incomplete fragments. Some of them never return, leaving gaps in my self-knowing.

Returning memories brings guilt and remorse. As though for every person I've killed across my lifetimes, I killed a piece of myself.

*

The first hint of climax comes an hour before dawn.

Still locked in half-fused stasis, I remember those incidents from long ages past. Remember Moarne, and how I had used Primador to free myself from the fungal memory-eater.

We are briefly alone in a screened chamber. Magister Militum Ricimus stoops over me. Loyal to the last. I force a degree on concentration sufficient to move my lips, my larynx, my vocal chords. I whisper so low that only he can hear. "Kill me, please. I can no longer bear this pain of living."

"Rurik Varangian" he says, "you are my Warlord. Is this truly your bidding?" He was a warrior. It was not his task to reason.

"It is. Earn the gratitude of my damned soul. Kill me. End this vile torment."

Steel whines as he unsheathes his engraved two-handed longsword from a scabbard filigreed with tortoiseshell and mother-of-pearl. The chill perfection of a finely hammered blade. An old-civilisation steel blade from before the ice. He holds it in both hands in a kind of reverie, swings and poises.

Then locates the point in the hollow of my neck, just inside the collarbone.

I breathe, "Thank you."

His sword-arm is a blurred streak as he thrusts in one deep penetration through my vital organs.

The regret on his face turns to horror as I seep up into him.

By the time the Warlord's body is discovered, Ricimus has slipped away, a thick-set figure loping through shanty alleys, he ditches his distinctive tight-fitting honey-coloured armour, and loses himself in the sprawling encampment. Not to be seen again. If the Magister had been recognised on the streets of Ruagh, he would be summarily executed, despite whatever protestations he made, so he never used the codes agreed with Umika to collect his Assassin's reward.

With Warlord Rurik Varangian dead, the fragile tribal coalition falls apart into feuding factions. They turn from attacking the pearlescent towers of Ruagh to warring among themselves. Small groups desert and wander away. Until the leaders turn, seeking easier targets. In the confusion, Varangian's woman prisoner uses Sicarius' poignard to stab and wound the bald Chirurgeon, then she takes a chest of alchemist's gold and makes good her escape on a horse, to live out her days in relative prosperity.

There is dancing and celebration in the streets of Ruagh as the siege is lifted. The Warlock and the Theologian carry the wounded Chirurgeon and present themselves at the gates of Ruagh, requesting sanctuary. Unaware of their role in manipulating the siege, they are granted asylum and given a tower in which to practise their hermetic arts. The city returns to something approaching normality, harbouring refugees and seeking to reduce the suffering in the devastated communities beyond its towering walls.

For a further century I watch Ruagh thrive and even prosper, despite the darkening skies, they trade with islands to the south, harvest the wealth of the sea, until it all ends when black plague decimates the people. The last of those who escape hideous plague-death flee, leaving the streets empty. For a thousand years the city stands deserted. Members of the Astartian sect move in, clear accumulations of windblown debris and crawling weed, and establish a peaceful academic community there in the harbourside area. But eventually they leave too, and the ruins return to their interrupted slumber.

Finally, the release of waters from melting ice at the dawn of the next interglacial raises the sea level, and Ruagh is inundated, swallowed up by the waves, to vanish from human memory. To become a myth. Until even the myth is forgotten. But I remember. I reign in my horse along the new shoreline. I sit on a rocky outcrop of ancient stone that is like the desiccated bones of the world, and gaze out over the stillness of the tide that conceals what remains of the pearlescent towers.

This is a story with no real end. In the clear evening air the stars are strengthening.

And when I think of Moarne, my eyes mist, I feel that terrible desolation of loss and remorse.

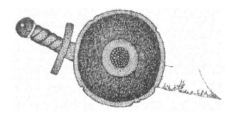

TO RAISE THE SHINING WALLS OF IREM ONCE MORE

A TALE OF THE INLAND SEA

Tais Teng

In the middle of the night, with the almost full moon westering, King Arimel heard his name called. He sat bolt upright, a miniature crossbow in his hand, one wound up and ready to discharge, for Arimel was a warrior who had been born without a drop of royal blood.

A glance to the left, one to the right, but the other two embroidered pillows remained empty: even the lustiest and manly man sometimes needs to spend a night alone.

"King Arimel," the voice repeated, and it was a most delectable voice, one so feminine that it couldn't have emerged from mortal lips.

"Show yourself, jinna!" he cried. He lowered his crossbow. The quarrels hadn't been blessed by any priest and wouldn't hurt one of that iron-skinned tribe. It was an oversight he would remedy as soon as the sun rose.

The darkness condensed, became luminous. A girl stepped from the mist: her skin was pale and gleaming as the finest ivory, her lips the lustrous red of blood corral, her eyes shining opals.

King Arimel felt his manhood shrink, the dread of any mortal confronted with a creature made of so much finer material than mere clay. Kiss such a luminous being and all human females would forever fall short, become ugly as monkeys.

"Do you like what you see?" that wondrous creature asked. She licked her lips and that it was with two forked tongues only made her more desirable, more excitingly exotic.

"Very much, Great Lady," Arimel said. "But I know your radiance would burn out my eyes if I gazed too long on your loveliness."

"That is well-spoken," she said. "Don't fear, my king. I didn't come to sleep with you, even if your fine feather bed looks delightfully soft. I came to warn you: an assassin is climbing up to your window. He holds a strangling cord between his teeth and as a devotee of Kali he knows how to use it. Another is reaching for the knob of your door right now. His other hand holds a throwing knife and he could hit the eye of a rearing cobra at sixty passes."

"What should I do?"

She laughed, a tinkling as of glass bells. "You are the warrior. You should know."

He grinned back. "I do. Thanks for the warning. Gasping for breath and gutted like a fish... Well, there are nicer ways to wake up."

A shadow darkened the moonlit sky beyond the window, and he raised his crossbow. A muted twang, instantly followed by a thud and the window was empty once more.

The door swung open, and he rolled to the left, threw one of the pillows. A knife intercepted the soft target, and a storm of feathers swirled through the room. A second knife nicked his right earlobe, and he hissed in annoyance. For an enemy to claim first blood was humiliating. Still, any knife artist only owned two hands and those must be empty now.

He jumped, his calloused heel hitting the breastbone of the assassin, driving the jagged shards of a broken rib in his heart.

He rose. The girl was standing at the window, looking down. "Dead before he hit the ground. You are clearly the man I was looking for." She folded her arms. "I just saved your life."

"True." It would be churlish to deny that claim. "I owe you. Ask what you want in exchange. But I won't offer you my soul."

"What should I do with a human soul? We jinn are made of roaring fire and swirling sand: the last thing we need is your feeble flame. No, I need a companion, a brother-in-arms. There are places where no jinna can go, too well warded with awful spells or sheathed in yellow copper."

"I see."

Jinn were made of magic and copper sucked their life force away and negated their spells. Long ago their capital city Irem had been built with walls of copper, to stop most enemy conjurations. Most, but some magic was too powerful to stop.

The great King Salomon had used Michael's flaming sword to smite their city. A blow so mighty that it tore a crater from Jorsaleem to Basra, the ancient Inland Sea that now fronted Arimel's palace.

He put his boots on, hung a brace of throwing darts over his shoulder.

"You want me just to depart? Leave my palace and my *hareem* with seventy-three lovely wives? An empty throne will be soon filled, Great Lady. I have nine brothers roaming the dunes and while none is as accomplished as me, they are formidable warriors."

"You have been the king of Shimrabath for nine years now. Don't deny that it is starting to bore you. All your possible enemies cower in fear. The best they can do is send an assassin now and then." She spread her hands. "What if you lose your kingdom? Wouldn't it be fun to conquer it again and cut off the head of one of your traitorous brothers or nephews?"

"This city is soft as marzipan and her aristocrats have sherbet for blood. How can a wolf dwell among sheep without becoming fat and indolent?" He walked to the window. "When do we leave?" The Inland Sea became an undulating silver snakeskin in the moonlight, endless and mysterious. "Do I step out of the window and we fly away like eagles? Or will you summon a bronze horse to gallop through the sky?"

She smiled. "We must be more discreet. I'll take the shape of a mortal and we'll board a ship. You'll be a simple Tuareg, with me your humble slave-girl."

He frowned. "Slave-girl? Are you sure you can play that part? All tales insist that jinn are deeply arrogant and exceedingly proud."

"But also that we love to lie and deceive. This would be like playing a part."

Shimrabath lay far to the South, a city founded by expatriate Sidonians. For every altar of Ormazd, there rose two fanes dedicated to iron-bellied Baal Hammon. The priest nowadays only burned babies on the solstice, though, and often not even then, being satisfied with a black rooster or a suckling pig. In the king's eyes that smelled of decadence. No priest worth his name should forget the power of blood and pain.

They emerged from the palace at first light, the sky pink as a rose petal. A dozen ships lay ready to depart, their prows decorated with winged sea monsters or mermaids with broad smiles showing their shark teeth and sucker-studded tongues.

"What is our destination, Lady?"

"Don't call your slave that."

He turned around and she had become hideous. One eye was milky and her hair a stringy and repulsive matt, like a mixture of wet straw and seaweed. A bulbous nose that leaned to the left and one foot swollen and dragging completed the picture.

"I am afraid that simply won't do. Look at my clothes and boots, my weapons which are the best money can buy. I am clearly a successful pirate or at least a mercenary captain. I wouldn't want to own a slave girl this ugly."

"Ah. Perhaps I went a bit overboard." Her dead eye cleared and her hair lost its dullness, became curly. The nose straightened.

"Better," he said. "My vizir would never have bought you for my *hareem*, but you are perfectly alright for a pirate."

"To answer your question, we're crossing the Inland Sea. There is a certain wandering island. A wizard built it on the back of a turtle."

"Like in the tale of Sindbad? It looks like a palm island but dives the moment any hapless traveller sets foot on it? Drowning every sailor?"

"She is a bit more active than that. The moment the turtle spies a ship in her territory she paddles in her direction, fast as a trireme. She next bites the offending vessel in two and munches on the pieces until only wreckage is left. Her attendant sharks take care of any survivors."

"And the wizard? Is he still alive?"

"Before King Salomon ascended to the Paradisio he handed his great-grandson something that belongs to us. Our most precious possession." She hesitated, clearly unwilling to tell a mere mortal such a secret.

"Go on."

She closed her eyes, grimaced. "Good. It is the Key. The Key to Irem. When Salomon walked with the archangel Michael through the fused sands he found the Key. It was the only part of Irem left, imperishable, too strong even for the divine fire of Michael's sword.

"Our emir and a thousand of our most powerful sorcerers had used it to conjure Irem from the sands. Every tower and palace, the Great Library with dragon-hide scrolls, all fountains and gardens, the herd of bronze horses that galloped through the sky. We can resurrect Irem if we recover the Key. Copper walled Irem and all the jinn who died that day." Her voice was wistful and for just a heartbeat she grew supernally beautiful again. "Steal the key back and we are in your debt. All the jinn. No wish will remain unfulfilled. We'll make you emperor of all human lands. Grant you a thousand years of life. Anything!" Her opal eyes blazed.

Arimel laughed. He felt like fourteen again, after he had skewered the liver of his uncle and the whole tribe shouted his name. He might be dead soon, turtle food, but right now the whole wide world lay at his feet again, like an immense unrolled scroll. "Let's get that key first."

The jinna walked past the galleons, the mighty ships with gilded bows and a dozen wind-ghosts each. The enslaved spirits would fill the silk sails with their magic breeze until a ship could sail against the wildest storm nature could breed.

Lesser ships followed, single masted feluccas with no more than a single wind-ghost.

In the second harbour, unprotected by the long moles, half a dozen Frankish ships lay moored.

The Sunset lands disdained magic of any kind, Arimel knew. No wind-ghosts for them: when the winds fell still, they rowed. Every sailor and slave.

They were ingenious, he had to admit, their sails complicated as the war-kites of Han, catching the slightest breeze. Hero steam-vats drove Archimedes-screws, huffing and puffing and belching black smoke, like the sulphurous breath of demons.

The jinna pointed. "This one." She turned her left thumb and the runes on the bow flickered, changed into proper Arabic letters. "Odin's Excellent Spear."

"A good name," Arimel said. "One of my war brothers had some Northland blood. Odin is their war god. His spear is a living snake that always hits her target. A poisonous snake that kept on flying once she was thrown."

"I thought they didn't do magic?" the jinna said.

"Magic isn't for mortals. It dirties their soul. The Three-Headed Hound of the Afterlife will smell it on them and tear them apart."

"Perhaps that is true? We Jinn don't do any afterlife. We prefer to live forever." She marched up the gangboard of the ship and Arimel had to run after her to arrive first.

"Don't do that!" he hissed at her. "A slave should never walk in front of her master."

"Sorry," she said, mockingly adding: "Master."

Arimel hired one of the bigger cabins for himself and his servant. There was a single mattress. One of them could sleep on the floor.

"I don't exactly understand how we'll reach the turtle," he said to the jinna. "It was circling the central mountain you told me. No captain will steer his ship in that direction. We bought passage to Jorsaleem, and our ship will be hugging the coast all the way."

"They don't command a single wind-ghost and an Archimedes screw gobbles fuel. It will only work for a short while. The wind and the currents are all they have. Both are easily manipulated if you are a jinni."

He didn't intend to sleep with the jinna, even if she had been willing. A man has his needs, though.

On the fifth day he stood looking at the sunset next to one of the better-looking female sailors. They had played backgammon for two hours and he had let her win to get her in a good mood. Silver and gold coins meant little to a king and less to a warrior who was accustomed to grabbing what he needed.

He took her hand and it was nicely calloused: a strong woman, with her face tanned to exotic mahogany, her hair bleached by the sun and the salty breeze.

She didn't snatch her fingers away but returned the pressure. "I wondered if you made love to your servant?" she asked. "She seems nice enough."

Arimel nodded, then belatedly remembered he should shake his head to indicate a negative. "I am a warrior from the deep desert and each of us has to obey several taboos. One of mine is sleeping with a slave: I am only allowed to bed a freeborn woman."

"Ah, that is why you were making eyes at me even when I don't look half as pretty and quite a bit older." She smiled and for a moment that made her quite beautiful. More beautiful than the jinna in fact because there was no magic in it, just who she was. "My name is Asgild by the way. Your cabin or mine?"

"My mattress is probably bigger, and I'll send my servant away. And you can call me Arimel."

"Any relation to the king of Shimrabath?'
"I wish!"

When he woke the next morning the wind had fallen still. Not even the slightest breeze ruffled the sea which reflected the single cloud in the sky like a dull mirror. The crater wall painted a misty silhouette in the distance, a blue only slightly darker than the sky.

"No matter," the captain shrugged. "We'll row."

"That means me," Asgild said. "See you later, my stallion."

In the afternoon the sea suddenly grew rough. Whirlpools appeared all around the ship and the captain had to order the oars shipped or they would have snapped like dry reeds.

There was still no trace of wind, but from the waters a dank miasma rose, redolent of the abyssal muds.

"I don't like it," Asgild said. "This isn't natural."

The ship started moving on the new, rapid current, turning like an aspen leaf in a mountain stream. The crater wall sank beneath the horizon and only churning water surrounded them. From the corner of his eyes Arimel saw the jinna smile. No, not a smile, but something closer to a smirk.

Night fell and the sky was filled with enormous stars. As a traveller across the trackless desert waste, Arimel knew his constellations. They were all still there: the Plowman, the Tiger and the Ogre with his Mace, The Laurel Wreath, but some stars had changed colour or brightened and Aph-Roditeh, the Evening star, was nowhere to be seen.

"What exactly is happening?" he asked the jinna.

"This is our sky and our sea. I pulled the ship just this little bit aside from your reality. Time flows differently here, faster. In the morning we should arrive at our destination."

She was right. If he looked at the blue star closest to the bow spit he could see her move. The constellations rotated through the sky.

No one manned the steering wheel. All sailors crowded together at the altar at the bow, praying and cutting themselves, dripping blood on the statues of their uncouth gods.

Asgild came to join Arimel and the jinna.

"So much strangeness," she said. "Are we dead? Sailing through the Afterlife?"

"Why ask me?" Arimel said.

"Because you and your servant are the only thing that is truly different this journey. And a king knows things a mere citizen doesn't know." She pursed her lips. "I recognized you the first day. There is a scar on your left thumb, just like the king. That is one coincidence too many." She turned to the jinna. "You are no slave girl. You walk like a free woman, like a princess. And your shadow sometimes points in the wrong direction." She folded her arms. "Kill me if you want to keep your secrets."

"No need," the jinna said. "We are almost there."

A feeble sun was indeed struggling up from the mists, a blood-red orb devoid of any warmth.

"Almost where?" Asgild asked.

"The Island of the Turtle."

"The turtle that devours ships. I heard about her."

"We have to board her," the jinna explained. "She'll attack the ship and then, while the sharks deal with the sailors, we'll join them. Who notices two more sharks? Just before we clamber ashore I'll change us back. There will be no magic to warn the sorcerer, nothing to tell him I am a princess of the jinn."

In the distance an island rose from the sea, surmounted by a tower sheathed with yellow copper plates. A village of palm leaf decked shacks clustered around the foundation.

Yellow copper, Arimel thought. *Jinn proof. The reason why she needed me. A jinna can't even touch the gate without losing her magic.* "He keeps soldiers in that town?"

"Cannibals," the jinna said. "They form his third line of defence. The sharks divide their spoils with them and always let some half-drowned sailors crawl ashore." She nodded. "There'll be feasting in the village tonight, great spits turning above glowing coals."

And suddenly the distant island wasn't distant anymore. A head rose from the ocean, waterfalls cascading from her mighty beak. The jinna touched Arimel's shoulder and he saw his skin turn shark grey and rough as sandpaper.

"Wait!" he cried. "Change her, too!"

"I thought you already married seventy-three queens? No matter. I'll consider this your first wish."

The head rose above the ship, struck.

Arimel jumped down from the rail and had grown fins and gills before he hit the water.

Three sharks didn't join the joyous massacre but swam to the shore through clouds of blood and strips of torn silk.

The moment Arimel touched the keratin shore his tail retracted and his fins turned into limbs.

He stood up on unsteady legs and discovered he was still clad in his lightweight armour, with his sword at his side, his bow across his shoulder. His clothes and boots should have been sodden, but they seemed completely dry. Well, magic was magic. Not a warrior's concern.

"And now?" he asked.

"We walk to the tower, which I obviously can't enter. You kill him and take the Key." She smiled. "And everybody lives happily ever after."

"You mentioned cannibals?" Asgild said. He had been right in his assessment of her: she was as tough as any of his sisters, ready to roll with the punch and hit back hard.

"They are savages. They carry maces and fire-hardened bamboo spears. Our warrior here still carries his bow and yesterday I put a spell on his quiver. He won't ever run out of quarrels and they'll always hit their target."

Arimel frowned. "Won't the sorcerer notice that?"

"He smells the casting of a spell. Not a spell that is already in place."

The cannibals fled like dormice at their approach. They had perhaps seen swords before but never in the hand of a living man. Like all scavengers, they preferred their prey dead, not alive and eager to fight.

The path to the tower was paved with skulls, a nice touch if you wanted to discourage visitors, even if it made for unsure footing. The sheer number also showed how long the turtle had been swimming around the central mountain.

The tower gate rose to seven man-heights and was incised with the most elegant and awful spells the archangels had taught Salomon. Aside from the poisonous copper, it would dissolve a jinn who touched any of them in a puff of smoke.

"Well, this is as far as I go," the jinna said.

Arimel handed Asgild his sword. "I am afraid that my bow is too attuned to my touch to be of much use to you. Also, I rubbed the bowstring with a poison that I made myself immune to."

The woman raised his sword to test the balance, then described a swishing figure-eight through the air. Yes, she would do.

He looked up at the fastening of the door. The massive lock seemed intricate as a Gordian knot but just above it, a copper ear stood poised, ready to listen to a visitor's password.

"Ay," Arimel said, "I have never been very good at enigmas. Any sphinx would leave me stuttering."

"It is probably just meant to keep jinn out," Asgild concluded. "The passwords would be something no jinni can ever say without burning her lips. Something like: I embrace Ormazd the Bringer of Light and call His Chosen Warrior Salomon my Master, perhaps?"

The gate swung open.

The stairs were coated with ankle-deep dust. It had been a long time since anyone had walked these steps.

They crossed a hall filled with jewelled trees and amphorae filled with black pearls.

"Don't touch them!" Arimel warned.

"Do you think me daft? My fingers would fall from my hand, black with pestilence. If I cradled that bird of paradise in my arms it would shriek so loud my eardrums would burst and next peck out my eyes."

Arimel nodded. "You clearly listened to the right tales."

The next room was filled with a lake of gleaming quicksilver, and they ran across the stepping stones, holding their breath against the poisonous fumes.

Five more rooms which had been booby-trapped in the usual ways and then they found a door not made of silver or gold or even flaking mother-of-pearl but carved from the burly wood of a weeping willow.

"This is it," Asgild whispered. "The dwelling of a sage who has chosen wisdom above jewels and worldly goods."

Arimel almost overlooked him. The man sitting on the throne was so shrunken and wrinkled that he could have been a mummy. The ancient raised his head.

"Finally," he wheezed. "A stalwart warrior and his maid. Kill me, good people. Kill me and take the Key. All my treasures will be yours. The Great and Awful Turtle will obey your every command."

"You want to die?" Arimel said. "But the great king, he made you immortal!"

"He ordered me to keep the Key safe. Me and my children and their children's children. Forever, world without end. I was never meant to live on and on, never finding the solace of the grave. I have lain with a hundred maidens, but my seed always refused to quicken in their wombs. No children or grandchildren, so I had to stay as a guardian."

He rose and spread his arms to bare his breast. The key hung from a chain, a copper spiral that endlessly kept turning, like the World Snake biting his own tail.

Arimel raised his bow and an arrow stood quivering in the socket of the sorcerer's left eye. To make doubly sure Asgild lopped off the head.

The outer gate swung open at their approach: the tower knew his new masters.

"The key?" the jinna called. She had taken her true form, a sensual beauty that made Arimel gasp for breath.

"So much loveliness," he whispered. "Such a pity to spoil it."

The little copper knife he had hidden in his boot the

morning they departed, spun through the air, hit her. She instantly vanished, popped like a soap bubble.

Asgild gaped at him, her mouth open in shock. "But she promised you immortality. She would make you king of all the lands under the sun!"

"The Fall of Irem was the first tale my father told me," Arimel said. "How our ancestors fought in the army of Salomon and defeated the perfidious jinn for once and all. I am not turning that back."

"And the Key?" Asgild asked.

"I am putting it in the most secure place possible." He fastened the shining amulet to an arrow. His bow sang and the arrow rose in the sky, higher and higher and then flashed down. Just before it hit the sea an enormous head rose and snapped it up.

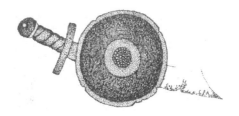

FULGIN THE GRIM: RETRIBUTION

Ken Lizzi

Fulgin the Grim leaned upon his axe. The scene unfolding in the dell appeared all too familiar. Fulgin wanted nothing to do with it. And yet he must pass this way.

The cart path cut its rutted route through the thinned, interlinked coppices that traced the bottom of the dell and climbed its flanks. Something about the place engendered in Fulgin a burgeoning recognition, a familiarity of location that juxtaposed with the sadly commonplace nature of what he observed below.

The trees provided ideal concealment for the footpads who had emerged onto the track to surround a lone figure leading a suddenly balky sumpter mule. Fulgin could not see if the traveller was armed. Even if he were, five against one seemed insurmountable odds for a tinker, peddler, or practitioner of whatever itinerant trade the traveller pursued.

Fulgin unslung the targe from its comfortable resting place upon the bedroll hanging at his back. He hefted his axe, his calloused fingers closing comfortably around the worn leather thongs that wrapped the lower two-thirds of the haft. The two-foot length of hornbeam slotted into a single-edged, bearded axehead of blackened steel, its edge maintained by Fulgin to a sharpness that could split a wisp of goose down.

As usual his knees protested when he forced his booted feet into a run. As usual he endured the discomfort and pushed himself to a faster pace. Fulgin had entered the dell from over the northwestern brow and so let the slope add length to his strides, though that did demand a deliberative navigation of the beech trees and elms that preponderated among the coppices. The westering sun remained hovering behind him at the mouth of the dell, providing a lambent, rose-hued light to guide his steps.

His bootheels struck the path, the wheel ruts carved into it still ridged and hard-edged in late summer, not yet softened by the impending fall rains. Ahead of him, fewer than a score of paces away, the scene had altered little. The mule, its headstall now gripped by a bandit, brayed its annoyance and discontent. The centre of attention for the remaining four footpads — the mule's erstwhile owner — held a quarterstaff horizontally, as if that provided an impenetrable bulwark. The brigands stood arrayed in an arc across the path. From behind they appeared to assume posturing attitudes of amused contempt and derision: hips cocked, weapons resting on shoulders. For was not this their supreme moment? Did they not savour the exultancy of banditry; the feeling — temporary though it might be — of power and authority?

For the moment ignoring the footpad occupied with the pack beast, Fulgin closed the distance, swiftly and with such silence as he could maintain. He angled his steps to his right. The targe — the modestly-sized circular shield of oaken strips faced in hammered bronze — boasted a spike protruding four inches from the centre of the boss. Tightening his fingers about the grip at the rear of the targe, and ignoring the expected arthritic flare in his thumb, Fulgin punched the spike into the back of the nearest footpad, one of the two standing in the path. At the same time he uncoiled a backhanded swing at the brigand holding the right flank of their line, needing to open his hand for a split second to allow the haft to slip to the slightly widened butt in order to achieve the necessary reach. The edge of the blade, driven by thickly corded shoulder and triceps muscles, sheared through the vertebra immediately above the shoulders, leaving the filthy coat of brigandine the man wore untouched.

The flesh tugging at the spike and the resistance of muscle and bone met by the axe aided only fractionally in slowing his charge. Fulgin the Grim found himself five paces beyond the action and into the trees before he could stop and turn around.

The first man he'd struck was attempting, with poor success, to feel between his own shoulder blades, no doubt puzzled at the pain he felt. Periodic jets of blood pulsed from the wound to soak into the parched earth of the track. The second footpad remained standing, unmoving. Then, as Fulgin began to stride back into the fight, the man pitched face forward like a felled tree.

"Let that mule go, Yoncy, and come give us a hand," said the bandit at the far end of the path. There wasn't a quaver in his voice, no hint of fear arising from the near instantaneous death of two of his comrades. A hard man, no doubt, unconcerned with the fate of even his closest boon companions. But Fulgin had encountered his sort often enough. Courage — or a sort of inborn, stupid fearlessness — provided no great advantage in a death struggle.

"He's done for Bross and Sonty, Mhoxio," Yoncy said from his position by the mule. His voice failed to manage a convincing degree of bravery. He sounded young and scared. And that too Fulgin had heard, and knew if offered no safety.

"Yes, Yoncy. And if you don't want the same to happen to you, get over here and help."

The third of the remaining trio had spoken, and he sounded much like Mhoxio. Fulgin noted a physical similarity as well. Both were bearded, sandy-haired, rangy men, wearing poorly patched coats of brigandine and carrying swords, now no longer held casually across the shoulder. Mhoxio gripped a rust-pitted falchion while the other bore a basket-hilted broadsword, its edges glinting, catching the rays of the dying day.

Fulgin did not wait for Yoncy to join, leaving the youth to fumble about for the spear he'd dropped in order to restrain the sumpter mule. Instead Fulgin made straight for the bandit with the broadsword. He feinted with the targe. Most men will flinch when a bloody spike is thrust at the face. The unnamed brigand, however, was not most men. Instead of stepping back, he hacked at the targe, as if parrying a sword thrust. That result worked for Fulgin just as well — distracting his foe with his left hand, leaving his right to do its work. He hacked through the footpad's sword arm at the elbow, the axe cleaving through bone almost effortlessly.

A red torrent splattered against the face of the targe. Fulgin moved to his right, lest the crimson spray blind him. He nearly collided with the owner of the mule, who remained in the same spot, staff still raised. Perhaps close proximity to another was all the man required to stimulate his nerves, for he at once sprang to life. As Fulgin moved to keep the newmade amputee between himself and Mhoxio, the traveller edged toward Yoncy, whipping his staff into a blurring circle like a man well versed with quarterstaff play.

"Mhoxio," the wounded bandit said, pressing his gushing stump against his side. But that single name seemed all he had the strength for, and he sank to his knees.

Mhoxio snarled at Fulgin, revealing a scant few blackened teeth in a filthy, bearded face. He spat, then glanced at the man desperately attempting to staunch the exodus of his life blood. For a moment Fulgin thought Mhoxio might run. He did not. He came forward, unleashing hammer blows at Fulgin with the single edge of his slightly curved sword. Fulgin fended them off with the targe, hearing steel ring against bronze, feeling the impact run through his arm and shoulder. Flakes of rust and chips from the falchion's edge flashed across Fulgin's vision. He gave ground, content to catch and turn each strike until the opportunity to counter presented itself. He did not have to wait long.

The affray brought Fulgin backing past the first man he'd struck, the one he'd punctured with the spike of his targe. At some point the wounded man had felt the need to sit down. As the fight crossed before him, he spoke, crying "Mhoxio, help," and reached out to grab Mhoxio's leg.

Mhoxio snarled again, cutting backhanded into the wounded man. The blade chopped into neck and collarbone, and temporarily resisted Mhoxio's effort to tug it free. Fulgin sank the axe into Mhoxio's head, bisecting his face from forehead to chin.

"I offer my thanks for the rescue," said the traveller, appearing a moment later as Fulgin carefully cleansed his weapons of gore. "I am Ghorsyk of Burgens, itinerant purveyor of luxuries and sundries. I'd hoped to reach Verusk by sunfall, and thus lessen the risk of banditry. Alas, I miscalculated my mule's speed."

Fulgin's head — with its grey-brindled mane of dark hair and the lined face set into its habitual hard expression — jerked up, onyx-dark eyes focused on Ghorsyk rather than the blood-soaked cleaning rag.

"We *are* near to Verusk then?"

"Aye. Through the dell, over that rise, and — if we're quick — through the gates to the inn where I will purchase you a roast capon and a flagon in partial repayment of my debt."

The gate guards of Verusk, lax and uninterested, allowed the pair in even though the gates were nearly pulled to. The inn — a tile-roofed, two-story affair of river rock and timber — proved accommodating. After attending to his mule and the sequestering of his 'luxuries and sundries', Ghorsyk joined Fulgin, who was already deep into a flagon of a rich, brown ale, redolent of cardamom and honey.

Fulgin began to wish he'd waited for the capon — and the accompanying onions, parsnips, and small meat-filled pasties slathered with sour cream — before getting into his cups. Yet after the fight, after the journey, after so many other obstacles...he needed the drink.

Ghorsyk was fulsome and forthcoming about himself, about his travels, travails, and trading. Fulgin was content to let him speak. 'Garrulous' did not describe Fulgin the Grim. Yet he could feel the ale suffuse him with a sense of well-being, and when Ghorsyk asked for his benefactor's name, Fulgin complied with but a moment's hesitation.

"Fulgin the Grim? I cannot say I've heard the name," Ghorsyk said. "What, may I inquire, brings you to Verusk? Do not think I failed to notice your interest when I mentioned the name. We merchants depend upon the shrewdness of our surmises and upon our skills of observation."

"Business of my own," answered Fulgin the Grim.

"No doubt. But as I owe you a life debt, your business is now my business. Come, let me replenish your tankard. Wench! Another flagon."

And so, rather to his surprise, Fulgin the Grim heard himself beginning to speak. It was, he realized, only fit that he relate the story now. Now or, likely, never.

"I was not always Fulgin the Grim. Nor even Fulgin," he began. "It was some ten years ago, I was young — no, don't interrupt, Ghorsyk, or I'll turn mute and as stubborn as your mule. I was, I said, young. An armsman for the Kaznac of Verusk, and married. Married to the fairest, most desirable of women: Cortabella. The happiest man from snow to shore. Alas, what cannot last, will not last. Or so I have come to learn.

"The fame of Cortabella's beauty reached the ear of a certain magician of the blackest sort: Drucar. Drucar the Blithe, as he styled himself, though when I first saw him I could not fathom why. He stooped. His grin seemed forced, yellow teeth showing in a sallow face beneath thinning hair. The richness and elegance of his robes, cotehardie, and velvet cap could not hide a man in his declining years, though he made a pretence of youth and good humour.

"Drucar came to my cottage, announced himself, and entered, along with a half-dozen men armed cap-a-pie. He could not take his gaze from Cortabella, nor did he make an effort to do so.

"The details remain sharp. Painful. I will not disturb your appetite with them, Ghorsyk. At some prearranged signal, Drucar's armsmen overbore me without a word and held me down upon the table. After which Drucar employed his diabolical arts, his entourage observing silently. I could not understand his incantations. I recognized none of his arcane instruments, nor the designs he inked on the floor in cock's blood and etched upon my walls with a silver knife. The only note of familiarity was the homely scent of beeswax and the exotic fragrance of sandalwood from the candles placed at precise intervals about the room.

"All I can tell you are the results of his diabolism. For he explained it to me. He became quite jolly as he worked, and talked freely. To be brief: he drained twenty years of my life from me and absorbed those pilfered years into himself.

"It was an experience I find hard to describe, Ghorsyk. Imagine every deeply personal loss you've ever suffered, the grief you've endured at every death of kith or kin, all distilled into a single, drawn out, physical pain, yet one that still carried with it the distinct heartache of those individual losses. Nothing could be worse.

"And yet...He then conjured a creature from the Pit, a winged abomination. This demon — though clearly suffering from the compulsion of Drucar — leered at me, revelling in my woe. At Drucar's command the demon grasped my weakened, unnaturally aged body in its talons and flew far away. Across leagues. Across unknown lands and vast seas, to abandon me at last upon an islet at the far end of an archipelago of terrors.

"I know the question you would ask, Ghorsyk. Why didn't the magician simply kill me himself? I was pinioned, tied, unable to fight. And he had a silver athame to hand. I asked him that very question when the demon appeared. He told me, and I can only assume he spoke the truth. He said that his were the hands that had transferred my life force as if siphoning wine from a cask into a demijohn. If he killed me he'd sever the magical link, or siphon. But the link was only at risk if the magician himself broke it or if it was broken in close proximity to the magician. So he would spare no concern for my continued well-being once I was out of his sight. And then he commanded the demon to drop me into certain, mortal peril far, far away.

"I wondered, when I had a few lucid moments during that foul passage — moments without terror of the heights we flew or the speed at which we traversed the earth and seas — what would happen if I severed that link, if I killed the magician. Would the siphon reverse? Would my youth be returned. I have often wondered the same since. But not for some time. I have been much too busy trying to stay alive.

"Thus have I been occupied for *ten years*. The rock in the empty sea where the demon deposited me was home to monsters. As was the next in the chain, a slightly larger hummock of land I reached in a boat fashioned from the carapace of a marine abomination I slew. The larger land mass simply meant larger monsters. I fought my way across the archipelago, surviving unspeakable creatures, swamps, precipitous cliffs, pirate strongholds, and the abodes of witches. It cost me five years to complete the trek, then most of another to traverse the sea in a ship that suffered the foulest of fortunes, blown off course, twice run aground, and at last sunk in sight of the mainland.

"For nearly five more years I fought my way across the western lands with their barbarian empires, corrupt city states, matriarchal witchdoms, and petty principalities. But ever I bent my steps east, drawn ineluctably back to the Cordillera Seigniories. Back to Gnomon Spire."

"Gnomon Spire?" Ghorsyk repeated, startled out of his impatiently maintained silence. "But that's just a day's easy walk over there." He gestured with a hand in a generally south, south easterly direction, slopping ale over the brim of the tankard the hand grasped.

"I know. I may have become unrecognizable over the past decade, but these lands appear unchanged. Our landlord, for instance, has put on three or four stone about the middle, yet I could not mistake him. Me? He would not believe me if I offered my old name.

"I have returned. At last. But one more short journey awaits me."

The fief of the Kaznac of Verusk consisted of two parallel, upland valleys, running generally north to south. At one time it had seemed all the world to Fulgin the Grim. Now it appeared an insignificant backwater. The Kaznac's stronghold — seeming a weak, poorly defensible watch tower in comparison to the mighty citadels and vast, circumvallated fortified cities Fulgin had encountered during his wanderings — sat atop a bluff at the northern end of the town of Verusk in the western valley. Gnomon Spire towered just beyond the southern termination of the eastern valley, outside the Kaznac's remit in lands of dubious allegiance. The Cordillera Seigniories extended from white-topped alps to the north down to a forking peninsula in the south, with long inlets stepping down in series of luxuriantly vegetated precipices to the warmth of the sea. The geography lent itself to such unclaimed pockets as that claimed by Drucar the Blithe. The Seigniories' secluded vales were defined by juxtaposed ridges and sheer buttes linked by saddles. The erratic terrain produced odd declivities occurring at the already questionable borders on the ever-shifting maps of the dozen or so polities squeezed into this country of peaks, combes, high glens, jutting eminences, and sheltered dales.

Fulgin crossed the length of the fief at a leisurely pace, keeping to woodlots and boulder-strewn sheep pasturage far from the dirt tracks that served for such commerce and visitation as Verusk required. He could still push himself, handle hardship and exertion. The last ten years had hardened him, adding strength and endurance even beyond that he'd enjoyed as a young, energetic armsman. Yet the hardships of those years had also worn him down, added as they were atop the stolen twenty years. An accretion of injuries added to the indignities of age had taken a toll. Aches, stiffness, an increasingly sore lower back, and twinges of arthritis all spoke to the wisdom of patience, of arriving at his longed-for destination in a rested condition.

He inventoried his gear as he walked, turning his thoughts from the nostalgia that each familiar scene threatened to invoke. It required little mental effort to squash sentiment; nostalgia bordered on happiness. Fulgin the Grim had known none for ten years.

His axe he'd honed that morning, after breaking his fast on bread and bacon. His targe remained dinged and dinted, but none of the stout oaken boards had suffered so much as a crack. His knee-high boots, reinforced with strips of iron, carried him steadily onward, despite the occasional protest of knees and a stiffness in the right hip that cropped up during steep ascents. The kilt he wore sandwiched squares of steel sewn between a coarse fabric weave and a leather backing. It covered him from mid-abdomen to past the tops of his boots. His torso he guarded with a coat of blackened steel scales riveted to an inch-thick vest fashioned from the hide of a grey behemoth Fulgin had encountered in far southern lands where the climate alternated between torrid and torrential. A simple, leather-covered, narrow-brimmed kettle hat protected his pate. A knee length tunic of wool, dark and heavy from the fuller's art, and a cloak of the same waxed against the elements, completed his kit.

In no way did Fulgin the Grim resemble the young armsman he had been, resplendent in gleaming mail and the

Kaznac's colours of azure and gold. Fulgin brooded upon this transformation over his small, concealed fire a scant four miles from Gnomon Spire and the abode of the man responsible.

Dawn cast the shade of the slender spike of stone across the end of the eastern valley. The spire rose, gnarled and twisted, a hundred feet or more. The shadow it cast offered the locals a convenient way to measure the passage of time and thus lent the aberrant geological feature its appellation.

Below Gnomon Spire, built up against its western face, sprawled the manse of Drucar the Blithe. A band of trees marked the bounds of the Fief of Verusk from the lands claimed by the magician. Beyond the trees peasants beholden to Drucar worked fields watered by a meandering, lazy rivulet. Beyond the fields, vineyards climbed the gradually increasing slope to the low wall surrounding the manse, a wall commencing at the northern side of Gnomon Spire and ending at its southern. Or the other way around.

From his concealment in the belt of trees, Fulgin thought the scene presented a falsely idyllic picture. He watched carefully as the eastern sky shifted from pink to pale blue, searching for evidence of the traps and guards he knew the magician must employ. Yet his observations proved fruitless. Smoke drifted from the manse's chimney pots. Movement within the grounds spoke of ordinary activity. No chimera took flight to hunt for intruders, no basilisks slithered over the walls to despoil the vines. No troop of armoured horsemen rode forth.

It appeared serene. Safe. Too simple. And so Fulgin the Grim waited with stoic patience for nightfall. He had already waited ten years.

Lazy clouds drifted across the face of a new moon, providing sufficient light for Fulgin to distinguish the track from the fields. He failed to note the creek and wetted his boot. Again he waited, allowing the boot to dry enough to avoid squelching when he walked, then continued on. The first check, he surmised, would be the wall.

The track began to ascend. He felt his right hip hint at an impending protest at about the time he entered the grape vines twining about trellises on either hand. Eyes fixed on the end of the track and the gate twenty yards distant, Fulgin failed to see the darting motion. He felt his kilt rebound from his thigh in a manner inconsistent with the rhythmic swaying induced by his gait. Glancing down, he saw by the sickle of the moon the coiling length of a snake, its fangs entangled in the outer layer of fabric, its venom doubtless expended harmlessly against one of the steel platelets beyond. A rapid backhand of the axe beheaded the serpent.

With slow, careful movements, Fulgin grasped the severed stem of neck immediately behind the spatulate swelling of the head and extracted the fangs. But even as he tossed it aside, a slithering rasp alerted him that the dead snake had not patrolled the vineyard alone. Fulgin leapt and whirled, hearing the creak of his knees as they bent and straightened. The strike of the second snake passed a whisker beneath his boot. Fulgin landed on the writhing creature, his heel grinding and twisting while his axe descended again and again, hacking the coiling and twitching length into gobbets.

Warily, he passed the remaining rows of vines on either side, listening for the sound of scales on dirt. No further serpents struck at him.

The gate neared. A gate was a weakness in a wall. It was also a bottleneck, a point of observation. A trap. Pounding on the gate and demanding that Drucar show himself might appeal to a sense of drama. Fulgin the Grim possessed none.

The wall itself would prove no barrier for a determined, armed force. The younger version of Fulgin, confident and spry, would have merely leaped up, grabbed the lip, and pulled himself up and over. Fulgin the Grim had accumulated too much hard-earned wisdom. Drucar the Blithe would not allow such easy entry into his manse.

First check.

Fulgin paused, considered. Then he continued, following the northward curve of the wall until it terminated at the base of Gnomon Spire. While the wall was plastered smooth, the spire remained rough, its sides offering a profusion of protrusions and indentations. While it did not precisely invite climbing, Fulgin had faced worse ascents over the last decade than that presented by Gnomon Spire.

He climbed. In but a few moments he was level with the top of the wall, then above it. The new moon glimmered upon a scatter of pale green tiles that formed a sickly viridescent pattern atop the yard-thick coping of the wall. If it was indeed a pattern. Fulgin couldn't decipher it. It hinted at dreamlike geometries or the calligraphic expression of some inhuman tongue.

Anchored by his feet and a solid handhold, Fulgin groped for a fistful of loose grit and gravel. He tossed it onto the wall. The bits of dirt and pebble were not even afforded a chance to bounce and rattle. The green tiles emitted a pallid jade luminosity. The grit flashed into superheated vapor, the larger segments of stone hissed and took on a short-lived red glow.

Fulgin did not set foot atop the wall. Instead he crabbed along the face of Gnomon Spire a few feet past the wall, then dropped, bending his knees to absorb the impact as he landed upon a smoothly cropped swath of grass. He restrained a grunt as his knees protested and the targe slung across his shoulders smacked him smartly on the back.

It seemed an opportune moment to transfer the targe from back to hand. Then Fulgin unlimbered his axe while he squinted into the gloom, espying what awaited him.

This northern section of the grounds looked to be some sort of formal garden, with a lawn broken into sections of tended flora, and here and there what might be a fountain or a statue. Not more than a dozen paces from Fulgin rose one wall of the manse. But he could see no door, no lower story windows that might grant him ingress.

A flutter of cloud drifted across the moon. Fulgin waited for it to pass. The lunar illumination seemed stronger when it reemerged. Farther along the garden a pale glimmer suggested a pebble-lined walk or shell-paved promenade leading from the gate to the formal entrance of the manse.

Fulgin took a cautious step in that direction. As he did, a pair of statues revealed themselves to be something else entirely.

Though both came on without speaking, it was clear neither were supernaturally animated sculpture, nor magically powered automata, but rather men of flesh and blood. Men armed and armoured. Fulgin did not wait for them to approach and bracket him. He did not wish to yield the initiative. He pushed his legs into a short sprint toward the foe on his left. The movement brought the front of the manse, foreshortened, into view, and along with it the effulgence of lamplight from upper story windows. Fulgin's brow furrowed as the light brought the features of the nearing armoured figure into relief. He recognized him. The day Durcar upended his life would remain forever etched in his memory. This man before him was one of the six men who'd overpowered him and lashed him immovably to the table.

The man hadn't changed, had remained unaltered by the years.

If the guard recognized Fulgin he gave no sign. He did, however, seem to recognize an intruder and grasped the hilt of his sword, preparatory to unsheathing it. Fulgin did not grant him the time. He delivered a powerful blow at the juncture of neck and shoulder, hacking through steel links, leather, and diapered cotton padding, then on through the clavicle. Blood welled and spurted, black in the moonlight. The guard fell, dropping his sword hilt to clutch at his wound. A plaintive, almost canine whimper emerged from his throat.

The second man had closed silently. He had drawn his sword as he'd come; a simple hanger, single edged and possessing a narrow knuckle bow of bronze. The guard — also known to Fulgin the Grim's unforgiving memory — offered no clever feints, no swordsman's tricks. He came on directly, unwaveringly, hacking at Fulgin with an animalistic ferocity.

Fulgin responded with equal ferocity, though governed by wisdom and martial experience. As was his nature he fought with a silence that matched his opponent's. Only the ring of metal on metal might reach an observer's ears. Or of metal on wood. Or into flesh.

Fulgin received a graze along one ear lobe, and a scratch along the forearm behind his targe. But he repaid the latter with a clubbing swing of the targe that caught the sentinel's swordarm and lowered his guard long enough for Fulgin to deliver a blow with the power of shoulder and hips behind it. The stroke sent the quiet sentry to the turf, his head tumbling and rolling to disappear into the orderly array of a flower bed.

Yet another of Drucar's minions approached from the shelter of a vine-draped pergola as Fulgin made his way through the garden toward the stairs leading to the main entry. As the sentry passed from shadow into a beam of light from an upper window, Fulgin saw him sniff, as if catching a scent. Fulgin sprang at him, beating aside the sword with his targe. The soundless guardian hopped backwards, Fulgin's axe scraping along the links of his mail shirt. He came back with a speed the two serpents in the vineyard might have admired. Fulgin caught the thrusting sword point with his axe on the backswing, then bulled forward, targe foremost, trying to piece the armour with the shield's spike. The links held, though Fulgin pressed hard. A faint growl emerged from between the compressed lips of the sentry. The edge of his sword rang against the overlapping scales over Fulgin's ribs. The stroke was delivered primarily by wrist and elbow; Fulgin barely noticed it. The two combatants were nearly corps-a-corps, close enough to breathe in the tang of sweat. Fulgin slammed the butt of his axe haft into the guard's face, feeling bones and cartilage give way. He hooked a foot behind the guard's heel and the man went over backwards. Though the guard raised his sword, he was unable to block or deflect the descending axe blow that burst mail shirt and sternum. He emitted a pained, confused exhalation, almost a bark, and then died.

Fulgin grunted, breathed once deeply, then continued on.

Three more awaited him at the five steps leading up to the entry porch and the thick, deeply recessed door behind. Cressets cradled smoking torches that lit the scene in shifting red and orange.

Fulgin beckoned Drucar's minions. Better to fight them on level ground than suffer the disadvantage of fighting up the stairs. Two obliged, the third remained where he stood.

The scrap was brutal, confused, and longer than Fulgin would have preferred. At one point Fulgin found himself buried beneath both men, one astride his torso, trying to find a gap between armour scales to slip the point of his hanger through, the other sprawled across his legs, attempting alternately to saw through one of Fulgin's boots and to regain his feet, managing to accomplish neither. Fulgin awkwardly levered his targe between him and the guard on his chest. He maneuvered the spike beneath the man's chin and pressed. The sentry dropped his sword, grasped the rim of the shield in both hands, and endeavoured to push the targe and the threatening point down and away. Fulgin gritted his teeth and threw his strength behind a single, massive exertion. He both heard and felt his wrist snap. The pain coursed through him, but he held firm until the guard collapsed, gurgling and clutching at his spurting throat.

Fulgin kicked at the second man. They both rolled to their feet, Fulgin regaining positive control of the axe that had been trapped beneath his thigh. He cradled his left arm against his chest, then closed with the guard. He kicked away a low line thrust then buried the lower half of the bearded axehead into his foe's throat. The guard's life blood gushed forth and his eyes grew dim and staring, appearing remarkably canine. Dog's eyes.

The remaining minion waited at the top stair, just below the landing. A low growl sounded from his breast. Fulgin responded with a louder growl, venting the pain that radiated from his broken wrist. He sprang up the stairs, shifting to left or right randomly. At the last step he feinted left, then hopped to the right. The downward sword stroke fell wide, glancing first from the brim of Fulgin's helmet, then sparking from the quartz-flecked stone of the stair. Half blinded by the helmet abruptly tilting across his vision, Fulgin acted half-through honed instinct, half through remembered spatial relationships. He hooked the inner curve of his axehead behind the guard's ankle and pulled. Already off balance, the man teetered, throwing his arms wide. Fulgin threw his left shoulder into the guard's thighs. Keeping his feet would have asked too much from a trained acrobat. The guard tumbled, sprawling, the back of his helmet striking the door as he fell. Fulgin did not offer him a chance to recover, but chopped repeatedly into chest and abdomen, the axe crunching through mail accompanied by the tortured screams of bursting metal rings and a short-lived howl of pain from the guard.

His eyes too, glittering in the light of flickering torches, looked too large; like the hurt, uncomprehending eyes of a beaten dog. Fulgin the Grim felt no pity.

What foul deviltry had the black magician performed, Fulgin wondered. Were these dogs somehow transformed into men? Were they men infused with the souls of dogs? Drucar had sucked the vigour of youth from Fulgin and funnelled it into himself. Perhaps he could perform a similar transference for his minions employing animals. These men hadn't appeared to have aged. Perhaps they'd accepted — endured — transfusions of lifeforce from canine to man. Perhaps frequently repeated; after all dogs did not enjoy a man's lifespan. If so, at what cost had these men gained longevity? The cost of humanity? Of speech? A gradual replacement of a man's soul with the combined souls of beasts?

Fulgin the Grim took the baldric from the corpse. It was an awkward task, performed one-handed, like removing a rope from about a heavy, wet sack of grain. He slipped free the frogs attaching the scabbard, then hauled the baldric over his own head and fashioned a sling for his left arm. The action dislodged his helmet, revealing that the chinstrap had snapped at some point during the fracas. He crouched over the corpse, settling the dented kettle helmet over the unblinking face. Then he opened the pouch at the dead man's belt and retrieved a large iron key.

Leaving the bodies and his shield behind with the same indifference, Fulgin contemplated the door. A heavy door knocker in the form of a dragon's head looked back impassively. Stealth, he realized, no longer presented itself as an option. Silent Drucar's minions might have been. The fight had still produced a significant amount of noise. The household must be aware of his presence. The thought of knocking crossed his mind without leaving a trace of whimsy in passing. Fulgin the Grim had left mirth behind.

The lock yielded easily to the key. Fulgin lifted the door latch and pushed with his foot at the base of the thick panel of oak. The door swung noiselessly open.

The entry hall stood dim and quiet. Lights from the second floor — reachable by a grand stair at the end of the hall — offered scant illumination. Fulgin received the impression of luxury, of costly display, of doors past the stair and beneath the mezzanine that led to other, darkened parts of the manse.

Fulgin moved quickly across the polished wooden floor, keeping his teeth gritted against the pain that throbbed in his wrist, a pain that shifted into insignificance the sting of minor cuts and scrapes he'd incurred fighting Drucar's guardsmen.

A yowling hiss sounded as he set foot on the lowest step of the broad stairway. A woman, her youthful features disfigured by a teeth-baring snarl, emerged from the shadows beneath the mezzanine. She wore a white cap over her hair and a tight black shift, over which was tied a white apron. She threw herself at Fulgin. She struck at him with hands curled as if she possessed claws. With the fist gripping his axe Fulgin backhanded her, sending the woman sliding on her back across the slick surface of the floor. She did not rise.

There had been a time he would have refrained from striking a woman. Fulgin the Grim felt no remorse.

More servants appeared as Fulgin mounted the stairs, some coming from above, some from below. They did not coordinate their attacks, coming at him singly, or — perhaps coincidentally — in pairs. They hissed like cats or squealed like sows. Cooks, manservants, scullery maids. Not fighters. Fulgin did not bother employing the edge of the axe, content to strike them down with the haft or the weight of the flat. Whether the blows killed or merely stunned he did not much care.

Double doors awaited at the top of the stairs. More doors beckoned to either side. But from beneath the double doors emerged the warm, golden glow of innumerable candles and the odour of beeswax and sandalwood.

Fulgin's boot slammed into the join of the doors, sending each half slamming against the wall to either side. He paused only long enough to take in the scene.

At the far end of the room, upon a section of the floor raised a foot above the rest, stood Drucar the Blithe. About him glittered dozens of candles. A robe of midnight blue velvet was cinched about an expansive middle. Blond curls emerged from a close-fitting velvet cap, from which hung a jaunty pheasant's feather. He clutched a silver blade in one hand, though he wore a sword belted outside his robe. His other hand held a paintbrush, from the end of which poised a welling crimson drop. Fulgin could see a partially completed circle of incomprehensible design on the platform. The body of a midnight black cat, its throat slit, lay crumpled just outside the partial circle.

An array of padded, gaudily upholstered furniture cluttered the remainder of the room. The illumination cast by the candles on the floor was supplemented by tapers in tall silver candlesticks set at intervals around the floor and in the corners, as well as a chandelier depending from the high ceiling, in which glowed the steady light of a dozen lamps.

And reclining on her side upon a couch that filled a wide window niche, was Cortabella, propped up on one arm and watching.

Fulgin did not wait for Drucar to finish his conjuring circle. He doubted he could tackle a demon, even with two good hands. With a grunt he pushed himself into a sprint across the floor, dodging and leaping settees, chairs, and low side tables of gilded marble.

Drucar was backing out of the circle, even as Fulgin arrived — Fulgin scattering candles and grinding his bootheels across painted symbols, smearing the darkening, copper-smelling paint into the sigils carved into the floorboards.

"You," Drucar said, pressing his back against the wall. "I recall you. The years have not been kind." He laughed as he spoke, seemingly unconcerned.

Fulgin refrained from responding. Drucar appeared now a man in his fifties, as did Fulgin himself. But whereas Fulgin's age showed in the grey salting of his hair and the bristles on his square jaw, Drucar's showed in the droop of chin and a sallowness of skin. Where Fulgin stood erect, flat of stomach, Drucar stooped and his belly sagged. He had not taken the effort to maintain the vigour of his stolen youth. Doubtless he intended to simply repeat the process with some other luckless victim. Perhaps he'd done so many times. Who, besides Drucar, knew how old the black magician truly was?

Fulgin raised his axe. Drucar plucked a sealed vial from a pocket of his robe. He tugged loose the stopper, then drained the contents down his throat, jowls shifting as he gulped.

Drucar drew his blade, a splendid specimen of the sword maker's art; a broadsword with a pierced steel basket guard and a straight, two-foot length of gorgeously damascened steel. "There, armsman. You may have a bloody axe in hand — though it appears one hand is all you can rely on — but I have just imbibed the expertise of a dozen master swordsmen."

The uncharacteristic swell of the sword's oversized basket hilt allowed room for Drucar to execute an elaborate moulinet. The magician grinned, offered a mocking salute, and then attacked.

Fulgin gave ground. The speed of Drucar's onslaught caught him off guard. His calves encountered an obstacle and he went over. He toppled into a backwards somersault, his strapped-up arm directing him to the left. A renewed spike of pain ignited in his broken wrist. He rolled up again onto his feet as the magician's blade hacked into the stuffing that padded the stool he'd stumbled into. The flashing edge missed him by the slimmest of margins and scattered an explosion of horsehair. Fulgin sprang backwards and to one side, risking another collision in order to break the immediate threat of Drucar's relentless pursuit.

With the speed and deadliness of Drucar's magically assisted assault firmly fixed in his mind, Fulgin resumed steadily backing from the chamber, keenly aware now of the existence of furnishings barring his path. Should he collide with or trip over another piece again, Drucar would be upon him in an instant, either with edge or point. It was clear from

Drucar's footwork, from his shifting from high line to low line, from his balance, his rapid recoveries from thrusts and feints, and the care he took to avoid overextending himself that he had indeed absorbed the talents of an expert swordsman. The initial minute was fraught; Fulgin escaped lightning lunges and cuts coming from unexpected angles by hair's breadths. The scales of Fulgin's armour absorbed more than one blow, and a wickedly fast lunge passed through a gap in the layered protection of his kilt and pinked him above the left boot.

And all the while Drucar the Blithe quipped, jested and capered. Fulgin uttered not a syllable.

Then they passed out of the doors and onto the landing. Fulgin continued to retreat. He put on a burst of speed, though favouring the wounded leg. He backed rapidly down the stairs, maintaining a spacing that neutralized most of the advantage Drucar held attacking from above. Fulgin took care not to trip over the inert forms of Drucar's animal-souled servants, feeling with the heel of each boot before committing to a footstep.

Then onto the ground floor. Fulgin could hear Drucar's breathing. It became increasingly audible. As Fulgin back-pedalled in a wide turn about the entry floor, the black magician's breathing grew laboured. By the time they'd twice circumambulated the floor Drucar was panting. By the third he was wheezing and his attacks and gambits became infrequent.

"Wait. Sir, wait, I beg of you." Drucar stepped back out of axe range, bending at the waist, off hand resting on his hip. "Killing me will not return your youth. It is far too late to sever the link. Your stolen lifeforce has been consumed. There is none of it left to recover."

Fulgin the Grim said nothing. It was his turn to advance. He came on as inexorably as time.

Drucar gave ground, forming a dancing, expert defensive

pattern with his blade that deflected each of Fulgin's attacks. But the effort it cost the magician was evident, and each escape was a nearer thing than the last. At last he caught a heel on a maid still lying senseless, and fell backwards. He raised his sword and held his free hand up, palm out.

"No. Stop. I can...I can return your youth. Take it from another. Only spare me."

Fulgin the Grim sank his axe into Drucar's leg. The black magician screamed, dropping his sword and clutched at the spurting gash with both hands. Fulgin took his head with the next stroke.

Upstairs Cortabella remained upon the divan, waiting.

Close up, Fulgin could see beneath layers of paint and powder the contours of the face he remembered. The blush of her beauty had long since faded. She did not rise to greet him. No smile of welcome, or relief, or pleasure touched her artificially reddened mouth.

Cortabella frowned at him, crow's feet etching the corners of her eyes.

"You. Why did you have to return?" she asked, her voice bitter and accusing.

"Cortabella," Fulgin said, "I returned for you."

"Well, I didn't ask you to. Did you fail to notice this manse? Not a cottage, this. Didn't you see the grounds, the tilled lands, the vineyard? The rich furnishings. The servants. I am a lady. Lady Cortabella."

"You were my wife."

"The wife of a penniless armsman. Drucar gave me something more. And he loved me, in his way. What could you ever give me?"

Fulgin stared down at her, feeling the pain in his wrist intensely. He would need to splint it soon. Yet his face revealed nothing.

At length he spoke. "I can give you your life. I can even leave you this manse, instead of burning it to the ground. Perhaps the wealth it represents will be sufficient for you to attract a new, younger paramour. Some tangible benefit will be necessary, I fear. For, alas," said Fulgin the Grim, tilting his head and squinting his eyes in critical appraisal, "the years have not been kind to you."

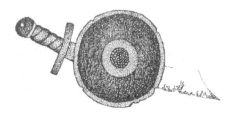

SNOW IN KADHAL
Jaap Boekestein

It snowed in the desert city of Kadhal. Instead of the nightly warm rains the city of the Weeping God was assaulted night and day by thick blankets of snowflakes, storms of rock-hard hails and floods of biting ice-rain. During the days the sky was grey and cloudy, and when the sun broke through, it had far too little power to restore the usual dry heat.

The Kadhalese suffered the natural phenomenon with infinite bad temper and plenty of complaining. Public wells needed to be cut open daily, the flat roofs of the city had to be cleaned of the thick layers of snow. Some had already collapsed. Kadhal's citizens dressed in all the clothes they owned and still were miserable. Several had frozen to death in their unheated houses. Coal was expensive, fur was priceless, heat was a scarce commodity. The citizens of Kadhal were unhappy, moody and little inclined to have fun. Most of them, anyway.

The laughter of the children blared triumphantly through the street.

"Kad's balls!" Mayl screamed furiously. "May piss run from your nostrils!" She waved her fists furiously – and completely in vain – at the young boys who laughed at her from a safe distance. Her lengthy blond hair and fair skin made the fire dancer a natural goal for the latest form of terror in the streets of the Imperial Capital: throwing snowballs. One of the cold projectiles had hit her knitted hat, three her dress and one, a master's throw, had landed right in the ever so lightly exposed curve of her neck. Of course the flakes melted immediately, and they glided down with icy fingers under her bodice, both at the front and the back!

Still cursing, Mayl entered The Shaved Monkey. It was busy in the pub. The cold drove the citizens off the street and out of their houses. Pubs weren't heated either, but a mass of warm bodies made life a little more bearable. The smell in the pub was almost palpable: a mixture of human bodies, beer and brandy, cooking smells, the smoke from pipes and the few oil lamps. After some scrutiny Mayl discovered her half-sisters Asca and Mayl standing in a corner, sipping their brandy. Their common father Visal Twentyfingers had a wide taste in wives and thus his three daughters were as different as night, day and the time in between. Dark-haired Asca was the eldest, and she danced with swords, just like her mother. Mayl's mother had been from the barbaric north where the people were pale, blonde and blue-eyed. Mayl had learned the fire dances from her mother. The youngest, and smallest, was Cyrel with reddish hair, a nasty streak and a taste for bad men. She danced with the snake she had inherited from her mother.

"You look flustered, had a lovely snow kiss?" Cyrel taunted Mayl.

"When we're outside, I'll show you, you evil dwarf!" Mayl's mood was bad. Mother had often told her about the blizzards and ice fields of her homeland. In those stories it all seemed wonderful. Cruel perhaps, but with a wonderful quality. But fancy stories were no more but fancy stories. Snow and ice were not beautiful at all. They were cold, uncomfortable and treacherous.

"Stop!" ordered Asca, without having to think about it.

Some things never changed. Making sure her younger siblings didn't end up clawing each other's eyes out was a daily task. Why was she the only one with some common sense? Mayl was a dreamer and Cyrel was just nasty. *It's always up to me we earn some coin and not blow it all on booze, men and dresses.* Asca asked: "Mayl, did you bring the lute?"

"What do you think this is? A bag of tubers?" Fortunately, the snowballs had missed the embroidered velvet bag with the lute.

"Do we really have to go all the way to The Twelve? That tavern is at the other end of the city, all the way through the cold!" Cyrel complained. "I'd much rather stay here."

"Do that, and Mayl and I will split the dance money together. Or do you have a gig around here?"

Cyrel didn't answer. At this moment, dance jobs were scarce. And what was available yielded very little. Cold weather made the people miserable and frugal. It was that Asca had arranged a dance at some veteran's party, otherwise it would have been tight with the pennies this week. "I'll go with you," Cyrel said after a short heartbeat. "But The Twelve is a boring place and far away too!"

Asca didn't reply. Every pub without sell-swords, fights or gambling were boring, according to Cyrel. The Twelve lay outside the Ninth District and wasn't frequented by camel drivers or bravados.

"Can't we take a cab?" suggested Mayl. "A carriage is better than walking."

"That will cost us almost everything we'll earn tonight. Maybe for the way back, if the tipping is really good."

"Hmpf!" was Mayl's answer. It sounded she had to venture out into the cold again. *Kad's balls.*

"Hmpf!" Cyrel agreed.

*

Magic, snow and ice. It provided a breeding ground for apparitions that usually were too weak to come alive in the desert city of the Weeping God. Until now. Until someone called them...

The room was small and crowded, an insignificant temple hidden in the impenetrable heart of a slum. A dozen figures knelt before a throne of blankets and pillows where an ancient bald male sat with a head that looked the most like a walnut. The fat eyelids, flat nose and iron-grey skin of the priest betrayed that he was born far away to the north and east, on the mysterious, icy plateau of Kesbo where ice-demons devoured imprudent souls and magicians could shake the mountains. The tapestries carried the effigies of the terrible gods of Kesbo. There was Dhurrhan the Eater with his bright red skin and green tusks; there was the Bittermaiden whose beloved weapon was poison and for whom the marrow and the brains of the dead were a delicacy; and Iniiaka, the veiled snake that ate the sun every night and gave birth to the moon.

The believers murmured in trance, a monotonous sound reminiscent of cold strangling winds, deadly ice fog and freezing blood. The priest raised his bare, sticky arms. "O Father Dhurrhan, o Mother Bittermaiden, o Aunt Iniiaka, your children beg you! Your children are begging you! Help us carry out our revenge!"

The grey sky above Kadhal stirred and it started to snow harder.

*

"Kad! I hope it's warmer inside the tavern than outside!" Mayl's teeth clattered and she could no longer feel her nose and ears. She wiped the snowflakes from her eyes with her bloodless fingers.

"It must be, colder isn't possible!" Asca remarked as she adjusted her bag with dance gear and her flute. The Twelve was a two-storey tavern with shutters painted cheerfully red and white. There was real glass in the windows, and through the small squares – held in place by strips of lead – shone inviting lights. Snow was accumulated in the corners.

Cyrel said nothing but hurried to the door. She carried her snake Sjli with her, tucked away under her coat and bodice, but she worried. Sjli couldn't stand the cold at all. Before she went inside, she shook the snow from her hat, annoyed.

Asca and Mayl didn't hesitate half a beat and followed Cyrel inside.

The snow stopped falling.

*

Almost thirty years ago the platoon of soldiers climbed the rocky slope that led to the shrine. Although the stones were cold and slippery due to the inevitable ice, no man fell and no sound was heard. These were Runter's Men, the special unit of the Fourth Army Corps that was used for the most dangerous missions, the most difficult raids. However, there was no mission tonight. Officially, they were three valleys away, in their encampment. They weren't at all in the vicinity of the Temple of the Seven Winds. If the holy place was to be plundered, it certainly would be robbers, although no Kesbonese robber had dared to steal from a priest since times immemorial. After all, who dared to harass their merciless and very vindictive masters? Only unbelievers would be so stupid.

The Kadhalese climbed over the wall without being noticed. There were no guard posts. Why would there be guard posts?

The first one to die was a bald-shaven novice who was on his way to refill the lamps in the chapel with a jug of oil butter. His throat was cut skilfully. The jug didn't even get the chance to fall and break. More deaths followed. Of course there were shouts, of course there was fighting, such was inevitable. But the shouting was quickly silenced and the fights were short. There were no deaths among the Kadhalese.

Loaded with gold, silver and loose gems, Runter's Men returned to their camp in a forced march. A week later they were ordered to break up and leave. The Fourth Army Corps was needed to fight an uprising in the Noquies provinces. The Empire left the icy highlands of Kesbo and wouldn't return during the reign of the next few emperors.

*

They came from far, but they came. Full of hatred, full of malice, wanting revenge. The Hungry Father, the Bitter Mother, Aunt Beast. They looked down on the building that was the focus of their wrath. It was destined that the twenty-nine remaining men were gathered in one place. Gods didn't make plans, they made realities.

Dhurrhan the Eater opened his teeth-filled mouth and with his breath, he froze every window and every door shut. Escape was now impossible.

The Bittermaiden shook her terrible hair and waved her skirts. A storm wind surrounded the tavern. No living could still approach the building.

Iniiaka rolled around the tavern, tighter and tighter and

tighter. The coldness of her blood penetrated every crack, slid with thousands of groping feelers along walls and shadows.

On the back of the unusual weather the gods of Kesbo had arrived in Kadhal.

*

"They're all old geezers," Cyrel grumbled as they changed into their costumes.

"Veterans with money are always old," Asca replied. "Young guys spend their money more easily."

The three sisters chuckled that memory. Their breath was clouded.

"In the main room it really must be warmer! My fingers are freezing off!" Cyrel continued.

"They aren't really looking at our fingers." Asca put a shawl around her shoulders even though it wasn't really part of her costume. But it was also so cold! Even inside.

"I don't care. I only hope they have a fire."

"Ha! We will heat their blood!"

"But *I* want to be warm!"

"Don't complain! You both have still some covering left!" Mayl objected. "I'm there in my dance costume!" By now she was completely dressed and covered with the special, secret paste of her late mother. But her fair skin was one and all goose bumps and she had put a blanket around her shoulders to stay warm. It hardly helped. The cold seemed to go right through everything. For the very first time she did her fire dance, Mayl regretted that she didn't feel the warmth of the flames. The paste and her inherited magic disposition prevented such, but it would be very welcome right now. "Hurry up! I want to start as soon as possible!"

"I am already done. Almost." Asca adjusted the lute. She turned a string and tried the instrument again.

"I'll keep Sjli with me!" Cyrel's statement was a mix of concern and challenge. Woe to the one who said she had to abandon Sjli! "It is too cold to leave him behind. He hardly moves."

"Some advantage of this damned cold," Mayl murmured, so softly that Cyrel couldn't hear her. A quarrel right now would only mean that it would take longer to start her dance. Her teeth were chattering and she stamped her feet. Kad, the cold was terrible!

Asca said nothing at all. As long as Cyrel kept up with her flute, she could wear Sjli as headdress for all she cared.

"Hurry up!" Mayl cried out. "I'm freezing!"

"Yes. Yes."

"Yeeeeesss!"

"Well, come on then!"

*

The worshippers in the underground temple rocked back and forth. The priest shook and bowed again and again. They knew that their supplication had been answered. They knew that the Hungry Father, the Bitter Mother and Aunt Beast had come to take revenge.

Deep in their frightened hearts, they hoped that there was enough blood to satisfy the hunger of the gods. Otherwise, that hunger would be satisfied with their own lives.

Calling gods was always dangerous.

*

"Yee! Yee! "

Swirling, dancing, waving her torches, Mayl came up. Her arrival was received with joy in the banqueting hall. In a corner Asca and Cyrel played the lute and the flute. All the lights in the room were extinguished so that Mayl could shine all the better.

It was clear that the men had left their soldier's days a while ago. Hanging cheeks and bellies, grey hair. Once soldiers, now affluent citizens with well-running affairs or annual fees, caring women at home, children and grand-children, servants. Not every soldier ended with missing limbs as a street vendor or doorkeeper. Some had good money left from their service in barbarian regions. Especially Runter's Men! Their bowls and plates were filled with roasts, the glasses and mugs brimmed with wine and brandy, and in the centre of the room an exotic young girl danced, reminiscent of glory days long ago and far away.

*

The cold sneaked through the tavern as a master assassin. It penetrated loam and stone, wood and dust. Slow, unnoticeable, unstoppable. Iniiaka squeezed the life out of everything she encountered. Small at first: lice, cockroaches, scorpions and other vermin, but gradually bigger: the mice in the walls and under the floors, and then the rats in the cellar. Sliding, strangling, nothing escaped his grip.

The Bittermaiden stroked her fingers through cracks and crevices, found roads and openings and squeezed lamps. The robe of the Bittermaiden was Darkness.

Dhurrhan the Eater devoured. He devoured every dead-frozen life. Small first, but gradually bigger. They were small snacks, appetizers. The main meal was yet to come.

*

The believers and the priest grinned. Their hearts filled with fierce joy. Revenge was near.

*

Mayl shivered and danced. She spat fire, letting flames lick her legs, belly and arms, but she only felt the cold. The floor sucked the heat from her feet and legs, the air was syrupy and seemed filled with countless – and invisible – of the smallest needles that could be imagined. Cold! Such a coldness! Mayl started dancing faster, trying to evoke some warmth.

Asca squeezed her eyes tightly several times to stay awake. Her fingers slid effortlessly over the strings of the lute, but they seemed to be separated from the rest of her body. She felt a lazy buzz about her, which was almost impossible to fight. It was also dark in the room, just like the night. Crazy, she didn't feel the cold anymore. It was really pretty pleasant...

Without losing her tune, Cyrel shifted once more. Her buttocks felt like stone loaves! Under her shirt Sjli moved against her belly. The serpent seemed agitated, as if sensing prey, or an enemy. Once in a pub a dog had attacked Sjli. It had been a rat-biter that was used in the fighting pits. The owner of the mongrel hadn't wanted to curb his dog, and Cyrel had finally stopped the mutt with a blow from a jug. Luckily that night she was in the company of a professional wrestler. It all ended in a fierce fight, but Sjli and she had gotten away undamaged.

Cyrel looked around. Was there a dog or cat somewhere that Sjli was so excited about? Kad! When they were done here she would sit on a hot griddle until she had feeling back in her behind again!

The audience looked attentively at Mayl – no wonder, the old men they were. Moreover, there was little else to see in the dark room – but the cold also had them in the grip. Their breath was white, their coats buttoned up, their hats pulled down deep, scarves and headscarves to close the last gaps. Like the mummies of forgotten rulers of yesteryear they were sitting at the banquet table, only the eyes, nose and mouth free. The rest wrapped up, wrapped around like mummies. Frozen mummies.

*

The gods of Kesbo knew no joy, only satisfaction. And the expectation of satisfaction.

The Hungry Father, the Bitter Mother, Aunt Beast knew it wouldn't be long now. The souls of the temple scouts waited. The feast would soon begin.

*

Mayl's teeth chattered and she tried not to shiver. *Cooooooold!* It was an incredible cold, a bitter cold, a burning cold. How could mother have lived in a country where it always was like that? Mayl's dance with the torches was over. It was a spectacular sight and usually warmed her up. Not this time. All the warmth was immediately sucked out of her bones by the cold draft in the hall. *Like the caresses of a corpse*, shot through Mayl's head and she shuddered at that thought. *Where did that come from? No time for stories. Concentrate on the dance!*

The men at the table were quiet, they knew more would

come. There was a deadly silence, the silence of a tomb, throughout the whole tavern. Snow in the corners made no sound. Ice in the water jugs didn't make any noise. Dead creatures in holes and corners made no sound. Lost souls made no sound.

It's time. Mayl nodded to her two sisters. She was ready for the finale, the dance for which she was famous. The dance she had learned from her mother and which only she could perform throughout Kadhal, or maybe even the empire. Her fire dance.

The flute cut sharply, fragile through the silent tomb – *Tomb? Room! Room! A dark room, that is…* – and Mayl took the first steps.

Where is Asca? The lute was silent. The flute alone carried the melody. From the corner of her eye, Mayl saw how Cyrel gave Asca a firm poke. She was sleeping! The stupid wench was sleeping!

With a shock Asca woke up and a few seconds later the sound of lute added to the flute.

Relieved, Mayl continued her dance and clapped her hands in rhythm.

As was intended, the spectators joined in. Slowly, because Mayl danced slowly. For now.

*

The priest and the believers rocked back and forth in the same enchanting rhythm, as the snow fell silently. Voices roamed from high to low, like the howling, freezing winds that swept between the mountains of the distant Kesbo.

Slow, slow, slow. Slower and slower. Insidious, smothering, killing. The revenge that came all the way from the highlands was bitter and cold, dark as the endless night that waited at the end of time.

Slow, slow, slow. Slower and slower.

*

Mayl's mother was called Snayl and once she was the youngest fire dancer at the court of the king of Rhunney. There were intrigues, an old king whose position would weaken when his holy fire dancer disappeared, there were greedy foreign traders who thought they could get gold in far Kadhal for the king's fire dancer. There was fear of killing the fire dancer. She was holy. No, you couldn't kill or harm the king's fire dancer. Especially not if she would fetch good money in faraway Kadhal. Such was Snayl's fate, mother of Mayl. Oh, and there was a thief in Kadhal who freed her and took her in, but that was another story altogether.

Rhunney, land of ice and fire, wrapped in eternal struggle with itself. Awesome ice walls moved ever closer to crush it, to suffocate. But the fires from the underground deeps, the liquid rock and boiling water sources held back the ice and cold. And the fire dancers steered those hot subterrain veins, they called and seduced the molten stone, the power of fire. That's why they were holy.

What did Rhunney, land of fire and ice, have to do with the mysterious plateau of Kesbo? Nothing. They were far apart and shared no history, no language, no faith, nothing.

Except the ice and the snow of course.

*

"Yee, yee!" Mayl danced the ritual steps she had learned from her mother. Everything was as it should be. One misstep and the dance wouldn't work, or worse, the dance would work but her protection would be insufficient. Mayl could vividly remember the painful lessons of her mother. Fire blisters for every mistake. She didn't make mistakes with her dance anymore. "Yee, yee!" Slowly, but always a little less slow, Mayl danced. Every step, every turn just a little bit faster.

The focus of all life in the tavern was Mayl. She was a flower, she was the sun, she was warmth, she was alive. Lute and flute played, the men clapped. Faster and a little bit faster every time.

*

A shiver, an unrest, a dissonance felt by the worshipers of the gods of Kesbo. The rhythm faltered and for a moment the rocking accelerated, the murmur of the believers became uncertain.

The ancient priest snarled and reassured the worshipers. Nothing could stand in the way of revenge on the robbers! Nothing could stand in the way of revenge!

The worshippers doubled their efforts to overcome this unexpected hurdle.

*

Iniiaka the snake hissed, the Bittermaiden with her deadly fingers and skirts of darkness hissed, Dhurrhan the Eater with red skin and green teeth hissed. In Kesbo they would have wiped out the shameless opposition and let the soul of the witch suffer an eternity. This, however, was Kadhal, city of the Weeping God Kad, city of heat and dust. Here the gods of Kesbo had to fight to make their will a reality.

And they fought.

*

Step by step Mayl danced faster, every step a little, little bit quicker. There was only the music, the dance, the rhythm.

Faster, faster.

She followed the rhythm, the rhythm followed her. Subtle magic lured the almost frozen veterans back to life. The men clapped. Rime hung from beards and moustaches, ice covered the drinks, the roasts had frozen on the plates and dishes. They clapped as if their lives depended on it.

Sweat droplets immediately turned into small, white ice beads that bounced away. Mayl danced, but it didn't work. She followed the rituals, she seduced, she lured, but the warmth didn't come. The smouldering fire that normally grew in her with every pass she made, didn't want to come.

It wasn't possible, but it became even colder. The air itself seemed to freeze.

*

The priest and the faithful hardly moved anymore. Their voices were frozen together to an almost inaudible hum. They knew what was at stake: their revenge.

*

Mayl moaned. It became almost painful to move. With every step she took, the floor seemed to bite at her feet, with every movement she made, eternal ice winds were caressing her skin. Her eyes were almost closed.

I have to dance.

She no longer heard any sound, nor music, nor clapping, nor cheering. Maybe there was nothing more to hear. She saw nothing more, only darkness surrounding her. Darkness and the cold.

*

"Mine," said Iniiaka the snake, as gods spoke. She wanted to crush the insignificant mortal.

"Mine," demanded the Bittermaiden. She wanted to strangle the life out of the dancer with her cold fingers.

"Mine," Dhurrhan the Eater ordered, and that was that. He was the Father. He would devour the fire witch with skin and hair. Her bones crunching between his teeth, crushing her soul between his molars until there wasn't even a memory left of her.

*

Once started, an avalanche can't be stopped. A thunderstorm begins with the first raindrop, a blazing fire is born from one spark.

Step. Step. Mayl didn't even know if she actually danced. She floated in darkness, independent of everything that had to do with life. She had to... She would...

Step. Step. Step.

The first part of the dance was completed, the ancient fire ritual had reached its peak.

Mayl caught fire.

The fire embraced her, waved around her, played over her body, her hair, her clothes. It was heat, it was life, it was light.

Screams of surprise and fright were heard among the spectators – Suddenly full of life, as the hall suddenly bathed in light.

Mayl smiled, swirled around. The flames couldn't harm her. With the dance she could call up the flames and during the dance the flames were her friend. As long as she danced.

*

The three gods from far screamed, battered, burned. Their hold on power was broken, but their goal wasn't broken. They were summoned for revenge and revenge would be carried out.

The cruel gods of Kesbo were not picky.

*

The ancient priest didn't get the chance to scream, nor did his followers. The intense coldness ripped open his heart, shattered him, devoured him. The same happened with his followers.

In human terms it took a moment. Measured by the rhythms of the soul and suffering it took forever. Then everything was over.

The three gods disappeared from Kadhal. Their task accomplished.

*

While pennies and even thalers bounced across the floor, Mayl finished her dance. Managing the flames had to be done carefully. Fire was wild, playful, greedy. Given a chance it would escape and devour. Fire had to be kept on a leash. Carefully Mayl continued and little by little the flames on her body became smaller and smaller.

For the first time in many weeks she felt warm inside.

*

That night it rained in Kadhal. It was a warm rain.

The next morning ice and snow had gone from the city of the Weeping God.

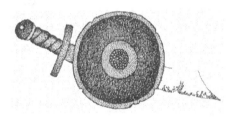

VOYAGE TO VANCIENNE
Gavin Chappell

Fit the First: Across the Glass Desert

It stretched as far as the horizon, an endless field of powdered diamonds, a vast expanse of glittering dust that winked malevolently in the sun's pitiless gaze. The air shimmered in the baking heat, nothing moved beneath the blazing heavens. Not a breath of wind stirred the sparkling grit, nor did even a vulture circle in the endless azure heavens—Death himself had forsaken this barren waste. All that broke up the monotony was the dusty road winding its way across the hostile desert. Along it, two mounted figures rode in weary silence.

Their steeds, strange and ungainly, were flightless birds with feathers of scarlet and jade and amber, plumage more fitting for some lush jungle than this ceaseless vastness of glass and quartz. The mounts trotted in cumbersome fashion, clawed feet kicking up pulverized crystal which hung in the hot air a few seconds before settling in glittering heaps.

One of the riders was a woman, young and stern, who sweltered in a byrnie of browned iron with breast and backplates, while a war-hammer hung heavily from her saddle. Beneath her morion, her severe face was set in an exasperated expression. Her name was Elenara Moonstar, and she had once flown on the back of a hippogriff, high above the world in the sky's icy embrace. Now her gut roiled with the jarring of the avian's clumsy canter, and her brow was dewed with sweat. An oath formed itself upon her lips.

Her companion, a slender man of perhaps thirty summers, wore a shabby hooded cloak and rode with an offhand ease that seemed at odds with the first rider's rigid posture. His name was Talon, by some called the Cutthroat, by others the Rogue. A long, sharply honed dagger hung at his side. He grinned as their mounts kept up a constant stream of inane twittering, a cheeping, trilling parody of human speech.

"I'm a birdie! Birdie-birdie-birdie! I'm a birdie! Wow!"

Their voices were high and shrill; the song went on intolerably as the two travellers trotted across the Glass Desert.

Elenara's lips a cold line, she turned her ice blue eyes on Talon, and addressed him. "When we set forth from the Holy Lawberg, we rode unicorns caparisoned in cloth-of-gold. Lord Zennor himself presented us with our mounts in token of his esteem, since we rode on such a parlous quest. And yet now we sit astride these mangy avians, subjected to an endless song too absurd to reiterate. Tell me again why I am subjected to such indignity."

Talon chuckled leniently, as if at the petulant whining of a sulky child. "Everyone knows that these birds parrot men, Elenara, much as parrots do themselves. Doubtless our feathered steeds were taught their song by the children of that merchant we met at the last oasis." He looked unusually grave. "Diseases lurk in this desert that will strike dead the most noble unicorn as fast as the mangiest nag. These birds," he thumped the side of his own mount affectionately as he spoke, stirring up a cloud of gleaming powder, "are somehow immune. I sold the unicorns for a fair price and bought these avians with the proceeds of the sale."

Elenara Moonstar gritted her teeth and seized the reins tightly. Casting her gaze skyward, she considered how far she had fallen since those days—not so long ago!—when she had flown at liberty upon her hippogriff. "Cursed is this land," she murmured. "The sun scorches us, the air itself emanates death—and yet you laugh."

Talon shrugged. "Laugh, or go insane, I suppose."

"Birdie-birdie-birdie," Elenara's mount trilled maddeningly.

"Let us halt, at least," said Elenara, her voice breaking. "I weary of this infernal warbling."

Talon was riding in the forefront. "Very well," he said, sawing at the reins. As soon as the bird jogged to a halt, he dismounted, tethering it by burying one end of the reins under a glassy rock. Elenara imitated him, staggering as she leapt down, such was her discomfort. Her sinews ached, her proud posture was bowed from long hours in the saddle. She stretched, rubbing at her back and hams beneath her mail. Her scorn-filled eyes did not leave Talon, who had taken out his long dagger and was sharpening it with a hone. Perched on a glassy rock he looked insouciantly into the distance, as if fascinated by the glittering immensity.

"You must be sore after all yon riding," he commented, concentrating on his blade.

Without making a reply, Elenara filled a cup from her waterskin. She sipped primly, her face blank, though inside she burned with loathing both for the wasteland and for her seemingly oblivious companion, who seemed so at ease.

"Don't you mean to drink?" asked Elenara, half in accusation.

Talon shook his head and sheathed his sharpened

blade. "I wet my lips at the oasis. It's not long before we reach the caravanserai at the Wells of Kubasek. Water is worth more than gold dust in the Glass Desert."

Elenara Moonstar recalled the rain whipped skies, the powerful wings of her noble, feathered mount, and snorted. "Ere I joined this quest, I flew over such barren, fruitless wilds without a qualm. Would that my hippogriff yet lived."

She poured some water into her cupped hand and held it out to her mount. The bird dipped its beak in greedily, tilted its head back in an awkward fashion to swallow, then resumed its irritating song.

Talon's mount joined in enthusiastically: "Birdie-birdie-birdie! I'm a birdie, wow!"

"Silence!" Elenara thundered, two spots of red appearing in her cheeks. For an instant, peace reigned over the shimmering desert, until it was broken by a resentful, "I'm a birdie!" from Elenara's mount.

Talon chuckled as he swung himself back up onto his avian. "If you're rested, I suggest we ride."

Elenara scowled, but unwilling to be abandoned in this dead place, untethered her own creature. They rode together in awkward silence, the desert stretching interminably before them.

*

Shades of night were pooling amongst the crystal boulders. The day's savage heat had yielded to a bitter chill that froze their marrows. Elenara's spirits had lifted as the lesser moon shone on a distant grove of thenar trees whose black silhouettes marked the site of the caravanserai. At last they would be able to rest and refresh themselves after a hard day's journey.

The desert wind brought a waft of cooking meat and a catch of singing voices. Yellow lanternlight spilled out into the darkness as they trotted through the open gateway. Slaves hurried forward, taking the reins of the avians, and Talon went to bespeak them rooms. Elenara flung the slaves a couple of gold coins, then as they led the mounts away walked stiffly into the cool interior of the white walled building. Fountains played soothingly in the middle of a courtyard. The idol of a horned goddess sat in one corner, incense smoking before it, but unusually Elenara made no obeisance. She wanted nothing but rest.

Talon rejoined her and they were ushered into the dining chamber, where groups of travellers feasted beneath a vaulted roof. A slave girl asked them their desire, and Elenara requested an herb salad, Talon a roast yak haunch.

"Wine can be purchased from the tapster," the girl added pertly, and Talon vanished into the taproom. Elenara sat at their table in demure silence, watching as pilgrims, clad in long red robes embroidered with strange patterns, clustered around a big templar, a hearty companion who kept the pilgrims entertained with merry badinage and a fund of comic anecdotes.

Elenara yearned to be one of that ebullient company, though she feared she would blush and stammer at the templar's bawdy jests.

The slave girl appeared with food, but Talon had not yet returned. Frowning, Elenara arose, leaving her frugal meal untasted. In the taproom, she found Talon quaffing wine and laughing with a villainous looking crew as he rolled dice on a pitted tabletop. Catching her frosty glare, he groaned, pocketed his winning, and rose regretfully to his feet.

The gamblers guffawed. "Ye be in trouble, shipmate!" one bellowed. "Be that the wife?"

Fit the Second: Templars and Pilgrims

Elenara had scarcely stepped back into the dining chamber when Talon reeled after her, his clattering bootsteps breaking into the hum of conversation. In one hand he held a wine flagon, in the other, two cups threatened to slosh their contents across the reed strewn floor. The patrons turned to watch his progress with sardonic amusement at his unsteady gait.

"Elenara, I can explain!" he called, breathing heavily.

She halted midstride in the archway, a pale eyebrow lifted as she turned purposefully. Her smile was a death's head rictus. "Explain?" she inquired, with seeming light-heartedness. "Why, what's there to explain? You're disgustingly drunk, that's all."

Talon struggled to suppress a belch. "Not a bit of i'," he protested, his face flushed red. "I've not even finished my second cup."

"You were supposed to be fetching our drinks," she replied with a hard edge to her voice. "Yet I find you gaming with brigands and drinking yourself into a stupor."

Talon hung his head. Some distant cousin of shame flitted across his face, but it was swiftly followed by feigned nonchalance. "A kind man invited me to his dice game," he said, giving an awkward shrug. "I could hardly refuse his hospitality, now could I? It would have been very rude!"

She gave a long, exasperated sigh and returned to their table. The templars and pilgrims were no longer watching them, and now their laughter drifted away into the low murmur of the chamber.

Talon set down the carafe with a casual flourish, spilling wine on the roughhewn table as he filled their cups. "Some of those men are seamen," he added, sitting down.

"They're on their way to take up berths rowing a wing-ship bound for Vancienne. With a little luck, we might..."

Elenara's eyes became malevolent slits. "Where did you get the money?" she asked, voice as cold and steady as an unsheathed blade.

"What was that, by Zorn?" asked Talon, but his words were drowned out by a roar of laughter from the pilgrims.

"You heard what I said," she replied as the laughter died away, her voice hard. "Where did you acquire the gold?"

His fingers twitched as they curled round the cup, but he forced a carefree smile as he set the drink to his lips. With a shrug, he said, "A little luck at dice."

Her hand flashed out before he could take another sip. She seized him by his tunic collar, pulled him closer with a strength that belied her slender, girlish physique. The distinctive chink-chink of gold drew her attention. Elenara's lips compressed to a thin white line and she slipped a hand inside his cloak, bringing out a weighty purse that bulged with much more coin than could be gleaned from a brief dice game. Snapping it open, she gazed wide eyed at the gleam of gold within.

Talon's grin faltered. "My winnings," he said, his tone bland, but his eyes those of a cornered rat seeking a bolt hole.

She tossed the purse onto the tabletop, and as it landed with a heavy thud she crossed her arms, regarding him as balefully as any basilisk. "You had no money when we set forth from the Lawberg. How came you by this gold?"

He shrugged, picking a little at the roast yak haunch on his trencher. "I'm a man who knows how to make a little money."

Her eyes narrowed. "Did you steal it?"

"Has anyone reported a robbery?" he countered, snatching a swig of wine.

Curtly Elenara halted a slave girl as she passed. "Has anyone cried theft of a purse of gold?" she asked.

The slave girl shook her head. "No, ma'am, no thefts have been reported."

Talon grinned. "You have an exceptionally suspicious mind. You should trust me a little."

"You sold our unicorns," she spat. "And traded them for those miserable birds. What became of the rest of the gold?" She pointed at the purse. "That!" she said savagely. "That's what happened to it."

Caught out, Talon scowled. "Oh, very well," he said with a resentful shrug. "So I made a profit on the deal. What of it? I know how to make coin. If you'd not spent all your time in castles in the sky and riding hippogriffs..."

"Those unicorns were the property of Lord Zennor," she said haughtily. "Any money left over from the sale should have gone to me, as his envoy. You're a thief. A thief and a fraud and a cheat."

Talon's grin grew colder. "But that's why you dragged me into this! Because I'm...." he gave a low, dirty laugh, "...evil."

The words struck deep. The silence that fell between them was pregnant with unspoken truths.

Memories flashed through her mind, images she couldn't suppress—her return from the blighted world of Ebonvale, clinging to her dying hippogriff as the black sun blazed. Her once noble companions twisted into grotesque parodies of themselves, faces warped by darkness, majestic steeds transformed into manticores.

The words she had spoken to the councillors of the Lawberg drifted back into her thoughts. *"Evil cannot be fought, for those who fight evil can do so only by committing evil acts themselves. By fighting Evil, we join its ranks."*

Lord Zennor's cold yet kindly gaze had seared itself into her mind. *"If what you say is true, child,"* he had wheezed, *"we have no defence against the Dark Ones. Our every endeavour will be futile."*

Lord Zennor's words had still haunted Elenara when she discovered Talon in the catacombs beneath the Lawberg, fighting a losing struggle with an arachnid monstrosity. She had slain the distracted creature with a single blow of her war hammer, and dragged Talon to face justice for his tomb robbing.

She could still hear the cold authority in Lord Zennor's voice as he addressed Talon. *"We need evil to fight Evil. We have chosen you as our assassin. You will travel through the dimensions to the world of the Sons of Darkness, there to gain access to the halls of the King of Darkness. You will slay him…*

"A geas has been cast upon you—a sorcerous compulsion. You must fulfil this quest, Talon, or die in the attempt. You are bound by forces greater than your will…"

Talon had laughed, but Elenara had seen the fear in his eyes. He knew as well as she did that his geas could not be escaped. Absently, her hands brushed the amulet at her neck…

Her attention was drawn by the raucous laughter of the pilgrims. A large man, broad shouldered and clad in the mail of a templar—the one who had so entertained his companions earlier—rose from his seat and, to her surprise, sauntered over.

"A paladin, by Ti," he said, with a guffaw. "What brings one of your kind to this out of the way spot?"

Elenara met his eyes, her composure unshaken. "A small matter of business," she replied with a quiet smile.

"And you, templar? You are on pilgrimage?"

A broad, brawny man, his strong face was burnt brown by outland suns. Two clear brown eyes blazed in a solemn face framed by black hair cut into bangs. His stern mouth was graced by a long, drooping moustache. There was a cruel, sardonic twist to his lips.

"Corvalan, of the temple of Ti. I am escorting these pilgrims to the holy city of Vancienne, and the temple there. A dangerous journey. Plagued by brigands and worse."

"By a strange coincidence, our journey will take us to Vancienne and beyond," said Elenara. "My companion and I are journeying to the Lap o' the Gods. This is my guide, a common man of the streets named Talon."

"Will he be able to guide you across the Sea of Many Islands?" Corvalan asked Elenara. "Or indeed over the crags of the troglodytes? Listen to me, my lady," he added, placing a gauntleted hand on her mail clad forearm, "it is my duty to protect those in need. May I invite you to join our party?"

Talon glared at the templar's gauntleted hand. "I'm not just a man of the streets. I know the Glass Desert well, and the Sea of Many Islands too." His face was ruddy, his eyes bloodshot, and she saw he was spoiling for a fight. "I can get high and mighty Elenara Moonstar to her destination quicker than any tinpot templar."

Ignoring Talon's boorishness, Elenara favoured the templar with a sunny smile. "It would be an honour to accompany you while you escort your pilgrims to Vancienne."

"And just who precisely is this?" A whey faced youth had joined them on silent feet, the squire who had sat at the big templar's side. He looked from Elenara to Talon, a vicious glint in his watery eyes. His sulky gaze lingered on

Talon, who glared back, unintimidated.

"A fair damsel in need, Florian," Corvalan boomed. "I have besought her to join our company, and her little friend."

"Her? And yon rat-faced gutter thief? They can fend for themselves!"

Corvalan's voice hardened. "Hie thee to our chambers. Go!"

"A good squire in his way," he added as Florian slunk away, "but he has much to learn. Welcome to the pilgrimage. Together, we shall brave these untamed lands."

Fit the Third: Moonlit Flit

Soon the company were seeking their beds. By some odd fluke, the chamber Talon had bespoken was beside that taken by the templar Corvalan and his squire. As Talon and Elenara approached their door, Corvalan was entering his own rooms, and he paused to greet them heartily. Elenara offered a tight little smile, concealing her thoughts beneath a mantle of courtesy. Talon, less afflicted by courtly customs, affected not to notice the templar, busying himself instead with the door lock.

As they entered their chamber, they heard, filtering in through the thin walls, the muffled sound of Corvalan's stern voice addressing his squire in disapproving tones. Disregarding it, Elenara halted a few paces in, looking around the small, dimly lit chamber in puzzlement.

"Is this all there is?" she asked disbelievingly.

A large, roughhewn double bed took up much of the chamber, its worn frame creaking gently to itself like a senile grandam. Beside a narrow arrow slit that looked out onto the shadowed courtyard below stood a ladder-backed chair.

In the far corner was a small, unassuming, narrow doorway.

"Nay," said Talon with a cheery grin that comforted her no whit. "The bath chamber is through yon door. It's most luxurious. You have a bath to yourself, if you can pay the extortionate deposit I coughed up."

"Is there no bathhouse for womenfolk?" stammered Elenara.

Talon laughed. "They do things differently in the caravanserais of the Glass Desert."

Elenara bit her lip, her desire for cleanliness struggling with propriety. "And there's only one bed," she observed gloomily, her cheeks pink.

Before either could say any more, a creaking of bedsprings and passionate moans and grunts drifted from Corvalan's chamber. Elenara's already rosy face grew crimson, and she busied herself nervously with the clasp of her cloak.

Talon stifled a laugh, jerking his head towards Corvalan's chamber. "Never have suspected it of him," he chuckled, "although I've heard rumours about these templars."

Elenara's eyes glinted with fury. "What do you mean?" His attempted jocularity faltered under her cold stare. "Sir Corvalan is a man of chastity like all his kind. Templars or paladins, we are all sworn to have no unchaste relations with the opposite sex."

Talon's grin widened, his tone took on a mocking note. "Chaste? You are? Remember we're sharing a bed. What would Lord Zennor say?"

"You have been working up to this outrage ever since we left the Lawberg!" Elenara said, her cheeks burning. "Last night at the oasis you sat uncomfortably near. I must make it clear, I am sworn to celibacy."

The squeaking of bedsprings was reaching a crescendo,

creaking in time with bestial groans and high-pitched squeals. "Like Sir Corvalan the templar?" Talon inquired sardonically.

Her face was grave. "Aye, like Corvalan, we knights of the Palace and the Temple are all vowed to chastity. So your plan is futile."

"Plan? I had no plan!"

"I know you for a liar," she said. "We will not share this bed. You will turn your eyes to the wall as I disrobe, and sleep in yon chair by the arrow slit."

"For Zorn's sake!"

"No doubt you have known many trulls easy with their favours," she said superciliously, lifting her chin, "but my chastity is sacred to the gods. If a man were to take it, he would be a better fellow than you."

Silence had fallen next door, but as if in response to her words, the bedsprings began another concerto. "Like Corvalan, I suppose?" Talon repeated sardonically.

She nodded gravely. "Sir Corvalan is a worthy man. Yet he is a templar and I am a paladin. Both of us are sworn to chastity."

An ecstatic moaning grunt shuddered through the walls. "Are you really sure about that?" Talon inquired.

She coloured again. "Sir Corvalan's squire serves more than one purpose. He accompanies Sir Corvalan so that the paladin can sate his manly lusts without breaking his vows."

"Vows? Of chastity?" Talon hooted. "He's breaking those for the second time this evening and it doesn't sound like he's planning on stopping!"

"I see naught wrong with it," said Elenara haughtily. "Now turn your back whilst I remove my armour and take my bath. You will sleep, as I said, in the chair."

"Wait a minute," he said, as he heard her shrugging

herself out of her jingling mail. "If Sir Corvalan sates his bestial lusts with youths... does that mean you sleep with maidens?"

"It is none of your concern!" Her breastplate fell to the flagstones with a loud clang, followed by the lighter ring of her mail and the almost inaudible thud of her hauqueton. Opening the door to the bath chamber, she flung back, "I must needs endure your companionship, but I am not obliged to answer your prurient enquiries."

As Talon settled into the uncomfortable chair, the soft splashing of water from the bath chamber drifted into the chamber, mingling with the lingering, rhythmic creaks from Corvalan's room. Despairingly he laid his head on his hands and prayed for sleep.

*

Hours passed in the silence of the night. Talon's uneasy sleep was punctuated by fitful dreams, each more absurd than the last. He dreamed of ships with feathered sails gliding across the skies of crystal deserts, pursued by cities that soared like ghostly leviathans.

The next he knew was a gauntleted hand on his shoulder, shaking him awake. "We move at once," whispered Elenara Moonstar.

Moonlight spilled through the arrow slit, illuminating Elenara as she stood over him, her face a pallid mask.

Talon groaned, still half asleep. "You want me to join you in bed?" he mumbled optimistically, rubbing his eyes.

"Nay!" she hissed, her voice full of vexation. "We must depart. I have thought long and hard."

Bewilderedly, Talon peered at her in the darkness. "I don't understand. We're supposed to be riding with the pilgrims."

Elenara's voice trembled with emotion. "We cannot! Imagine how shamed I would be, were we to ride with Sir Corvalan and his companions mounted on... on those birds!"

"Oh, I get it," said Talon with a bleary giggle. "We've got to get up in the middle of the night for the sake of your pride? So no one important sees you riding birdie-birdie-birdie? Oh, go back to bed."

But Elenara Moonstar would brook no argument. They moved in silence, gathering their belongings in haste. The lesser moon hung low in the sky as they slipped from the postern gate, the still air was heavy with the scent of powdered glass. The birds, those ludicrous steeds, waited in the stables, their avian eyes glinting dully in the gloom. Talon couldn't help but laugh under his breath as he saddled them.

By morning they were a long way down the road.

*

Four dawns later, the salt tang of the sea hung rankly in the air. The road wound past rugged cliffs of ochre stone, and as the two riders rounded a bend, a distant view opened up before them—an expanse of rolling jade green waters veiled in mist. In the offing stood several islands, grey pillars of smooth basalt crowned by verdant pinnacles of vegetation.

In the bustling harbour at the edge of the ocean, vessels rode at anchor, their masts like skeletal arms reaching toward the heavens. Among them, a strange vessel caught Elenara's eye. Its sails were unlike those of other ships— these were vast wings of canvas, extending from the ship's hull like the pinions of some great and terrible bird.

"How very strange," Elenara murmured, gazing at the ship in awe. "I've never seen a vessel like it."

Talon grinned. "Yon's a wing-ship. They use those great flappers to cross the sea, especially when dodging the floating cities." His voice took on a conspiratorial note. "This sea is unlike any other. Strange things roam these waters."

Elenara was about to ask her companion how he knew so much about the coming voyage when a group of riders galloped up—pilgrims on yaks and zebras, their leader unmistakable.

Corvalan, clad in burnished mail, leapt down. "So there you are!" he called, striding toward them. "You've led us a merry chase. Here you are, where we were going all along. Oh, but you can't escape us!"

"Birdie-birdie-birdie!" chirruped one of their mounts.

A deep crimson blush spread across Elenara's face, and Talon could only shake his head, his laughter echoing across the harbour as Corvalan's voice boomed triumphantly.

Fit the Fourth: The Wing-Ship

Early the following morning the wing-ship *Gallimaufry* embarked upon her voyage across the misty waters. The vessel's wings cut through the haze, their ceaseless rhythm as tedious as the tolling of a distant bell. Belowdecks, the rowers Talon had met at the caravanserai toiled in stifling near darkness, bent over their looms, hauling on ropes and pulleys that worked the intricate mechanisms.

Elenara Moonstar, emerging from her cabin, felt a wave of nausea as the ship swayed gently beneath her feet. The wings beat with a steady, hypnotic rhythm that rapidly grew monotonous. She felt unsteady, out of place in this alien element of sea and sky, mist and fog.

Skeletal crewmen, with bones as pale as moon-bleached driftwood, moved about the deck, their feet clacking like castanets. Too intent on their arcane nautical duties to heed her, they scanned the horizon for signs of danger.

"Hail, my lady," said a strong, rich, hearty voice.

She turned to see Corvalan approaching. The huge wings were beating faster now as the mage-captain piloted them across the mist hung waters. "Your companion does not accompany you," he commented, a small smile beneath his drooping moustache. "Does he have the sea sickness?"

Elenara scowled. "My companion suffers no such ailment. Indeed, he boasts that he was born upon this ocean, though I have learnt to mistrust much of what he says. Nay, he drank deep with the rowers last night and lies still abed."

Corvalan chuckled thunderously. "So that is why he is absent! Florian is afflicted with a most wretched malady of the belly. I left our cabin seeking a change of air. A foul miasma hangs over it." His face darkened a little, as if some memory haunted him. "Would you walk with me, Lady Elenara?" He laughed sardonically. "Or will you flee me, as you did at the Wells of Kubasek?"

Elenara suppressed a frown, little wishing to be reminded of her earlier folly. She gestured for him to walk alongside. The two knights promenaded along the deck, their mail clinking softly as they took deep breaths of misty air. The wings of the *Gallimaufry* thrummed overhead like the slow, ponderous flapping of some titanic bird; the mist hung thick, diffusing the weak morning light into an eerie, ghostly glow.

"I truly must apologise," she said, breaking the companionable silence. "Our sudden departure from the caravanserai was not without its reasons."

She was too ashamed to explain and yet she would not insult him with a lie.

Corvalan regarded her with a knowing smile, although his eyes, deep set and shadowed, revealed little. "I'll not pry, madam. I was troubled for your safety, however. I have heard rumours of subhuman nomads of the Glass Desert who rob lone travellers unwise enough to journey without company. You successfully evaded them?"

"Our steps were dogged by stalkers," she admitted. "But during the night Talon located their camp and seemingly despatched them. Ask me not how, I heard naught of it ere morning."

Corvalan's brow furrowed, his face set in a pensive grimace. "He is stronger than he looks, your runtish companion," the templar commented. "And more dangerous. Why do you accompany him?"

"He is a cunning guide," Elenara replied evasively. The truth, she knew, was far more complicated. Talon's methods unsettled her, but she could not deny that they had survived because of his ruthlessness. And he was the only man who could hope to prevail against the Sons of Darkness.

They had reached the stern, where the mage-captain stood by the great steering oar, his gaunt figure silhouetted against the swirling mists. His face, obscured by a wide brimmed conical hat, surveyed the waters for'ard. They were passing to port a small archipelago of islands and a stretch of open, if misty, sea stretched before them.

Corvalan's voice was low but persistent. "What business takes you to the Lap o' the Gods? It is a remote mountain pass, known only for..."

Before he could finish, the mage-captain bellowed a sulphurous curse, audible the length and breadth of the vessel. He had a spyglass clapped to his eye and was gazing starboard.

Elenara wheeled, a chill prickling at the base of her neck. Something was moving out in the mists—something vast.

The mage-captain leapt down from the poop deck and pounded upon a gong that hung from a wooden stanchion. The clanging echoed across the ship, skeletal sailors poured out from the hatches to take up positions on deck and in the rigging, bony feet rattled on the deck strakes with a clatter like rolling dice.

Elenara and Corvalan rushed to the rail, eyes wide with astonishment as the thing in the mist took on greater definition. It was huge.

Emerging from the white shrouds of mist like a dark harbinger of some forgotten aeon was a monstrous shape, great and hulking. As more and more of it hove into view, Elenara realised that it was not a ship, but rather a colossal turtle, propelling itself dreamily through the water with flippers the size of sails. Upon its broad, weed encrusted shell stood an entire town—huts and houses and even sizeable mansions, the walkways running between them winding up towards the highest point of the shell where stood a high, weed covered tower.

The mage-captain's eyes blazed. "She hasn't seen us. All hands to the looms! We'll escape yet."

The wings of the *Gallimaufry* began to flap at greater speed, desperation goading the rowers onwards. The mage-captain wrestled with the steering oar, calling, "Ho! Big man! Help me at the helm. Hard-a-port!"

The templar Corvalan joined the mage-captain, his heavy frame straining at the oar as the ship veered to the left. Looking over her mailed shoulder, Elenara realised to her dismay that the floating city had sighted them, that the monster turtle was now bearing down on them. It was then that she saw the shell's edge bristled with armoured warriors—savage, half naked pirates, their flesh tattooed with ancient glyphs, ready to board the vessel.

"You'll never outrun them, mage-captain," a familiar voice called from behind them.

Talon had appeared at the threshold of the cabin. He took in the scene at a glance. His eyes were still bloodshot, but he was invigorated by the danger.

"We've no hope of escape. If we were captured by them it would result in horrors unending. It's best to sell our lives dearly."

Elenara was astounded to see something in Talon's eyes she'd never seen before—steadfastness, even nobility. Corvalan let go of the steering oar and clapped the thief on the shoulder. "The runt is a hero in his own paltry way. Let us fight, then!"

Robed pilgrims emerged from their cabins, clustering fearfully on the quarterdeck, frightened eyes fixed on the gargantuan impossibility bearing down on their vessel. The mage-captain relinquished the steering oar, opened a locker, and began handing out halberds and partisans to the men who would fight.

Talon joined him. "The turtle's forced to remain on the surface of the sea by its masters who goad it from a cave bored deep in the shell itself. If we can enrage it enough, it'll ignore the pricking of the goad and dive."

The mage-captain nodded, his face grim. "Archers to the head! The rest, hold the line!"

The rowers heaved at the looms as still they attempted to outrun the turtle-borne metropolis. But now it was almost upon them.

Ballistae lined the shell-edge, and now they shot grappling lines clear across the closing gap. Grapples sank into the hull and the deck; teams of men turned capstans to haul the *Gallimaufry* closer. A drawbridge closed the gap, and armed pirates rushed wildly across it.

Clotted with gore, Elenara's war hammer met flesh and crushed bone, her arm moving with lethal exactness as she battled alongside Corvalan. Talon fought savagely with a halberd, felling pirates with brutal efficiency, forcing them back to their drawbridge. Florian gripped a billhook with white-knuckled hands, his face ashen, yet still he held his ground beside his master.

Pilgrims, womenfolk and children, loosed arrows at the turtle's beaked head. As their menfolk bought time, fighting and dying on the drawbridge, they transformed the reptile's brow into a pincushion. The creature let out a low, rumbling, irritable groan as arrows pierced its leathery brow. Slowly, roaring its anger, it began to dive.

"We're turning the tide!" Corvalan shouted, his voice filled with triumph.

Even as the turtle began to descend and the pirates fled for a doomed city, a loud crack split the air as the drawbridge broke. Talon turned to run with the rest, but as he did so the plank he stood on snapped, and with a startled cry he fell to vanish with a splash into the misty waters.

Fit the Fifth: Castaway

Elenara's breath caught in her throat as she stretched her hands futilely towards Talon. She stared at the stretch of water where her companion had disappeared, her heart pounding with a sudden, terrible dread. Dread not for herself, nor for Talon, but for the future of all worlds.

*

Free at last from its colossal assailant, the *Gallimaufry* rode out a tidal wave stirred up by the gigantic turtle's abrupt descent, wings flapping furiously as it flew towards the misty islands. The waters cast up a yeasty spray that drenched the deck in a cold, briny deluge. Saturated, Elenara collided with Corvalan's hard, mail encased torso.

"Talon!" she cried in disbelief, clutching at his armoured breast. "What's happened to him?"

The templar seized her shoulders in his iron grip, and his stern voice broke through the roar of wind and water. "He was lost overboard!"

The deck shook and shuddered, and when she looked back in the direction they had come from, Elenara could see only a huge swirling vortex where the floating city had been—a cauldron seething with shattered timbers, severed lines, all the remnants of a world dragged beneath the waves. Broken spars and snapped cables spun endlessly through the waters.

She swallowed a sob that astonished even her. What would she do without the thief? Her quest would be impossible! Talon had been opportunistic, devious—but vital. Now all the worlds were doomed to shudder beneath the tramping hoofs of the troops of Darkness.

*

Struggling impotently, Talon had been unable to stop himself being pulled down, down, down into the cold depths of the ocean. Dimly, through a tumult of bubbles, he glimpsed entire edifices ripped free of the shellback of the city, whole groups of people plunging downwards like shoals of fish, mouths agape in silent screams as they vanished into green shot blackness.

He tried to swim against the current, but it was almost impossible. Out of control, his bruised body was flung every which way by an irresistible undertow; his limbs were heavy and brine stung his eyes. He attempted to swim upwards, but his body was like a lead weight. It was then that he realised he was still clutching the halberd in clawlike hands. Relinquishing the weapon as if it were red hot, he watched numbly as it whirled away into the chaotic depths.

Yet still he sank.

Frantically he tried to determine the cause. Not the halberd alone—what else was weighing him down? His money pouch! Could a few gold pieces and the odd silver bit be dragging him down to a watery doom? Under other circumstances, the money, earned by cunning and duplicity, might have brought a greedy grin to his lips. But right now, mere survival was worth even more than other peoples' gold.

Clumsily, he unbuckled his pouch and, with a pang, watched as it spiralled down into the murk like some worthless offering to uncaring sea gods.

Still something seemed to weigh him down. He had rid himself of his wealth and his means of defence; what else remained? The shirt on his back? Or maybe... Hastily he unclasped his waterlogged cloak and let it drift away. His lungs were burning.

Free at last, he kicked upwards, swimming towards the pale watery gleam that must indicate the sun, high overhead. Yet still something, some inexplicable kind of weight, hauled him back into the greedy maw of the sea. As he fought it, his muscles shrieking in protest, he noticed the hull of the wing-ship cutting through the murky waters some way from his position. Changing direction, he swam hopefully in that direction, but in no time the *Gallimaufry* was out of sight.

His head broke surface at long last, saltwater streaming from his lank locks, cold air filling his lungs with sweet agony. Gasping amid the brackish water, he struggled to stay afloat: his tunic and breeks were heavy with brine. The sea all around him was clogged with detritus from the sunken city—broken spars, shattered beams, doors, fragments of houses, all bobbed on the waves.

Talon's heart sank. He had survived—but what now? The ocean was vast and indifferent, the nearest hint of land was a craggy isle several hundred man's-lengths across the misty waters. Atop it waved the fronds of a fringe of vegetation.

Nearer to him bobbed a broken length of wood. He swam over to what he soon recognised as a wooden gate pillar, intricately carved, perhaps once the gatepost of some mansion. Gratefully and wearily he hauled himself aboard with what strength remained in his exhausted frame. Slumping astride, half submerging the wood with his weight, he stared dully, with his sodden legs dangling into the water, looking hopefully, hopelessly around him.

The ocean still roiled like a maelstrom in the spot where the floating city had sunk, but the waters were gradually growing calmer. The *Gallimaufry*, now a distant shadow, raced away through the mist, its wings urging it on towards some hope of safety. Even as he watched, it was swallowed whole by the fog. Leaving him alone. Alone on this forsaken sea.

Close to despair, he clung to the drifting pillar like a babe to its mother's breast. How he hated it when things went spectacularly wrong! He wished he'd stayed at home now. But he had nowhere he could really call home. He was rootless, a wanderer born thirty winters ago in the slums of Tartaruga, one of the floating cities that prowled the Sea of Many Islands.

The pirate lords had ruled Tartaruga, waxing fat on raiding and marauding. For urchins like Talon, life had been a hand to mouth struggle to survive. He remembered how the tempest had come, how the turtle had been driven ashore by tidal waves, Tartaruga devastated. Surviving by a lucky chance, he had taken to life on land with equanimity, pursuing his customary vocation as thief, cutthroat, and general ne'er-do-well.

Gradually the island emerged from the mist, its cliffs towering above the water, clouded with mist and garlanded with weed. Talon paddled closer. Between the tug of the currents and his own trifling efforts, he drifted into a small, cliff walled bay at the foot of the crags. Fronds of vegetation waved like beckoning fingers from the crags. A distant roar echoed faintly, vast and primordial, born from the depths of ancient nightmare, and he shivered.

The pillar that had been his saviour was cast up by the waves upon a stony, barren strand.

Crawling off it, Talon took stock of his surroundings. The beetling crags ascended high overhead, lowering menacingly, dripping with moisture, wreathed with slimy weed. The strand where he lay was stony, lifeless but for a few sharp shells that lacerated his feet as he attempted to walk. The craggy sides, dripping with moisture, soared into the ever-present mist. Again he glimpsed the vegetation that thrived high above, recognising the distinctive broad leaves of thenar trees. An entire jungle flourished up there. If only he could climb those steep cliffs, he might survive—thenar fruit was piquant and nourishing.

Taking a deep breath, he seized hold of a huge, drooping frond of weed and used it as a rope to scale the rock wall.

It was a treacherous ascent, with handholds and

footholds few. On a slippery, narrow ledge a third of the way up the cliff face he ran out of options. The mists parted momentarily and a baleful sun glared down, as sweat trickled down his brow, steaming slightly in the tropical heat. High above him the cliff was sheer, without so much as a holdfast of weed.

It was then that he realised what had been weighing him down. Reaching inside his wet clothes, he hauled out his grapnel and a long line of tightly woven cord. Laughing bitterly, he probed his left hand into a handhold so small he had initially discounted it, then with his right began to rotate the grapnel in a tight circle.

Talon flung it, watching the grapnel loop high overhead and vanish out of sight. The line itself was so long he could have used it to climb back down to the beach, but he ignored that temptation. Doubtfully, he tested it. To his relief, it held.

It was long past noon before he reached the top of the cliff. Cries of strange birds and beasts rang out from the trees. Wearier than he had ever been before he sat down on a cool stretch of emerald sward in the shade of a thenar tree. He lay down and slept.

*

Nightfall brought new danger. Talon was awoken by a distant roar, followed by a pandemonium from amongst the trees. He rose on one elbow, heart hammering on his ribs like a frantic prisoner. Shadows pooled in the grass, moisture oozed from the broad leaves of thenar trees. From deeper within the jungle echoed the rapid drip-drip-drip of water splashing on the jungle floor. The lesser moon lofted high overhead like a silver sickle blade while the greater already peeked over the western horizon, staining the rolling waters of the nighted ocean with its pallid yellow light.

Again that roar broke the hush, closer this time, sending a chill down his backbone. Talon fumbled frantically for his long knife before realising, with sinking heart, that he had left it aboard the wing-ship. From deep within the trees the roaring came yet again; a sound so vast he could not imagine the beast that had made it. But it must be huge. How big was this island?

He had no answers—only the growing assurance that he was not alone. The roar came again, but this time fainter, as if the beast were moving away. Perhaps it was hunting something else.

Talon's belly growled, as if vying with the beast. He had last eaten aboard the *Gallimaufry*. And as the greater moon crawled painfully up into the sky, he saw, limned in its light, the fruit that drooped from the boughs of the thenar trees.

But before he could shake them down, a rustle in the undergrowth stopped him dead. From the shadows emerged a dozen small, manlike forms. The moonlight glinted from spearheads, transforming them by some strange alchemical property into yellow gold. Talon's heart pounded as he realized he was surrounded.

Fit the Sixth: The Dwarfs

Elenara beached the canoe at dawn. As she and her two companions came ashore, the sun crept over the high crags that lined the bay like the walls of a weed besieged fortress. The pale light cast ghostly shadows across the strand, the damp mist of the island clung to the rock like a shroud.

With a grin, Corvalan the templar slapped her on the backplate with a gauntleted hand, his voice rough yet hearty.

"This runt, my lady," he said meditatively, gazing pensively at the misty cliff. "Is he worth the trouble?"

"I very much doubt it." The third member of their party, Corvalan's squire, Florian, was gazing back at the water with a face like a frightened cat's.

Elenara's gaze was fixed on the heights. The cliffs were wet, swathed in clinging weed and speckled with barnacles. When she spoke, her voice was distant, as though her thoughts, like her gaze, were faraway, she murmured, "He whom you call runt is of immense significance to the cause of Good. It is imperative that we find him ere continuing our journey—whether he deserves it or not."

Corvalan hauled the canoe above the high-water mark. He dusted off his hands and put them on his hips and gazed up at the dizzying prospect. "And you are absolutely certain that he is on this island?"

"I know it," she said, touching the amulet Lord Zennor had given her. It was attuned to Talon's psychospoor, so even if they were parted, she could track him down. The geas should have been sufficient, but his lordship had provided her with this charm in case of such an eventuality.

"Then how will we ascend these cliffs?" Corvalan added. "They're high and steep, insurmountable but for the foul weed that infests them. And partway up, even the weed gives out."

Unspeaking, Elenara went to the foot of the cliff. "What's this?" she exclaimed, tugging at something half buried in the strands of seaweed. "Look, Sir Corvalan," she said excitedly, revealing a thin, frayed rope, knotted and worn by use, hanging down the side of the cliff. "A thief's rope. It must be Talon's. He was here. And he scaled the crag."

Corvalan strode over and inspected the strong, slender line, lips pursed in reluctant admiration. "But where is he now?" asked the templar.

Elenara shouted Talon's name several times, yet only harsh, mocking echoes answered her. She gripped tight hold of the rope, set her boots against the stone, and began to climb. With practised ease she ascended despite the slippery bladderwrack that disfigured the rocks.

The rope creaked under her weight, but held fast, and she soon reached the lip of the cliff, where she crouched. From her position, the island unfolded before her — a tangled mass of trees, dense and dripping with moisture. The thenar jungle was a primeval labyrinth, its green gemmed canopy glittering in the half-light.

The rope tugged and quivered beside her as Corvalan followed. Puffing and panting, the big man scrambled up to join her on the clifftop, his breath misting in the cool morning air. Together they surveyed the thenar jungle. "If the thief came this way, he has left no trace," Corvalan concluded gloomily.

Florian's terrified face appeared over the lip of the cliff and he dragged himself up to fling himself onto the grass. Here he lay shaking, gasping to himself, "Why do I always let myself in for this?"

"The mage-captain gave us the space of a single day to find your companion, my lady," said Corvalan, removing the grapnel from the root where it was lodged. "We can't waste time, else we will be marooned." He coiled the rope around his waist.

Not heeding the other two, Elenara set off down an animal track that led under the dripping eaves of the jungle. Corvalan hauled Florian to his feet and together they followed her.

The path was narrow, hemmed in by the thick trunks of thenar trees, whose baroque bark twisted into grotesque shapes as though frozen in mid-motion. Every time Elenara set a foot down it plunged into semi liquid mud; the air was thick with the odour of wet earth and something faintly acrid, like the breath of some unseen creature that stalked them through the shadows.

Their slow progress through the thenar woods produced no sign of Talon's passing. So much moisture dripped from the overhanging boughs that soon they were as drenched as they would have been had they gone out walking in a thunderstorm. The top of the island was like a shallow bowl, in which the trees grew thickly.

In clearings, jewelled insects danced in beams of sunlight that reached the jungle floor. From time to time, outlandish animal cries broke through the eternal sound of dripping.

A sudden crashing from the interior alerted them. They had reached the banks of a small stream, and Corvalan was investigating some animal tracks he had found in the soft mud.

"What d'you suppose yon spoor is?" he asked, marvelling. "If it is the beast that made these tracks, we're in parlous straits. They are the claw marks of some huge…"

As the noise drew closer the three of them sought shelter amongst the dripping undergrowth. From the underbrush on the far bank, something emerged. Elenara's first thought was that the newcomer was a child, and yet she realised that the girl was about her age, but stunted, like a pigmy or a dwarf. She was small and stocky, her mahogany flesh bare but for a brief loincloth. As she sprinted towards the stream, she cast terrified glances behind her.

Elenara was about to call out when something huge and green and scaled burst out of the vegetation, seizing the tiny dwarf in its fanged jaws.

From the undergrowth they watched in fascinated

horror as the huge, crested lizard, its scales gleaming like emerald in the dappled light, tore out the girl's innards, gulping them down voraciously. Abruptly, it turned and scuttled away into the jungle gloom.

Florian was first to break the deafening silence.

"A reptile!" he muttered hoarsely, his voice little over a whisper. "But of such size! Do you think yon monster devoured your friend?"

Elenara rose determinedly. "I know he still lives," she said, one hand on the amulet, feeling a faint throb. "We shall find him."

Without hesitation she crossed the stream by the stepping stones and Corvalan and Florian followed close behind. Flies were already buzzing around the girl's carcase, her blood stained the earth where the lizard had fed. The path had been churned up by its big, clawed feet, but it was not long before they heard shouts and curses ringing out from ahead of them, and the clamour of battle.

The trio exchanged startled glances, then Elenara broke into a run, the others following. Rounding a corner, they came out into a clearing, where the giant lizard was locked in savage combat with several dwarf warriors. Two of the small men already lay unmoving on the lush turf, shattered spears beside them, but the others fought remorselessly.

Elenara's war hammer was in her hand before she even realised it, and, yelling a war cry, she rushed into the fray. Almost at once Corvalan was at her side, his sword gleaming as he slashed at the beast's flank. Florian, pale and shaking, clung to the bole of a thenar, peering out from the safety of the shadows, his face white with fear. Overwhelmed by the sudden onslaught, the great lizard uttered a last, defiant, ear-splitting roar before crawling away into the jungle. Its prodigious form soon vanished into the all-encompassing gloom.

One of the dwarfs limped over to the two knights, addressing them in a thick, impenetrable accent. His skin was brown as leather that has lain in a bog a thousand years and he barely reached Elenara's midriff but boasted a grizzled beard. His words seemed to represent some kind of pidgin tongue. But it was clear that the dwarf—presumably some kind of chieftain—was inviting them to follow him.

The group marched through the wet, dripping woods, coming out into a larger clearing where reed huts stood amidst drystone walled fields of maize and tomatoes. The dwarfs ushered them into a low roofed longhouse, where they were led before a man who lounged upon a dais. The dwarfs prostrated themselves.

"Ah, Elenara," the man said cheerily. "And the templar, Corvalan. Oh, and even little Florian. Welcome to the island."

It was Talon.

Fit the Seventh: A Clutch of Eggs

Elenara's eyes blazed with barely suppressed fury. The air in the longhouse was thick with the scent of damp earth and pungent smoke from the fire that crackled on the hearth. The dwarfs, clustered in the shadows, watched with gleaming, beady eyes, their expressions inscrutable. Talon sat lazily on a reed mat, his posture relaxed, but his eyes sharp.

"What in the name of Ti are you doing here?" Elenara's voice shook with anger. "You have a quest to fulfil! You're under a geas to fulfil it or die in the attempt, and I find you lounging around with a tribe of dwarfs, enjoying yourself without a care in the world."

Talon scratched his head, as if baffled by her manner. "These little people found me and took me in. They've given me a roof over my head." He glanced at the grizzled dwarf. "Isn't that right, Pethig?"

Pethig made some guttural reply in his pidgin tongue. Talon listened, then laughed to himself. "Pethig is reminding me that we have a bargain," he said.

Corvalan, standing at Elenara's side, asked harshly, "What bargain is that, little man?"

Talon leaned back, stretched and yawned. "In return for their hospitality, they've asked me to steal for them certain eggs that can be found on the highest part of the island. These little people have big enemies, giant lizards who are rivals for control of the island. The dwarfs believe that the yolk of these eggs is sacred, and they will be able to vanquish their foes in one resounding victory that will make them masters of the island—if only they can get a hold of this yolk. The flying creatures that lay the eggs are very rare now, but one laid a clutch this year, and the dwarfs hope to obtain at least some of the eggs before they hatch, or before one of the lizards find them.

"Trouble is," Talon went on, his voice carrying a lilt of amusement, "the lizards themselves are attracted to the nesting area, and even if they haven't eaten the eggs yet, they will prove formidable foes."

"A clutch of eggs..." Elenara's gauntleted fingers traced the outline of the amulet at her breast, its faint pulse a reminder that their fates were entwined. "And if you get the eggs, will they let you go? The *Gallimaufry* is moored on the lee side of the island, but the mage-captain will only anchor for a short time."

Talon sat up straighter, eyes gleaming. "Is it? I'd like to get back to yon wing-ship, I must admit. I've felt the pricking of this cursed geas since I was washed up here... But now you've joined me, we can all find the eggs for the dwarfs. We can work together!" He turned to Pethig and the other dwarfs and a long conversation ensued.

At the end of it, Talon's face darkened. "Seems Pethig's not so trusting. He insists I stay here while you brave knights fetch the eggs. They'll let me go, and we can sail off into the sunset together."

"And if we don't?" Corvalan demanded.

"Pethig is adamant," Talon said, after another long discussion. "He'll keep me here until you return with the eggs. Then he'll let me go, let you all go. But if you don't do as he says, he'll, er, be forced to, er, well. Kill me."

Elenara's lips were a thin line. She looked down at the grizzled little dwarf, gauntleted fingers absently stroking the haft of her war hammer. "Since I value your continued existence highly, we'll do as he asks," she said resignedly. "By the Sword and the Ring, I swear that I shall go to the place where these eggs are to be found and obtain them. My word is my bond. I am a knight of the Palace."

Talon shrugged. "Pethig'll believe you only when he sees the eggs brought to this longhouse."

He stiffened in surprise when Elenara wrapped her mailed arms around him in a fond embrace. Talon could barely struggle. He was even more surprised when he realised the true purpose of this hug—the paladin had concealed something cold and heavy into his hand.

Talon nodded briefly and slipped it under his long tunic.

*

A quarter of an hour later the two knights and Florian were hacking their way through dense jungle, the ground growing steeper as their path wound steadily towards the island's northern crags. The thenar trees hung low with vines, dripping rainwater on the lush ground. Every step felt heavy, and the humid air pressed down on them. The only sound was the squelch of their boots and the crack of blade on bough.

Elenara paused momentarily to wipe a sheen of sweat from her brow.

"I don't trust these dwarfs," muttered Corvalan. "Nor do I relish fetching eggs like some scullion."

"Nor I," said Elenara, glancing round warily at the surrounding jungle. "It would be tempting if we were to snatch Talon and return to the *Gallimaufry* without wasting time with these eggs..."

"We cannot break our word!" said Florian primly.

"Nay, but Talon could," said Elenara, lowering her voice conspiratorially. "He lacks our knightly integrity. I gave him the means to escape, suggesting he break free as soon as he can, and join us. If he does, we can depart without squandering precious hours."

Corvalan scanned the trail behind them. "I see no sign of him. Frankly, I'm surprised that a paladin of your standing should be party to such an underhand scheme. You have spent too long accompanying this..."

Elenara wasn't listening. She had seen movement ahead, where the trees began to thin out; something darting through the underbrush. "I saw something crossing yon stretch of rocks..."

"One of these lizards?" asked Corvalan. He drew his sword. "Let us make haste."

They emerged from the trees to feel the sun beating down on their faces. A devil's playground of rocks and boulders led to the edge of the cliffs. In the distance the misty waters of the Sea of Many Islands stretched into seeming infinity, the horizon lost in the haze.

"What kind of creature would lay its eggs in such a

wasteland?" Corvalan asked as they made their way carefully across the rocks. "And where?"

"I should think it would conceal them," said Elenara thoughtfully. With her booted foot, she scraped away a scatter of stones, but the crevice they had hidden was empty. Corvalan, seeing what she was doing, joined her, picking rocks up and casting them aside, his broad frame straining with effort. Doubtfully, after much apparent deliberation, Florian picked up a small pebble and flung it towards the cliff edge. It fell short.

Elenara's fingertips brushed something smooth and cool. She cast aside a rock, catching a gleam of pale blue. Excited, she dug in the grit with her bare hands, revealing several blue mottled shells half buried in the grit. They were big—bigger than the eggs of a riding avian.

She picked one up and examined it, a troubled frown on her face. "These eggs," she murmured. "They are strangely familiar. I'm sure I've seen them before somewhere."

"Seen them?" Corvalan asked. "Surely that's impossible. Or have you visited these islands in the past?"

Before she could say any more, they all heard a scuttling noise. Corvalan wheeled round, his armoured bulk crashing into Elenara. The egg slipped from her hands and smashed. Vivid yellow yolk oozed from the shattered eggshell.

Florian cried out, his face white. "Look!" Corvalan gripped his arm, unsheathing his sword with his other hand.

Grinning at them from where it perched between two rocks, clawed feet sturdily gripping the stony flanks, was a giant lizard. Its dark green scales glistened in the sun, its crest waved in the breeze. A forked tongue tasted the air. It was watching their every move with cold, reptilian eyes.

But Elenara knelt by the broken shell, examining the

delicate, translucent embryo that floated in the yolk. The creature was small, fragile, but unmistakable. Its half-formed wings were folded against its body, and the sharp eagle beak gave it a noble look.

"Corvalan," she whispered. "See!"

Corvalan tore his gaze from the lizard. Elenara held the contents of the broken egg up to him. His eyes widened as understanding dawned.

"It's not a lizard egg," Elenara said softly. "It's a hippogriff."

Fit the Eighth: Lizard Thunder

Escaping the dwarf village was no easy task, even for a thief of Talon's undoubted quality. It would have been impossible, he had to admit, had it not been for the help of goody-two-shoes Elenara Moonstar, who had slipped him a very welcome parting gift while making her uncharacteristic show of affection.

His long knife glinted in his hand as he held its edge to Pethig's throat. The small warrior's eyes burned in their sockets as he glowered defiantly at his overlarge assailant. "What do you?" the dwarf leader demanded, guttural tones thick with fury. "You swore t' help us! You give us your word!"

"My word's not worth a bent copper piece," said Talon mournfully, "and besides, you promised to kill me if Elenara didn't return. You're coming with me until we reach the trees—and all your friends and relations are going to keep back, if they don't want you sporting a new grin. Understood?" He sketched the location of the smile in question—across Pethig's throat.

Pethig growled something urgently to the others, who

seethed with fury and indignation. Unwillingly, they parted, giving Talon a path to the gates. Mothers drew children to their bosoms, fearful but watchful, as the thief appeared in the middle of the village, still menacing Pethig. Dwarfs fled to the sanctuary of their huts, from whose entrances resentful eyes glimmered like angry fireflies.

Clods of dry earth powdered beneath Talon's feet before they reached the dripping eaves of the jungle. "They'd better not try anything," he muttered, his grip tightening on his hilt.

"You best kill me," said Pethig with dignity. "When me gone, they will hunt you down. You die, like all liars."

Talon laughed, a short, humourless bark. "I'm not going to kill you, friend. You're the best insurance I can get. But now..." He contemplated the gloom of the jungle. "...Sorry, but I'm going to have to let you go."

He relaxed his grip and gave him a little shove. "Run back to your people. But for Zorn's sake, don't come after me. It's death for any dwarf to go where I'm going."

*

Long before Talon reached the rocky outcrop, he already had a sense that Pethig's dwarfs were stalking him. Feeling the prickling of eyes upon his back, he broke into a jog. The sun blazed brightly as he burst out of the green twilight. Panting, he stopped short. The ground rose here and grew rocky, ending at the edge of a cliff. Beyond it stretched the misty waters of the Sea of Many Islands. His heart lightened as he saw, amid the barren rocks, Elenara Moonstar and the others. But threatening them was a huge, scaled monstrosity, hide rippling with muscles as it lashed its tail and roared deafeningly.

"Elenara!" Talon shouted desperately. But even as he started to run, he saw, emerging from the jungle, a band of dwarf warriors. They had followed him. And from the expressions on their faces they had not come with friendly intent.

Elenara turned to see the thief approaching. "Talon, keep back!" she cried, indicating the lizard. "I..."

Florian seized the opportunity to flee. With a sickening crunch the lizard bit off his head in a spray of blood. Then it leapt, bearing Corvalan to the ground, fangs and claws glinting in the sunlight.

The templar fought bitterly, only his mail saving him from laceration at the terrible beast's claws. Blood ran in the dirt as man and monster battled, before the lizard flung Corvalan to the stony ground. Lifting its head, it stared at the approaching dwarfs, forked tongue tasting the air pensively.

The lizard stalked towards them, long tail lashing, but before it could attack again, arrows whistled through the air. The lizard hissed, its hide bristling, before turning and pursuing the warriors into the jungle. Their shrieks trailed behind them as they ran.

"They're the wisest ones here," said Talon wryly.

Elenara examined Florian's headless corpse, her face green tinged, then turned her attention to Corvalan. So did Talon. "That's mine!" he said accusingly.

The thief unwound the rope and grapnel from round the templar's waist. Hefting it in his hands, he crossed over to the cliff edge. Down below, in the jade green waters, the *Gallimaufry* stood off so close it seemed to be almost within reach. Small figures could be seen at work down on its deck. With a smirk, Talon swung the grapnel over his head like a lasso and flung it.

The rope went looping over and over until it hooked

into one of the raised wings. "Come on," Talon said, securing this end to a convenient rock. "We can abseil down to the wing-ship then bid this island a fond farewell."

With Elenara's aid, Corvalan sat up, staring at Florian's headless corpse in despair, hand to his head. He seized the paladin's arm. "The thief is right, my lady," he rasped, his voice thick with emotion. "Our duty is aboard the *Gallimaufry*, not in this luckless place."

"Nay," said Elenara, who was gazing at the clutch of eggs. "I must remain here."

Talon seethed. "Yon lizard won't be content with chasing those dwarfs. It'll soon be back..."

"You don't understand," she cried. "These eggs..."

Talon seized Elenara's arm, but she fought him off. "Let the monster have them!" Talon urged her. "It'll keep it occupied. If it's between us and a few eggs... We've got a quest to complete, remember?"

"You fool! Do you not understand?" she said dispassionately. "They are hippogriff eggs! When my hippogriff was slain, it was thought the entire race extinct. Yet it seems that one came here to lay her clutch."

Talon stared at her. "Hippogriffs? You mean...?"

A loud roar split the air as the great lizard burst from the trees. Blood mottled its hide, arrows jutted from its crest, but it seemed to have been the victor. Elenara took several paces towards the eggs. Seeing her sudden movement, the lizard bore down upon her.

As Elenara Moonstar seized an egg, the great lizard sprang. She leapt aside and the creature thudded down among the rocks, but the egg fell from her grasp, cracking open. Now the lizard was between her and the clutch.

"Never mind the eggs!" Talon shouted. "Come with me!"

The three of them secured themselves to Talon's rope and leapt over the cliff. The wind howled as they zipped down the long rope, the sea below them looking like a jade-green mirror, the *Gallimaufry* growing larger with each passing second.

Back on the clifftop the lizard let out a roar of victory, crested head held high. Insatiably it began to feast on the hippogriff eggs, yolk running down its jaws like yellow blood.

*

A few minutes later the three escapees were on the deck of the wing-ship. The *Gallimaufry* shuddered as the skeletal sailors hoisted the wings and began steering it away from the island. The lizard and the eggs, the crags and the vegetation, faded from view, swallowed up by the mist.

Dourly the mage-captain came out from his cabin and several of the pilgrims appeared. "Ye found him, then?" the mage-captain commented. "Yet what of your squire?"

The mage-captain and the pilgrims listened grimly as Corvalan explained what had happened. Several of the pilgrims wept openly at the news. When the night came they lit candles and held a solemn vigil on the deck for Florian's lost soul, singing psalms and paeans as the wing-ship leapt the waves. A single tear was seen to trickle down Corvalan's rugged cheek.

Talon returned to his cabin, baffled and perplexed. Florian had never been well-liked, a green, untried boy thrust into the world of knights and quests—yet here, on this wing-ship, he was mourned like a hero. The thief wondered if anyone would ever mourn his own passing.

As night deepened, the ship sailed onward, leaving far behind it the island of lizards and lost hippogriffs, carrying its weary passengers toward the shores of Vancienne.

Epilogue

For many days they voyaged across the Sea of Many Islands, encountering no further incident. The waters stretched green and mysterious into the foggy distance, out of which loomed craggy islands much like the one they had escaped. Most nights found them anchored in placid, glassy bays amidst one island group or another.

At last the *Gallimaufry* moored off the wharves of Vancienne. Here Corvalan bade Elenara and Talon farewell, leading his pilgrims away towards the green domed temple on the height above them.

"May Ti's blessings go with you," the templar said, as he left them by the gangplank of the *Gallimaufry*. "I will be in the city a while ere I am assigned my next mission. We should look each other up, if you are still here, Elenara Moonstar."

"Now what?" asked Talon, tugging his new cloak tighter as a cold wind blew in from the ocean. The pilgrims had vanished up the winding way to Vancienne amid a heady miasma of dust, prayers, and incense. "Tell me you don't want to hook up with Sir Corvalan any time soon."

"We must hie ourselves to the Lap o' the Gods," said Elenara waspishly, "for yon is the location of the first dimensional gate. It will be our first step on our journey into the worlds of Darkness. But the troglodytes are up in arms, it's said, the mountains are unsafe for travellers unless they ride in large, armed bands. We must go to the Temple of Ti ourselves and ask that King Hiero renders aid."

They rode up from the harbour on their avians, which had been penned in the ship's hold for the whole trip.

During that time, one bird had developed a liking for the other. As Elenara and the thief ascended the narrow, winding stone stairway, Talon's bird kept trying to nip at the other bird's feathered backside, while the other raced ahead, squawking.

"Birdie-birdie-birdie," twittered the first.

"I'm a birdie!" trilled the other.

Elenara's face was as icy as a glacier in the Ice Mountains of the Far South. But Talon chuckled all the way up the harbour steps.

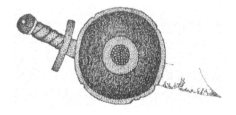

A PATHWAY FORWARD

A Chapter in *Tales of the Citadel*

Lyndon Perry &
David Bakke

1

The Citadel has nothing for us.

The whispered message that tickled the base of Tauric's skull raised hairs on the back of his neck. It was the first time the berserker spirit had spoken to him since he'd beheaded his master, the Grand Mage Skellen.

As he stared at the great manor across the salty marsh, the acolyte felt the truth of those words. The Citadel would never welcome him back. They'd put him on trial instead.

"I could return to my parents' farm," he suggested, wondering if the internal spirit of frenzy would continue the conversation. Whatever it was that ebbed just below the surface of his sanity remained silent. Tauric sighed.

Without a second glance, he turned his back on the wizards' keep. "If you won't speak, then you'll have to listen," he murmured, heading north into the wild country from whence he hailed. The weather was crisp, the late summer's warmth had already slipped south as the change of seasons pushed its way into the northern Angle Isles.

"Consequences, you see. I must face whatever punishment the new Grand Mage deems necessary. So I'll visit my family in Tarnepæth, then return to take responsibility for Skellen's death. I wonder who the high council chose to replace him."

No response.

It was just as well. Tauric did not care, his days as an acolyte were over. He would never again serve in the great manor; but neither could he return to the drudgery of herding goats and sheep. He wasn't the wide-eyed young man who'd left his home a year before.

He'd changed. He'd killed.

Yes. Lost in the battle lust deep in the low country of Korreth—across the Straits of Candalla in a land not his own, bent on some quest he'd hardly understood—he'd murdered the Grand Mage. But worse, at least in Tauric's mind…he'd succumbed to madness.

No.

The reverberated response served only to confirm his suspicions. Still, he could not deny the feeling that something had *joined* him. By some bedevilled sorcery he'd been enslaved to his master, yet Skellen's death had not released him from his bonds.

Whether madness or devilry, the berserker frenzy had not departed.

Devilry, I think.

"Oh, that certainly puts my mind at ease."

For the next three hours, Tauric hiked in silence, his ragged robe wrapped tightly around him against an incessant wind. He ignored the accompanying *presence* as best he could and focused on the path before him. It was familiar enough. He'd roamed these jagged hills as a youngling; its windswept moors and frigid tarns were a welcome contrast to the bloody plains of battle he'd left the week before.

Cresting a rise, he saw a scattering of goats in the

distance and his breath caught. He quickened his pace. Around the bend, a low-roofed hut came into view. The dwelling, sheltered by a rocky outcropping, had not changed. Of course it hadn't. The man stacking dried peat under a lean-to was his father; the boy and girl, now gawking at him, were still his younger siblings. The smell of smoke, of roasting meat, of animals and dung were all the same. He was home.

Tauric's heart ached with such anticipation, he shivered. It was as if he'd just returned from a journey of a thousand years. And when he saw his mother exiting their humble abode—looking his way, suddenly smiling—he nearly cried out.

Mœdar!?

The sensation of surprise and joy was so strong, his knees buckled. It took a moment to realize the thought was not his own. The word, the voice, echoed just beyond hearing.

"Yes, *my* mother," he grunted. What was the spirit implying? "My mother!"

"Tauric," his mother called, gathering her skirt, running toward him. His father, too, was hurrying his way; but Tauric was already falling on the ground, dipping into darkness.

2

A feverish dream reluctantly let go its grip on the former acolyte, and his eyes fluttered open. He blew out a breath and shook off the vestiges of fading visions—visions of ancient battles, of victories, great halls, and heroes. He sat up.

"You still snore," a young girl's voice said. Aisla.

"And you probably still pee in your sleep."

"She does!" taunted Keyon, pushing his sister and running from the hut. Aisla cried out and chased after her just older brother, throwing the goatskin curtain aside and briefly letting in the last of the setting sun.

Tauric's mother, Edy, opened the flap completely and entered the shadowed chamber, bringing with her an unlit lantern and a bowl of steaming stew. The room served as the family's evening gathering place, to eat and sleep, protected from the elements. Otherwise, life was lived out of doors.

"Smells good," Tauric said, accepting a pewter bowl filled to the brim.

"Tastes even better," his father said, entering the hut with his own cup of stew and some flatbread. Wigberht gave his son a wooden spoon and sat next to him on the slatted bed. He broke the thin loaf and offered half.

Edy lit the lantern and a few of the shadows dispersed. "Tauric," she said, her eyes shining with love and tenderness. "You made it home."

He tried to meet her gaze but looked away in shame. "I…"

After a moment, Wigberht said, "We know. The village knows. They want to speak with you on the morrow."

Tauric nodded. It was to be expected. He'd sent a raven before leaving Korreth. If the masters at the Citadel knew he'd killed their Grand Mage, all the surrounding villages knew as well. Gossip spread quickly in these parts.

It's what they didn't know—and what he couldn't tell them—that worried him.

"You should hear it first," the former acolyte said, after a time of thoughtful silence.

"Go on then," Wigberht said, not without pity.

"The Grand Mage is dead by my hand…" His father

nodded, his mother's countenance dimmed. "He took me in, Skellen did." His parents had been so proud. It was almost a year since Tauric had left. His two siblings were old enough to tend the animals, and with little enough food to go around, his parents had sent him to the wizarding city in hopes that he might serve one of the masters. That he was chosen by the Grand Mage himself was more than a dream.

"Skellen, he…he cast an enchantment upon me. A spell, an experiment, I think. It worked. I was his instrument, I did his bidding… I killed."

I killed.

Tauric shivered and his mother draped a rough woollen shawl over his shoulders. He appreciated the gesture, but it was not the evening's chill that stirred the tremor.

"Then you were out of your mind," Wigberht pronounced, settling the matter. "You were spellbound when you ended your master's life. Tell the village that, they'll understand. You'll find no love for the Citadel here; they merely want assurance no rogue dwells among them."

"How can I offer such assurance when I still feel his—" He broke off, uncertain as to what more he should say, or even what he felt to be true.

Edy asked quietly, "You believe you are still…enchanted?"

A slight nod and a sniffle. Tauric wiped his nose. He returned the bowl of stew half eaten.

Wigberht grunted. "You'll not want to mention that, m'boy. A powerful charm, a temporary madness is all. For most, that will be enough."

"For most?"

His father grinned and slapped his back. "As long as you don't start ravishing their sheep and howling at the moon, you'll find a place in the village."

Edy shot her husband a withering glance, and addressed her son, "You're exhausted from your journey. You'll be right in the morning." She glanced out at Keyon and Aisla stirring embers in the firepit, at play in their innocence. "We'll have no more talk of spells or sorcery."

Oh, but we shall, whispered the voice, sending another quiver down the young man's spine.

That night, Tauric met the berserker spirit in his dreams.

3

"I am Hælig," she said. A penetrating glare met Tauric's timid stare.

"I am Tauric," he murmured. "But I suppose you already know this." He was not surprised the reverberating spirit within his mind belonged to a woman; though truth be told, he'd tried hard to ignore its—*her*—presence ever since he'd first succumbed to the frenzied madness.

"My knowledge of this world is dim, my memories are still in shadows."

"This is not your world then?" He glanced around, realizing they were…beyond the physical realm, conversing in the borderland between the seen and unseen.

Hælig considered. "Same world, perhaps, but not my age."

Understanding dawned. He seemingly switched subjects. "And my mother?"

"So like my own dear mœdar."

The tenderness in her voice surprised him. And the word. *Mœdar.* An ancient word, from an ancient age. The Age of Heroes.

"At least four hundred years gone," he said, though he did not mean it to sound cruel.

The spirit nodded, saddened. In this shadowland of slumber, Tauric could see the young woman—just a few years his senior—shimmering before him, nearly tangible. He raised an eyebrow. Her features were striking, familiar...

"You're a warrior," he said, snapping his eyes away from her mesmerizing gaze.

Hælig wore a complement of leather armour: a studded cuirass overlaid by a sturdy gorget; her shoulders and arms protected by pauldrons, bracers, and gauntlets. Greaves adorned her legs which Tauric noted were long and toned. She was an attractive, fine-looking woman.

"I am Sealtmersc's protector," she offered, as if no further statement was needed for complete understanding.

Tauric's year of tutelage at the wizarding city gave him some insight. Seven manors currently ruled the Angle Isles, each manor led by a Grand Mage. But in the ancient days, seven major burhs boasted their own heroic protectors, hero mages who guarded and guided their village and its guild.

For nearly a thousand years, hero mages stood fast against barbarian hordes, wielding magicks few understood and fewer still could control. But the heroes' secrets were eventually found out, and four hundred years ago the seven guilds threw off their protectors in a violent revolt. The Age of Heroes had come to an end, and a new era of wizardry was founded.

"Sealtmersc?" Even as he said it, the meaning became clear. Salt marsh, of course. An ancient word to describe the surrounding swamplands over which their local manor had arisen. The Burh of Sealtmersc had given way to the Citadel Beside the Sea, just as the stronghold's hero mages had given way to a new age ruled by sorcerers.

A moment of hesitation and Tauric ventured, "You're a mage as well, then."

"Aye, but not like Skellen." To herself, Hælig repeated

her words like a revelation. "No, not like Skellen!"

She began to pace the boundaries between their worlds. Tauric followed after, though his movement felt meaningless in this land of shadows.

"Because he was a sorcerer?"

"Because his sorcery came from the chaos realm," she replied with urgency. "My mind is clearing, be it ever so slowly. I must reflect on what this means."

Tauric needed no such time to reflect. "It means he summoned you to inhabit me, so he could test me as a...as a weapon."

Hælig turned, pondering the pronouncement. The warrior towered over the former acolyte. He was small of stature; barely five feet and gangly of limb, his body still clinging to adolescence. A weapon, he was not. And yet Skellen had unleashed such a powerful berserker rage within him he had killed over seventy hardened Korreti soldiers.

"No," she said, her near tangible features shimmering with certainty. "Skellen did not summon me. He thought he was calling forth a fellow daemon. The sorcery he tapped was beyond his skills. Indeed, the thrones and dominions of Hades cannot be fully mastered."

Tauric cocked his head. "Fellow daemon?"

"Skellen was not who he purported to be."

"He purported to be the most powerful mage in all the Angle Isles."

"And yet I killed him."

"*I* killed him," Tauric insisted, though why he felt need to lay claim to such a deed he did not know.

Hælig scoffed, but without malice. "All right, then. *We* killed him. Which I take as a sign."

"A sign of what?"

"That our work together has just begun."

4

When Tauric met with the village elders the next day, he explained that he'd been taken captive by his master to the land of Korreth and war-maddened with a sorcerous rage. He'd been temporarily spellbound by the evil mage who had designs of power and glory beyond his iron grip at the Citadel. He'd killed his master in self-defence, he told them. He was no reiver or renegade.

Wigberht nodded in approval as his son wrapped up. "Aye, that's the long and short of it, I think. Victim of battle lust. But Tauric did us a service, he did. Saved us, I reckon."

"Are you saying Master Skellen was a threat to our village?" someone called out from the ring of listeners.

A handful of Tarnepæth's elders might lead their small cluster of farmers, herders, and tradesmen, but they'd hear every voice who wanted to speak, and there were plenty there who insisted on being heard.

"That and more, it seems," someone else countered. "You heard the lad, the Grand Mage wanted to conquer the whole of the Angle Isles."

"Now, that's not what he said—"

"Nay, but every damned wizard wants to rule the world."

Shouts of agreement echoed around the circle, prompting head nods among the elders. Conversations and side discussions broke out as the community freely shared their takes on Tauric's confession. Encouraging words drifted his way.

For the first time since returning home, Tauric felt the grip on his gut begin to ease. His friends, his kin would pass no harsh judgment on him. The same probably could not be said for those on the high council. He wondered, not for the first time, if he would stand condemned should he return to the Citadel.

Certainly you will, and then beheaded, came Hælig's whispered voice.

"Oh, thank you for that," he muttered.

"We stand with you, Tauric," one of the villagers said, accepting his ironic words of gratitude at face value.

An aged man next to his father motioned him forward. As Tauric rose to accept the decision of the elders, he barely noticed a hooded figure slip away from the circle and head down the path away from the small crowd. He was soon receiving pats on the back. A horn of mead was pressed into his hand, though it was only late morning. He grinned and gave his father a wink.

That evening, Aisla asked him what it was like to study at the manor by the sea and if he would become a great wizard one day. He smiled at her naiveté. High in the craggy hill country, dotted by standing meres, bogs, and shallow rills that led nowhere, it was childlike fantasy to imagine that villeins like themselves, mere commoners, could rise above their status.

Though it could happen, and did often enough, he supposed, to give some people hope.

But what was *his* hope? Did he have dreams and plans beyond the rocky outcroppings surrounding his home? To his younger sister, he gently demurred as he kissed her on the head and tucked her into bed alongside his brother, Keyon.

He would be no great magician. Upon reflection, neither would he stay long in these hills. Now that he'd crossed to the continent, he felt the call of something more. One thing he'd search for, a way to be rid of the ancestral spirit that had melded with his own.

Really?

"No offense, mind you," he said in a low voice. "And don't speak to me of a common path or that we must work together. I was not a willing party to Skellen's devilry."

"Did you say something, dear?" Edy asked.

"'Tis nothing, Mother." Tauric grabbed a blanket from a pile at the foot of the bed. "I think I'll sleep under the stars tonight; the chill isn't bad for the season."

"Take this fleece as well," Wigberht said. "Shall stave off the hoarfrost come morning."

"Thank you, Father."

A kiss to both his parents and Tauric made his way to a favourite rock shelf where he could observe the sleeping village below him. In the light of a three-quarters moon he watched tendrils of smoke rise from a scattering of huts and cookfires, and he contemplated his fate.

Hælig was silent, for which he was grateful.

5

Tauric awoke with a start, a shout from the warrior spirit reverberating out of his dreams into reality. The moon was beyond the horizon and darkness reigned; 'twas the dead of night when wights might roam or ghouls slip their graves.

Cries from the village rang clear through the crisp air, echoing Hælig's call of alarm. Rubbing the grit of sleep from his eyes, realization struck that Tarnepæth was under attack.

Below, he could just make out a series of shadowy forms stepping in and out of the collection of huts, hovels, and lean-tos. Scant starlight glistened off bits of armour and drawn swords which threatened any who offered resistance.

The soldiers were shouting, searching, making threats.

"Where is he?" one of them demanded. A few of the villagers were pulled from their homes and beaten when no ready answer was forthcoming.

A sudden and overwhelming urge to protect his kith and kin flooded Tauric's mind and spirit. Without question it was Hælig raising the battle frenzy within. Though he knew he had no ultimate say in the matter, he nevertheless gave in to the berserker rage. He opened his mouth and Hælig let forth a bloodcurdling scream of wrath and fury.

As he sprang down the rocky slope toward the enemy, Tauric noted with detached interest that he was still *present*—his mind sharing an internal space with his ancestral cousin. When he had fought the Korreti under Skellen's spell, he'd been an empty vessel, aware of his deeds only after the slaughter. His spirit then had been utterly subsumed within the lust of battle.

Tonight, it seemed he participated in the defence of his village, albeit as an active observer.

Our village, the woman warrior noted with relish, *our work!*

The urge to rain down death on these interlopers overwhelmed him. Though slight of limb and lacking in training, Hælig's preternatural presence provided supernal strength, and within moments Tauric slammed into an unsuspecting soldier. The man's sword was ripped from his hand as his shoulder was ripped from its socket. The guard screamed in pain, but his cry was cut short by the gash across his throat that ended his life.

Now armed with a longsword, which was quite long indeed in the hands of the former acolyte, Tauric cut and slashed through a small squadron striding his way. The sentries' armour slowed the assault somewhat, but Hælig's forceful blows hacked mercilessly through narrow joints and unprotected gaps. They fell quickly.

Tauric's heightened senses had informed him that about twenty raiders made up the original contingent. Five had already died. Though he was flecked with blood, he'd received but a few scratches from his adversaries so far. He was ready to take on the rest.

But now the remaining guards—*from the Citadel*, came the flash of insight—alerted to a counterattack from the villagers, gathered as one to form a battleline against their opposition. More than a few jeered when they discovered their opponent looked to be merely a young lad with a sword.

"It's him!" one of the soldiers said, breathing fast, though not with trepidation. "Master Skellen's errand boy."

"Be wary, men," another mocked. "He's said to have beheaded the Grand Mage with a single stroke of his blade."

The Citadel guards guffawed and relaxed their stances. "Put down the sword, laddie, and come with us. We'll not harm ye, will we now?" The men belly laughed once more.

Three were still laughing when their heads left their bodies. Two turned and ran when their minds registered what their eyes had seen. The remaining ten or so drew up their courage and stuck it fast to the tips of their weapons.

They circled Tauric and pressed their advantage. Hælig's spirit pushed her host to the limit, and Tauric leapt over an advancing soldier, impaling the man's skull on his way down. He snatched the dead man's short sword with his free hand and spun like a twisting bauble on a string, slashing and slicing the two soldiers next to him.

Blood splattered, entrails flew, fluids flowed forth in unrelenting streams from eviscerated bodies. Each fighter met his fate; one by one they died a gruesome death. However, the berserker fire could not be quenched. When the last man had fallen, Hælig screamed for more.

Tauric surged forward as he spied a few horrified villagers watching from a distance. They quickly backed away and Tauric jerked to a stop, screaming, "No! No! It's over, Hælig. It's over." Like an impending tempest, the warrior's spirit nearly burst with abandon, but then slowly relented. The storm had subsided, the threat had passed.

Tauric dropped his weapons and collapsed, emptying his stomach and groaning in exhaustion. A crowd rushed toward him. Wigberht and Edy pushed their way through and knelt beside their son. A deep gash adorned his brow, and his mother tried to staunch the bleeding.

"Fæder! Mœdar!" he cried but couldn't tell if it was him or Hælig who wept.

6

In the morning, the elders begged him to leave.

It was for the best, he knew. He'd never be accepted now that they'd witnessed his ensorcelled madness. What his kinsmen saw that night was far worse than ravishing sheep and howling at the moon. And if he stayed, he'd endanger those closest to him.

Though his mother tried to reason out a better solution, his father cut to the heart of the matter. "You're a wanted man, m'boy," Wigberht said. "There'll be no stopping the Citadel now."

Comforting words they were not, but Tauric accepted the truth of them. His mother wrapped up a bit of cold mutton, aged cheese, and flatbread as he packed his scant belongings in silence.

Aisla stared at her brother's bandaged forehead, tears in her eyes, while Keyon was more enthusiastic. "You're a warrior now! Think of the adventures you'll have, Tauric. When I'm old enough, I'll join you!"

By way of reply, Tauric simply ruffled the mop of hair on his brother's head. When it was time to leave, he couldn't bring himself to say more than a few 'Goodbyes' and 'I love yous.' Still, his parents and siblings hugged him tight; Edy snatching at his cloak even as he walked eastward across the rugged hillside, away from Tarnepæth and beyond the Citadel's province and rule.

It's okay to look back, Hælig said gently as they reached the final rise that would put their home behind them. Tauric turned. His family waved in the distance. He raised his hand and shuddered. Then he rounded a hill and abandoned all that was familiar.

When his mother had asked where he would go, he'd hedged his answer. "North, possibly. There are villages along the coast that have no manor ruling over them. I could learn to fish."

In truth, he'd heard of a small hermitage to the east where it was said a holy man dwelt. He tried to keep such thoughts buried, afraid Hælig might divine the hidden purpose of such a journey. As for his ancestral companion, she kept her own counsel, neither directing his path nor questioning where Tauric's feet took him.

The hills rose higher, and a misty fog enveloped them. Thick scrub and patches of heather decorated the countryside. Along the narrow path, a hardy yellow flower bloomed despite the elevation and encroaching autumn season.

After a few hours of travelling in amenable silence, Hælig murmured just beyond hearing, *We are being followed.*

The hooded stranger made no secret of his approach, and Tauric decided to wait for the inevitable encounter. He rested his hand on the pommel of the short sword he'd retained after the night's frenzy and faced the traveller.

The man drew within twenty paces and stopped. "You are no demon," he said without preamble. "What are you, then?"

"Of course I am no demon," Tauric replied. "I am a man, like yourself. Who are you, and what do you want?" His voice quavered as he nervously gripped the sword's handle.

He is no man, and he addresses me, Hælig said. *Ready yourself.*

"You are to come with me. The Demon Mage at Manor Hunesthall would speak with you."

"Hunesthall? I thought you came from the Citadel." Tauric was confused. Why would Hunesthall, or any of the other six great manors beside his own, seek an audience with him?

"Tell your host to remain quiet! And speak to me!" the cloaked figure roared.

I will speak. With my sword!

A powerful furore erupted within. Before Tauric knew what he was doing, he'd discarded his cloak and slid the sword from its scabbard. The stranger did the same, but before the weapon was raised for combat, the former acolyte raged and attacked.

The man fought like a demon, but the berserker frenzy that empowered the youth could not be overcome. With a skill beyond his wildest imaginings, Tauric stabbed, feinted, stabbed again. He swung from his right, pivoted, and sliced from his left. His blade tore through the man's simple armour, and the stranger was driven back, his sword arm useless, his chest and torso cleaved open. The warrior within pressed forward and the man stumbled, forced to his knees near the edge of a precipice.

Tell your lord…

"Tell your lord," Tauric gritted out, channelling Hælig's words…

…he unleashed the wrong spirit!

"…he unleashed the wrong spirit!"

A final arc of the sword and the stranger's head rolled from his shoulders and disappeared over the ledge. The fighter's body slumped and, with a push from Tauric's foot, followed its head down the side of the mountain.

Immediately, the frenzied fury subsided. Tauric heaved a heavy breath, his energy spent. "Who… what… was that?"

A daemon. An incubus from Hades itself.

"In human form? Like…Skellen?"

Yes. A gate has been opened and daemons run free.

"Demonic possession, then."

Something more. A sorcerous melding.

"Like us."

Possibly. Yet different.

Tauric shook his head, the implications of such a reality beyond him for the time being. "Who is his lord?"

Skellen.

"But he's dead. We killed him."

We killed its body. A djinn cannot be so easily defeated.

"Devils!" Tauric exclaimed. "Loose in this world."

A wizard's doing. We must find out who opened the gate.

"Oh, no, no, no. This is not my quest, this is not my fate." The nascent warrior wiped his sword and slid it back in its sheath. He took once more to the narrow path.

I've been released from the shadow realm for a purpose. Our spirits are united. We journey together.

"To what end? To track down demons and send them back to the abyss?"

Of course. But we'll want to first speak with the Demon

Mage at Manor Hunesthall.

"Oh, so we'll visit Hunesthall after all? And then what? Politely ask the masters there to cease their magic?" He huffed his incredulity.

That and more. The Age of Wizards must come to an end.

Tauric stopped, dumbfounded at the words that reverberated at the back of his mind. He turned a half circle and addressed Hælig as if she stood before him. "So that you can restore the Age of Heroes!"

If that is what must be done to overcome the chaos that has been unleashed upon this world.

"And, willing or not, I am to be your partner in this ludicrous pursuit." His truculent tone left no doubt as to his opinion on the matter.

It would help if you learned some fighting skills. And put some meat on your bones.

"What?"

Your small stature is hindrance enough. It would make the killing go smoother, and faster, if your body were better prepared for the battle lust. You'll recover more quickly.

"Smoother and faster. More quickly. Do you hear yourself? How about we think of a plan where we're no longer bonded? Where we can each go our separate ways?"

When our task is finished, perhaps. But for now, little brother, our pathway lies forward together.

Tauric glanced up the trail, the heavy mountain mist preventing a clear view of their passage eastward. He considered his options, which he quickly realized were few to none.

He was suddenly hungry. Spotting a rock to sit upon, he opened his small haversack and retrieved the meat and cheese his mother had packed.

"Give me a moment to regain my strength, and then

we'll think about our next steps." Hælig remained silent. Tauric sighed and muttered with just a hint of levity, "At least I don't have to share my supper with you." Then, under his breath, "Little brother. Hmph."

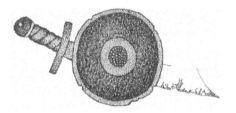

THE LEFT EYE OF PHUN MARGAT
Scott McCloskey

1

"Chu-toth, ga! Mar-gat, na! Chu-toth, ga! Mar-gat, na!"

So rose the chant, accompanied by pungi and drum. The rippled footmen, resplendent in their golden cuirasses and splint shin guards over naked legs, marched in time to the beat, bearing wicked pikes and stout, round shields to a man. They came in unchecked waves, phalanx upon phalanx, as they trod the land beneath their sandals. Their helms, plumed in bloody damask, were open-faced, that each man might display proudly the phun's personal brand upon his forehead. From the day of betrothal to their lord's service they were forbidden from ever glancing at their own reflection, for though they all saw one another, it was considered an affront for unworthy eyes to look upon one's own gift from the Master of All Sands. Those who drank from clear springs on the trail did so with eyes shut tight, for they would not be the first to have them gouged out where they stood by a loyal sergeant, who would surely be next did he fail to mete out discipline.

"Make way! Make way for Phun Margat!"

Situated due north of Shargo, its capital until mere days ago, the shanty village of Xaak was an inflamed waypoint of makeshift structures, used to the violations of marching men. Her paltry vendors, gaunt goat-herders, and sickly whores cared little for the change in power, for they enjoyed no benefit from their predecessor's benevolence and expected none now. Fear was their guide, and so they fled into their decrepit homes to wait until the men were watered and moved on. Those who were not fast enough were rewarded by a version of the Phun's mark reserved for commoners, cut into their foreheads by a footman's kukri.

The procession was but a splinter of the great stake now buried in the heart of Shargo, barely worthy of the solid gold palanquin eight men held aloft in its wake. Phun Margot graced no one with his presence; a whispered word behind curtains of amethyst silk was enough to bring the scorched, parched men to a sharp halt. They had been marching all day, yet their captain—a mighty-thewed man in a cloak of office—dared not speak of relief until his lord did.

"I die for you, o phun of phuns," said he, taking a knee to the curtains. "Your will is done. We have taken the place."

The phun had demanded this expedition almost immediately following the sack of Shargo, but the captain understood nothing of why. They had set off before the death rattles of the enemy had time to escape their steaming corpses, without any time to revel in the glory of victory. Now they were exhausted from a long jog to a place that sheltered wretches worth less than the shaft of one broken spear thrust into their hearts. He placed his hand upon his sword, expecting an order to put this sorry village out of its misery, but the command never came. More shocked was he when the curtains drew back.

The Wastelord Margat; he who had sacked the plebians, united the fingers of sand that still existed between the keys, and curled back the cracked lip of impotent rebellion, would show his face to a commander of mortal men? Or at worse, to these insects? The captain's eyes averted instantly to the dirty path he knelt upon, but it was too late, and he feared the worst for his transgression.

Within the palanquin, resting upon a satin divan, was the man himself—Margat *al* Margat, the swarthy, sweat-soaked spawn of humble husbandmen turned revolutionary. Swaddled in garish luxuries each worth more than the captain's life ten times over, the man Margat had developed a paunch to announce his debauched ways. Muscle lived there still in the arms and the legs, but this too suffered from erosions of plenty. The sharp moustache, its flax melted by the long, hot day, showed telltale signs of hidden grey. Margat's short beard was unkempt because he no longer cared to keep it, as it could do no good to hide the ravages of his brief, brutal life. Those few who had chance to look upon him could not say what sharpened edge or flatted maul had ravaged what was once the face of a man, though all agreed there was nothing natural in it—like the price paid to infernals from a fiery underland in exchange for power beyond measure.

Above it all was the eye. Though his left was a normal sphere of white and brown, Margat's right eye was no orb of flesh at all, but a bulbous, sharp-edged gem the size of a walnut that bled from its socket in crystalline red. The stories about where the eye came from ranged from a battle trophy to a demon's birthseed, but none knew the true tale, and all lived in fear of the mysticism that swirled within.

Phun Margat was a god among men; in public, he went always beneath a jewel-encrusted mask, chilling in its lack of expression. Tales told that the opulent accessory was wrought by artisans so highly prized that their patron had them all killed so that their work would never be duplicated. Further did the rumours claim that the phun's fourth son once looked into his father's eye without permission. Now he had but three. It was the phun's way to test his most trusted men on occasion by 'accidentally' revealing his visage to them, and so the captain told himself he had seen nothing. He instead stared patiently at the dirt, intending to do so for the rest of his life, while his master drank from a crystal decanter and secured that mask in place.

"I have seen it," the phun rattled like a sand twister. "I have seen the one with my own eye. She is here. You will bring her to me."

The captain balked. "...m-most glorious Phun, mere worms such as I have not your gift for sight beyond sight. If I could but know how the one you seek would appear to my pitiful gaze..."

"Bring *all* the women who walk on two legs to me," ordered the phun.

Grateful to be out of his master's sight, the captain barked orders at his men, who fanned out into Xaak on the scent of their quarry. A great cry of panic rose from the people, as they were systematically dragged from their homes at knifepoint.

Only one was silent. The one who already knew they were coming.

She had felt them nearly a mile off by the shifting wind that preceded them. Smelled the foreign perfumes of their alien land. Heard the baying of the jackals that ran alongside their march. In response to it all she huddled in a shallow larder, swearing to the father she loved that she would bring no harm to him by her presence. She owed him no less, for if it had not been for his efforts, her empty stare would have long since consigned her to oblivion in a world of sighted folk.

It was all in vain, and though she could not see it, she felt him die when the soldiers came. Heard his rattle. Smelled his coppery blood.

The larder was yanked open, and she was torn from its womb by the wrist and neck. She reached out, flailing her hands over her assailant's face in order to 'see' him, but was pushed away, tripping to the floor over her father's corpse.

"Prettiest one I've seen yet," one of two soldiers gargled. Knowing the layout of her home she took up a kitchen knife, swiping it wildly in the direction of his voice.

"What have you done to my father! Get out of my house!"

Her blade managed to taste his cheek but lightly, before the second guard stuck out his pike to trip her and she went down.

"A little slip in curls, and feisty too!" said he with amusement. "You hear that, Girl? I'm complementing you. You're the only one in this whole place who dared to fight back!"

The first touched his cheek, pulled away blood, then drew her up roughly and held her fast. "This one's broken, just look at her eyes. Surely we can have just one. I'd as soon bleed her for trying."

"They belong to the Master of All Sands," the other remonstrated. "She doesn't exist to us, or else *we* bleed."

The girl, whose name none of the villagers cared enough to know, was dragged to the square where the palanquin waited. There she was hemmed in with two score hags and jagged-toothed trollops; each shoved away and beaten at the behest of the phun until a mere eight girls remained.

Each was ordered on pain of death to avert her eyes while presented to the Wastelord, and this they did. When seven were sent off, Margat's plump hand stretched out to cup the chin of the last—the sightless daughter, so recently waifed.

"You are called Lannit, after my mother," decided he. It was not her name, but she dared not contradict him. "Tell me, what has become of yours?"

"Taken by the fever these five summers ago, my lord. M-my father...your man..."

"You have bled my man. I could give you to him."

Lannit shivered, but in memory of her father stayed her ground.

"Good. Look at me."

Lannit saw nothing, yet she knew the eye was there. It whispered to her. Called to her. As she climbed into the palanquin, it told her to fear.

"Water the men," Margat commanded. "We leave for Shargo in half a movement of the sunstar's shadow."

"What of these, oh Lord?" said the captain, waving to the seven in their ragged gowns and those villagers who cowered behind.

"Water the men," the phun repeated.

*

The fallen stones of the court at Shargo, burned by war, scorched Lannit's bare feet. Struck sightless from birth, she impressed the house guards by keeping pace with them by the mere feel of the windbreak as they led her along. They crossed the blasted palisade; their forms cast in ruinous relief by dwindling sunlight that spilled through the collapsed dome under which the old king had met his end.

They walked down a crowded thoroughfare to a once-majestic lane, where elite men stood by the door to a chamber of secrets. Within the blinded girl was given into softer hands, and Lannit felt the parting of air as a woman's palm passed rapidly before her eyes.

"She really can't see, Anja. What do you suppose the phun wants with a broken one?"

"Just look at her, Corrin. Not many men would be

interested in her eyes."

"What do you offer, girl?" scoffed the woman called Corrin, whose bangles jangled from delicate chains. "Will you even be facing the right way when our lord chooses a partner for the night?"

The room was filled with new experiences, like the scent of exotic perfumes and the shameless cadence of clean running water. The aloof voices of vapid women nattered over makeup, finery, and the day's idle gossip.

"You should mind your words, Corrin," scolded Anja playfully. "Rumour has it our phun left the scene of his own conquest to drag this one out of some muddy hole. There has to be *something* that makes her worth it."

Corrin oozed against a stone pillar. "Pah, just look at her. Skinny, sickly, and blind; bought and paid for by goat herders on three coppers a week. She still has all her teeth and knows some trick to keep the menfolk interested for a while, that's all. Don't get comfortable, girl. When Phun Margat sees how common you really are, you'll be gone."

Lannit slumped. She was not versed in any such tricks, but to lay her hand upon the phun in vengeance was a sentence of death. Perhaps there was no recourse but to learn.

"Come, let's get you cleaned up," said Anja gently. "You're the new girl. No doubt he'll ask for you tonight."

Divorced forever from her rags, Lannit felt the warm water slip high across her secrets with each step she took into the baths. Submerged to the valley of her chest she walked a dozen paces in every direction, measuring her steps as she marvelled over the sheer expanse of it all.

"You're a quirky one, hm?" Anja laughed. "When's the last time you washed your hair?"

Those who hoarded water in a sun-bleached burg like Xaak for any purpose beyond survival would be considered either wealthy or insane—and the place had no moneyed residents. Anja drew close, and Lannit reached out to probe her face.

"Is this how you 'see'? Look then. Look and find out what you need to be."

Anja wore a sheer veil, with ornaments in lush tresses spilling down her shoulders. Her smile was worn harshly into her cheeks, and there was nothing subtle about her comely figure. Lannit, being not so well endowed by half, heard Corrin's prediction again in her head.

"Whatever the phun sees in you, we'll just have to make it stick. It won't be good for anyone should he come away displeased."

It came to pass that Lannit, the nameless waif of Xaak, was turned into a lady. With colours crushed into her cheeks and silks sheer enough to make aesthetics blush, she floated about the chamber like a dusk-hued wraith. Her cascade of ebon curls was wrangled into order, and her boudoir lashes were curled to compliment her pouting lips. One more sense was lost to her, for she could smell nothing over the strong perfumes that rent her nostrils.

"You must never tell what you see when you 'look' at him," Anja warned. "Rest assured you will die screaming if ever you take your knowledge for granted."

For one full cycle of the moon, the Wastelord Margat called no other to his chamber but the enigmatic waif. By day the girl found her voice, bolstered by the servants and courtiers who gathered naturally around anyone who held the phun's attention. Opium and fine wine became her vices, but they were no escape from the harrowing nights.

"Look at me."

It was all he ever wanted from her, and so there was no opportunity to bedevil him with her wiles. The phun's apartments looked down upon the city from its tallest tower.

The breeze might have been relief from life in the sands, but every evening a lamp upon his windowsill burned choking, sorcerous sulphur.

"Look."

Her fingertips wandered the craggy tears that crossed his stubbly cheeks like a roadmap to damnation. Margat's right eye was a thing of wrongness; hard, sharp, and pulsing forever with unnatural warmth. Visions of infernal blackness danced into her 'sight' whenever she drew near, as though the bloody orb might rupture and devour her. When called upon to 'see' that awful sight, she wished that he would get on with it and make a woman of her, but this he never did. She took less solace in his preservation of her purity than had he taken her.

"See that she learns no face but mine," came his order one day. From that point on Lannit was never without the pungent odour of a nearby guardsman to see that she touched no one. Eating. Sleeping. Bathing. Walking the palisades with the followers she had gained. At length she took to caressing her own face liberally beneath the covers on the darkest of nights, lest she forget the contours of humanity altogether.

On a starry night she sat upon his bed, listening to the revelry far below as a chill wind elicited a grateful shiver from her naked back. She was ignorant of the conqueror's calendar and so the occasion was unknown to her, but so feral was the wild dancing and chanting as to call instinctual fear to her heart.

Margat *al* Margat, forgoing of a towel, emerged from his private bath to sit beside her. She heard labour in his breathing, as though he had run across the sands to horizon and back in a day.

"Look at me."

Automatically she reached up to touch him, but he batted her hands away. "Look at me," the phun seethed. "It is time you looked for *real.*"

The candles leapt with the rising wind. The chants of the revellers increased.

"It is the cougar's moon," said he. "The weak do not walk the streets, for if they were killed this night even their families would not blame the slayer. For the rabble it is a rapture of predatory might. For the powerful it is the time to call upon Karush Kor, the Hunter; the Rightsmith, who forges the Spear of the Left to turn the white sands red. Karash Kor, who for the worthy will slay any foe, no matter how impossible to reach. It is time. *Look at me.*"

The curtains billowed with a wind that rose to the beat of the drums below, and Lannit's heart raced with the tempo.

"M-my lord," she dared. "I...do not understand..."

"Look at me!" he demanded.

Though she saw nothing, Lannit stared deeply into the blood-red eye.

"*Oogat,*" said he, in the words of the ancients. "*Ark-a'an oogat, maliaux. Din al at duun.*"

The eye took shape; the first image ever to appear to her.

"*Oogat Ark-a'an! Oogat demforin! Arach-a! Arach-a!*"

Gods above, but she could see it. Lannit could *see* the eye!

So captivated was she by the first mortal image her retinas could record that she did not notice the wind that whipped her hair, nor his meaty grip as it closed around her throat. Thrust against the headboard she gagged and coughed, until a long knife bound in flesh—the Cougar's Tooth of blasphemous legend—plunged greedily into her face, driven by the raving cries of the mad warlock Margat.

The waif of Xaak screamed.

The eye shined brightly.

*

For six days and nights Lannit screamed, though the handmaids would have called it six hundred. Locked in her chamber she wailed and thrashed, destroying everything she could raise her hand against until the room was an empty husk. Her left eye, speared like a plump hog and pulled from its socket, had been devoured by her lord; thereafter replaced with one of bloody crystal just like his own.

Lannit could see for the first time in her life, and the blessing was a curse that nearly took her mind away. The alien shapes of the landscape; the foreboding towers that hemmed her in. The bleak, burnt sands that stretched to the horizon, and the gangly, misshapen, monsters once known to her as 'people' who walked upon it. Every image was refracted through her brand-new eye in nightmarish red, a dozen times over like the chambers of a honeycomb. All of them laid bare the truth behind lies told by her fingertips.

She sought to gouge the new eye out on her own, but an arcane compulsion prevented it. Thus in her most lucid moments, she resolved that if she could not remove her sight from the images, she would remove the images from her sight. She obliterated her every possession, tossing it out the high windows or smashing it against the floor, and shattered every mirror that mocked her with the pastiche of her disfigurement.

Meanwhile Phun Margat, who was not a patient man, waited.

On the seventh day, Anja picked her way through the battered furniture and shards of glass the servants were too afraid to clean up. The waif lay sprawled upon her mattress and would not open her eyes, so Anja set up a basin of warm water and sponged her there. When she was done she took Lannit by the hand, sat her up, and faced her to the window, so she might brush the girl's ratty hair and gather it into braids to make her feel human again.

"The wind is nice today. Doesn't it feel good on your face?"

Faces. Lannit no longer knew Anja's face. Anja had no face. There was only the face—the *eye*—of Phun Margat.

"The others, they ask after you sometimes. They want to know if you're alright."

"They want to know what I *did*," Lannit corrected. "They want to make certain they don't do the same."

"What...did you do?" Anja ventured.

"I looked at him."

Lannit opened her eyes. Anja gasped, her sack of makeup spilling out upon the floor.

In the days that followed, the waif of Xaak became a lady of the court. Her entourage followed her in reverent silence, for the crimson eye marked her as a personal favourite of a man so dangerous as to torment them even in their dreams. The Lady Corrin, who was quick to remind them all of the coquettish tramp Lannit was once taken for, vanished one day without a trace, though the act was not of Lannit's doing. It is said the eye looked down upon her.

2

Zhingari, the southland, was an existence of perpetual war; pockmarked by blighted fields and bloodied roadside shrines to the savage gods of old. Broken into fiefdoms these two centuries since the passing of the last great phun, her resource-starved citizens lived short, brutal lives, with two paths laid out for her children: find a lord to serve or be wiped out as an excess mouth to feed.

The land of Ghing-toh to the north, ('golden harvest' in the ancient tongue, though it now resembled no such thing) and its capital Shargo fared but marginally better. United under a single banner for far too long, her lords and ladies were ignorant gods in ivory towers of excess, whose people fought a war of their own against starvation. It was a soft place — its only defence a reputation of might and glory it had long outlived.

The two nations were neighbours, and though Ghing-toh was ripe for it, Zhingari was a land too divided to capitalize. That was until the rise of Margat *al* Margat, Master of All Sands, under whom conquest was a way of life. Those who did not fall upon their knees and accept his brand were hewn before the armies of the new great phun like so many blades of grass.

Lannit rode in a covered caravan, her entire face hidden by a thick veil. She preferred it this way, for much did she fear the twisted sights her new left eye would show her. She knew they were going north by the feel of the wind, and could tell by sounds of march the size of the platoon that protected her. Further she knew every intimate detail of the loose-tongued maidens who fidgeted upon the satin pillows around her, who were silent only so long as it took to swallow their wine. She envied their carefree demeanour, even as she found it insufferable.

On the fourth day, the dry heat turned so humid Lannit thought they had ridden straight into the fabled sea. It was said that in the wetlands of Kemor, no citizen went with thirst unslaked, and enough rain fell to leave the landscape lush and green. All of it stemmed from a millennial line of mighty seers, who were able to bend the very wind and rain to their will. A thousand years prior these seers rose a barrier of storms to repel any invasion, and war became nothing but a child's bad dream in their land. Insurrection too was unheard of, for there was no need to take what all were amply given. To those who choked on dry sand and suffered under the yoke of war such a place could only be found on the other side of death. Lannit knew it to be just a fairytale, until the caravan pierced the very veil of those dreams.

Lannit held herself, trembling beneath the awesome sound of cracking thunder. Driving rains beaded on her flesh and she lifted her veil, allowing the water from the sky to soak her face and dance upon her tongue. When the storms passed, drooping palm fronds tickled her from the open window as the caravan passed by. Walls composed entirely of water—called 'falls'—crashed with living terror all about. She might have fled screaming from the alien landscape, were she not so enchanted by its wonders.

"I am Goetran, Captain of the personal guard of Phun Margat *al* Margat, Lord of all Zhinghari and Ghing-toh!" announced the bald, bareheaded man in the lead, who wore a golden domino mask beneath his master's mark. "I am come to this place bearing gifts, with words of greeting from my lord to his most noble new neighbours. It is his sincerest wish that a border shared might be shared in peace, and so with great humility I submit myself and my men to the review of thy master, Prince Alrajiv Idrii, Lord of Wind and Rain!"

The turquoise tunics of the Kemorian soldiers were trimmed in shimmering silver, and their spearheads were swept like the breeze. Captain Goetran's counterpart spoke low to him, and soon they took each other by the hand. The caravan was escorted on by the Kemorian guard, and in a show of good faith, the Zhinghari troops marched with their pikes pointed down.

Kemor's capital, the great city of Tora-tur, teemed with verdant life. Though the others were blind to it, Lannit felt an oscillating hum from every mortared stone; as if the unwalled, sprawling metropolis were a living, breathing titan; resting in ages as a civilization rose upon it.

Lannit was escorted from her wagon and lined up with the other girls beside chests of precious riches. Each silk-swaddled lady held a gilded decanter of rich wine from whatever native land they hailed, all of which were now the sovereign property of Phun Margat. Lannit saw nothing from behind her veil, but felt the eyes of curious men upon her.

From a wide balustrade above, the robust voice of Prince Alrajiv addressed the gathering with words of greeting. Anja described him as a man of roguish beauty — tall and strong, with a young back and square shoulders. The Kemorian garb of office left little to the imagination, for these were a free people, comfortable with themselves and confident of their place in the world. Across his broad chest the prince wore naught but crossed baldrics, bejewelled to show his rank, and matched silver vambraces in the whispered style of Kemor's smiths. At his waist a thick girdle held up shalwar pants in regal blue, but though he carried a supper knife at his hip, no sword could be found there. His chiselled features, thin moustache, and razored goatee held court beneath a blue fez, tasselled in shining silver.

"My, but he's a handsome one," Anja whispered through her well-trained smile. "I could get used to this place. They bathe for *fun* here, so the stories say!"

Look at him.

Only Lannit heard the voice, and subtly she pulled down the veil so her left eye could see. Reflected in Margat's eye Prince Alrajiv was an ugly, horrible cretin; repeated a hundred times and bathed forever in baleful red. On the orders of the eye Lannit looked all about, taking in as much of the city, its layout, and its defenders as her place in line would allow.

The men of Zhingari—fearing any lapse in discipline— stood chastely at the ensuing revelry, while the prince's men danced and sang with ladies fair. Lannit declined all advances with poise, and evaded any question of showing herself to the commoners. The phun's plan did not include them, and he was watching her every step.

Halfway through, in point of ceremony, each foreign lady lined up with their decanters to pour wine for Prince Alrajiv, that he might sample all the best vintages of the south. Lannit took up the last place in line, as instructed by the voice in her head.

Spill the wine upon him ordered the eye when it was her turn, and she did.

"M-my prince!" said she in great embarrassment, but Alrajiv—who abhorred the distant title of 'king' and styled himself below it just to be relatable—laughed it off, taking her instead by one hand in his.

"Who are you?" said he kindly. "What do they call you?"

"I am Lannit, a waif of no importance," she replied. It was the only answer she could give, for since the eye was placed inside her she could remember no birth name.

The prince arched a brow. "With the way you cover your face, it is small wonder I now wear your offering."

"I...do not see," Lannit said in a purposefully demure voice. She had since learned tricks of her own, but was startled when the prince reached boldly towards her veil.

"Have no fear. Show yourself to me."

Look at him. Stare at him.

Her veil removed, Lannit looked deeply into the prince's eyes. A dark whisper, imperceptible to all but she, wafted on the breeze, filling the prince's sclera so that for one brief instant they showed pure black. The courtiers murmured at the sight of the blind girl with a gem for an eye, but the prince could not look away.

Lannit sat at the head table for the remainder of the festivities as the prince's guest. The red reflections of the people made her stomach turn, but the eye made her watch them until every face was committed to memory. When it was finally over she found herself walking through an oasis of palms at sunset, hand in hand with Kemor's only prince.

"The sands have no such thing as trees so tall," said she, and he laughed.

"Our land is one of many treasures. But how do you know their height?"

"I can feel them," Lannit lied.

"You are this way from birth?" asked he.

"Yes, my lord."

"Ah, but titles are for formal occasions. Please, I am called Simhé."

Lannit told her story, from saccharine days in poverty with her goodly father to the bitter taste of wealth. All her tales were true, save one. She told him the eye was but a bauble, crafted and gifted at the behest of the only good man left in the perilous south: the gracious and generous Phun Margat.

"It has many sharp facets," observed the captive prince. "Does it not hurt you? I could have it replaced with a smooth glass orb."

Refuse him. Do not let him take it.

"...no, my pri—Simhé. I have grown used to it. There

205

is no pain," she lied again, for the eye invoked constant agony.

The warriors of the phun left their gifts behind, and for a fortnight hence, Lannit repeated her walk at sunset with the prince. They traded playful banter, and whenever he smiled at her, she saw the barely perceptible flash of darkness deep in his eyes.

Time marched on, and Phun Margat waited.

*

The new girl, lithe and light with raven tresses, was called Enthuu. Lannit had not seen Anja since she became fifth wife to the prince's vizier twenty moons ago, but heard she spent her days at leisure. Emerged now to her yielding nape in the hot waters of a lavish outdoor bath, Lannit floated still as Enthuu saw to her care. Above them the trees made a lush canopy, letting through mottled bits of sunshine to play about the nubile forms of the beauties who lounged by the poolside. They were her new entourage; all ladies of the court, for the prince gathered no harem about him.

"...and so our blessing is carried down through the ages," Enthuu finished proudly as she bathed her lady.

"The prince is no sorcerer?" Lannit asked.

"No, but his blood-ancestors were. It's said that in the dark times, when priests of the savage gods rode atop fiery chariots at the head of bloodthirsty armies to threaten our lands, the seers of Idrii made a pact with nature itself. They gave their bodies and those of their descendants over as anchors to the verdant gods, so that even in the sands an oasis of this size could persist. 'So long as the anchor is rooted, the vines of life shall curl around it.' That's how the texts put it at least," Enthuu giggled. "But surely you would know better than I? Is his touch not so magical after all?"

"But the prince has no heir," Lannit observed. "What if he were to pass away?"

Enthuu's smile vanished. "Everyone thinks about that, but to speak it aloud invites bad omens. The world outside is an evil place, where the savage gods rule. We trust our prince will make the right decision. The problem is…"

"Yes?"

"Matters of the heart sway him. He desires to love and be loved. That is why the folk here show such confidence in you."

In the days that followed, the enthralled prince spent more and more of his time upon Lannit. During meetings of state she loitered in the halls, welcomed by the guard as her sharp ear picked up all manner of business in Tora-Tur. What she could see and hear, so could the phun.

"You are helpless no more," said the prince one day as he stood with her upon a high veranda. "This is a place of plenty, and that plenty is shared by all. Forget your old life and cherish all that you see, for there will come a day when you will be my bride."

And so, across the trials and victories of three hundred nights, their nuptials came finally to pass. On that night they took to private chambers, and it was a full cycle of the moon before they emerged again. Lannit became a woman, and the people of Kemor rejoiced.

Phun Margat, whose armies were no match for the wind and the rain, waited.

It is time.

Lannit had not heard the voice since before her wedding day—it had been so long that she had since drowned its memory in a syrup of bliss. She was a woman of Kemor now; her curls waved down her shoulders in the popular style, while her luscious form went about in the shimmering cloth, delicate baldrics, and jewelled tiara of office. She had taken to wearing an embroidered patch over her left eye, and even adopted a Kemorian name—Auqi—that she might wipe away all memory of her previous tribulations. The phun was silent to all of these changes, until Lannit's previous life had seemed nothing more than a terror of dreams.

You will kill him tonight.

Lannit sprang from her marital bed and writhed, her hands clamped over her ears, while her husband slept soundly.

"No...leave me!" She hissed. "Your plans have failed! I serve you no more!"

You have served me with more faith than the greatest of my warriors, and have proven three times their worth. Everything you have is thanks to me. The water you drink. The excess you enjoy. By your eyes and ears I have learned enough to hang a nation, and now it is time to pay.

"You cannot invade so long as my husband lives, and I will not harm him no matter your demands! Take your cougar-demon and begone!"

Kill him. Kill him and expose the fat underbelly of his soft soldiers to the hunt!

Lannit threw herself to the floor, beating upon it with fists of rage.

"Never!"

The Rightsmith forges the Spear of the Left to turn the white sands red. Karash Kor will slay any foe for the worthy. No matter how impossible to reach.

The princess of Kemor tore the patch from her face, though she willed it not. The blood red honeycomb bled into the world, infecting her with the curse of sight. Lannit screeched as she had on the day the cougar's tooth first tasted her flesh, and roused by her cries, the prince rushed to her side.

"My love! Auqi! What is it?" said he in a panic. "You are as a woman possessed!"

Lannit folded herself into her husband's arms. "Th-there, monster, you see?" she whimpered. "You will fail, for he is here to make me strong...together we will always be strong..."

"Of course," the prince agreed, though he knew not to whom his wife spoke. "You are my bride, my beloved. I will be always by your side."

"The eye, Simhé," Lannit managed through clenched teeth, "...y-you must..."

"Must what?" said he.

She wrenched away from him and scowled—the voice was hers, but the words were those of Phun Margat. "It's all a lie, cretin! *I* made your princess, from the moment you gazed into my left eye! You should have killed her that very day, but you show the mercy of the weak! It will be the downfall of you and your lands!"

"My love? What are you saying?" the prince queried in ignorance.

Lannit battled hard to reclaim her voice. "Take it out! You must put my eye out!"

The good prince hesitated, so the waif of Xaak took the battle to her invader. Inside her mind she fought in panic against her former lord, while her body pulled down rich tapestries, dashed stools against stone walls, and shattered priceless relics into incalculable fragments. Her husband sought to restrain her, but her strength was borne from the ravages of enchantment, and she threw him off.

"Dagger!" The mad princess raged. "Bring me a

dagger! I'll cut his bloody heart from my mind and devour it as he did my eye, with a bite for every life he's taken!"

Two guards arrived, roused by the fracas, though they knew not what to do in the face of such a scene. "Call the healer!" the prince commanded, and one rushed out on the errand. Alrajiv bore his love to the tiled floor with the help of the other, while Phun Margat spat vile exclamations from his own wife's lips.

"Black sorcery, my lord!" the guard shouted in fear. "A demon wakes inside her!"

"Turn her about and hold her fast!"

The man obeyed. In a rush, the prince tore down the curtains from his canopied bed, yanked out their woven cords, and used them to bind his love's wrists behind her back. "Healer!" he shouted again, as candles were lit and the halls awoke. "Bring the bedamned healer this instant!"

White foam, like that which crested the waves off the northern coasts, collected at Lannit's lips. The healer's entourage helped to hold her as the squat, rotund court physician performed his examination.

"Cut out the eye!" Lannit cried over and again. "Excise the Left Eye of Phun Margat!"

"She speaks the truth," the healer agreed. "It is a thing of curses and must be taken out lest it drive her to madness."

"Sight has brought me nothing but misery! Put my eye out!" Lannit pleaded. "Blind me forever! I must never see again!"

The healer drew forth a naked stiletto, but the prince demanded it instead. "This is my responsibility. I will do it."

Emboldened by her impending salvation, Lannit battled back against the red rage that whirled inside her like the storms that reigned over the Kemorian steppes. She rallied against the phun, whose influence had begun to ebb.

"He flees from me," she choked. "He knows he is beaten…"

Auqi the princess stood erect in the arms of the guards. She panted and wept, but her expression was her own again. The prince chose peace, and put his weapon down.

It was a decision that damned a nation.

On the cold edge of a shrill second, the cougar god Karash Kor ripped Lannit's defences apart. Driven unto instant madness by the very countenance of a savage god within her, the waif of Xaak cowered screaming in her mind's eye, her hands over her head, whilst her body tore away from the guards in one mighty stroke.

"Auqi! AUQI!"

She rammed the prince with the force of a charging beast. Too shocked to scream, he fell out the window from the tower room, missing the pool for the hard stones that surrounded it by no more than six handspans. The wet crack of his bones echoed throughout the avenues of Tora-tur, signalling the beginning of the end. His beloved leapt out after him.

Prince Simhé Alrajiv Idrii, Lord of Wind and Rain, was dead.

3

Lulled into lassitude by generations of peace, the Kemorians were no match for the armies of the phun. When the lightning stopped its cascade and the rains refused to fall, every Kemorian spear and coif of mail was ground beneath the marching feet and chariot wheels of forty thousand warriors, all branded by the mark of Margat *al* Margat. What few fighting men remained were rewarded by the savage gods with a quick death when the walls of their capital were breached. Kemor's riches were plundered; her people violated and left flayed open to bleed out upon the stones. Her pristine pools ran red, and her flowers wept.

The surviving Kemorians who were too young, too infirm, or too afraid of the parched sands to escape were branded with hot irons upon their foreheads to a one. Their homeland, like Ghing-to, became the property of Zhingari, and for the first time since the gods divided up the land, a mortal man had brought it all together.

But there was one possession that lay still beyond the reach of the Master of All Sands.

Phun Margat saw what Lannit saw and heard what she heard, but the sights had been dim and the sounds obscure since that fateful night she followed her husband on his doomed flight. He could not control her if he knew not clearly where she was, and so for every sun that set upon his regime, the phun's paranoia intensified.

"She lives," said he one day at counsel.

"Surely not, o great phun," a loyal man replied, but the phun shook his head.

"She draws breath still, I know it. The fool defies me, knowing that so long as she possesses my eye she will find no peace. Find her and bring her to me. Destroy anyone and anything that stands in your way."

"But my most glorious phun," a decorated man, brave in war, ventured fearfully, "the waters are polluted with the blood of our slaves, and we have barely enough left to strip this place. If we destroy any more, we will lack the hands to tend to that which your excellent presence has laid claim."

"Find her! Bring my eye to me or I shall take each of yours with hot brands!"

The people had everything to fear by the mere act of crossing their hearths for the day's new labour, for whomever among the slaves of Kemor could not answer for the whereabouts of their princess was killed outright. Even Phun Margat's expansive harem of comely girls were put to the sword for their ignorance, until but three remained. These pool souls were spared only because they had spent all their lives with him and had neither names nor personalities of their own to wield against him. They serviced him now as thoughtless automatons, their gyrations aethereal and lifeless. Never did he remove his mask in their presence.

"Wine," grumbled the phun as he looked out on a wilted Tora-Tur one night through Prince Alrajiv's chambers. One of his wraiths hopped mechanically to the task. "If she seeks to revenge herself, why does she not destroy my gift? The eye is no use to her. The right controls the left; there is no reverse. One day she will make a mistake, and I will see enough to know where she is. Then she will die by her own hand."

He could not fathom, however, why she had not ripped the eye from her socket and trod upon it as soon as his hold on her waned. Convinced by his personal demons that she rode at the head of a great army bent upon vengeance this very moment, he turned to his collection of venerable grimoires for an answer. He set out incense in putrid odours, filling the room with a ghastly reek, and sat upon a pillow to taste the bitter flavour of every chanted syllable that escaped his lips.

"Oogat. Ark-a'an oogat, maliaux dan din."

The flames of the candles rose.

"Deny me no longer, Huntmaster and Rightsmith. I do your bidding. I continue the hunt and claim for you the souls of the weak, but there is still one left to exsanguinate. Show me that one. Oogat arach-a! Arach-a! Show me that none are beyond the reach of Karash Kor!"

The images in his right eye became clearer.

"Yes! I hear her! I see her! Show me more!"

He saw his own room. Heard his own voice.

"What—"

The cougar's tooth, which ritual demanded always be present at commune with its god, bit thirstily into the jugular of Phun Margat. He fell backwards to the floor, and from his left eye looked up at the woman who straddled him. From his right eye, he looked down at himself.

"Congratulations mighty phun, you have found me," Lannit hissed, her words infected by trauma and madness. With both hands she drove the tooth deeper into him.

The phun managed words through gargles of blood. "N-no...this cannot be...y-you are no witch to defy my all-sight..."

"I am not," Lannit agreed. The princess was a shadow of herself. Leathery, emaciated skin draped over malnourished bones. Features gaunt and wanting. One eye, milky white, like a subterranean creature. The other blood red, faceted and gleaming.

"You looked everywhere but in your own stolen abode. I have waited so long...so long in the dark, in the walls where the spiders creep. Where nothing can see or hear clearly."

The phun tried to reply, but the tooth bit deep, severing his voice from this throat. Lannit reached down and tore the jewelled mask away, gazing deeply into his panicked face.

"Look at me!" the waif princess shouted. She yanked the knife from his neck, and as his blood sprayed out at her, plunged it into him again and again. "Look at me! Look at me! LOOK AT ME!"

The girls raised their poisoned voices in the phun's favourite song, masking his death rattles from the guard.

*

So passed from this world the Wastelord Margat *al* Margat, greatest of the phuns. The son follows the father, and so his three—called Gan Tet, Gan Maat, and Gan Tanboor—rushed to stake their claims. They quickly made war upon themselves as they picked their father's trophies apart like carrion flesh in a buzzard's beak. One kingdom became three again, though each one suffered under the hammer of barbarism.

Lannit, the waif of Xaak whose true name may never be known, died that day. In her place, Princess Auqi of Kemor fled into the sands, to the place where the ensign of the Idrii family still hung upon the ramshackle walls of the faithful.

Months hence, on a day lost to memory in a sallow hovel, the weathered Princess Auqi sat by a crackling hearth. The scent of cheap wine and opiates penetrated her nostrils, while her keen ears picked words of revolution from every tongue. By the swell of her stomach they built bastions of hope, for within their princess lived the new Lord of Wind and Rain.

She spoke kindly to him and in faith to his future subjects, but drew forth the ritual blade still hidden in her possession whenever her attendants were away. She wore a full blindfold now, embroidered in turquoise and trimmed in silver. Beneath it, where even her most trusted confidants were forbidden to see, her left socket stood empty. In the other lived the Right Eye of Phun Margat.

"You will restore their freedom," she cooed to the unborn as she palmed the other gem, "but know that I will never again live under the yolk of a tyrant. Should you ever stray from the path of righteousness, on that day I will give you a beautiful thing."

And by the Cougar's Tooth, she meant it.

SORCERY IN NEKHARET
Steve Dilks

1— The Grey Land

One minute the skies were clear, the moon hanging down over the parched land. The next they were covered in a storm of howling dust.

And in that storm the riders came.

On black camels they rode, shrouded in grey cloaks and wielding their moon crescent swords.

Their objective was the caravan that for the last two days had been winding its way across the Grey Land. They had watched it navigate the treacherous terrain, avoiding poisoned springs and the lairs of the near-men that dwelled along the cliff faces. Hampered by the storm, it had ground to a halt now and with ululating yells they descended on their prey. Blinded by dust, the guards wheeled their camels and looked to their weapons.

At the head of the caravan, Captain Jaliya swung his stallion round and drew his tulwar. His teeth were gritted as his eyes swept back along the trail. The gully in which they found themselves reared over them like the jaws of a trap. Looking at the camels and wagons of the train, he cursed to think its cargo would turn out to be his doom. If not for certain gambling debts and a hot-headed young wife, he would never have agreed to take this hellish trail. But it was too late for regrets now.

"Hold fast, dogs!" he shouted. "They're only men. Remember what that bastard Baron is paying your greasy hides for!"

Indeed, the pay to escort a caravan out of Yahrim through the Grey Land was triple what a normal guard could expect. Tax avoidance or illicit cargo—it was little concern to those willing to take the job.

Even as he spoke, a camel thundered by and a bowstring snapped. Captain Jaliya stiffened, one hand clawing his neck. As if by magic, the shaft of an arrow had sprouted above his hauberk. His mouth worked spasmodically as blood poured from writhing lips. His last thoughts were of an angry hot-headed wife before he toppled into the dust.

Halfway down the baggage train, a rider saw him fall. He was a big man, dressed in a cloak beneath which gleamed a steel ringed mail-shirt. Reining his camel around, he cursed even as his sabre left its scabbard. An arrow thudded into his buckler. Another glanced from his spiked helmet. The surly beast beneath him spat as he tugged on the reins. "Archers!" he roared. "Protect the train! The rest to me!"

The men did not need to see the scowling features and dark burning eyes of Bohun the Damzullahan to know it was he that had shouted. They obeyed his order without question. There was not one among the caravan that did not trust the ebon giant from the south lands with their life.

As the archers regained their wits, clambering to the top of the wagons to get a better mark, the guards on their camels drew into formation. Dipping their spears in a bristling steel wedge, they swung up their bucklers. Amidst the howling confusion more than one overzealous raider was caught and gored by those thrusting lances.

Hustling forward on his mount, Bohun flung back his cloak and raised his sabre. For a long moment he held it aloft as the marauders came thundering back into the gully. At the last moment, he let it fall and howling like wolves, the guardsmen surged to meet them. Arrows flickered in a deadly rain. Steel rang on steel and camels crashed together, their bellows punctuated by the shouts and screams of dying men.

Both raiders and guards died—their lifeblood sucked up and spat out into the dervish winds. Men hacked wildly and on his fighting camel, shouting encouragement into the tempest, was Bohun—the huge black warrior from the plains of Damzullah. How he, a warrior from the shadowy edge of the world, came to the lands of the empire with tempered steel and fury in his heart was a tale that bards sung from the shores of Grenell Bay to the marbled halls of Aviene. Lips a-snarl, the sabre in his hand sang its iron song of doom. It crashed against swords and shields, sending sparks flying and steel grating in a banshee wail. Men were heartened by his courage and redoubled their efforts. Then his camel took a lance deep in its side and it bucked, hurling him from his saddle. He was up in an instant, crouching low as riders surged all about him.

From out of the press a dismounted raider lunged at him. A crescent moon of steel slashed downward and he swung up his buckler. The blow all but tore it in half and wrenching it aside, the Damzullahan drove his sabre deep through the man's torso. Before he could drag it clear a camel backed into him and its hind hooves lashed out, smashing his helmet. A blinding flame filled his vision and he knew no more.

2— *Night wings*

His first impression of returning consciousness was the rush and roar of winds. Like souls screaming in torment, those winds plucked at his cloak and mail. He felt the sharp edges of a thousand tiny knives flaying his flesh, heard the wind's terrible moan as it tore into his skin and gnawed deep with a thousand needling teeth…

He voiced a soundless scream and reached up, clawing his way through an eternity of pain.

Gasping in a great lungful of air he sat upright and spat ash from his mouth. All around him corpses were strewn in the dust. Far off he heard a cacophony of sounds that were snatched away again by the wind. He rose and with one arm shielding his face, staggered to where he thought those sounds were coming from. He had gone only a few paces when he stopped. Strangely, it seemed now as if they were coming from behind him. Bewildered, he turned, crouching there among the whirling ash as it ripped at his cloak. Unclasping it with one hand, he flung it from him. He called out the names of his comrades but the words were lost in the storm. He shook his head, wondering if the camel's striking hooves had addled his brains. His sword was gone and he flexed his hands uselessly over the empty scabbard. For a moment there was nothing but the dust and the wind. He stumbled on, lost in the endless grey.

Then, through the storm, he saw something huge lined on the horizon. He made toward it, clenching his fist even as his left forearm shielded his gaze. The winds dropped at last, the swirling grey giving way to a vast black sky and a bone white moon. The stars glared frostily and where his mail was rent he felt the cold against his naked skin.

All his hurts were forgotten then at what he beheld.

It was a city—huge and foreboding, with black glistening walls that frowned on him from a dizzying height. Arms hanging limply, he blinked in wonder at its battlements and sky thrusting citadels. Black stained those citadels were, twisted in nefarious shapes with the glare of a pale moon hanging behind.

As a man dying of thirst is drawn to water, he staggered up to its walls. There he passed through obsidian carved gates to behold a city conjured from a dream.

Towers reared against the stars. Gazing up at them, Bohun saw the mouths of empty arched windows outlined as if in yearning rapture to the moon. He fancied he could hear the strains of an evil music drifting from those apertures, could hear laughter mocking sadistically from the shadows. But there was only the tread of his sandals on the ancient pave; the wind sighing mournfully along empty streets.

What manner of beings dwelled here? Giants, demons—gods? He did not know but he felt as if somehow he were being watched; appraised by a keen, cold intelligence.

Suddenly he felt something small glance off his mail. He jerked round, a low growl rumbling in his throat. He stood at the curving juncture of a street. On the corner was a grotesque statue that, for all its blasphemy, had a strange unearthly beauty. Beneath its feet, on a huge pedestal sat a man—a strange looking individual, ungainly but stocky with pale skin. His head was hairless offset by a short fierce beard. He was a hunchback, a stunted giant with great misshapen shoulders. He flicked another pebble, this time bouncing from the Damzullahan's chest to skitter across the pave. Black eyes twinkled mischievously. Annoyed by these childish antics, Bohun growled. "What is this? Who are you?"

The man did not reply at once but sat swinging his short thick legs. A black leather harness was clasped over a huge hairy chest and a tightly wound cloth girded his loins. He grinned impishly and shrugged one large hairy shoulder. The other shoulder was frozen up against the side of his head which titled awkwardly. "Phirum... call me Phirum." he said at last. "You come from outside. Fresh meat for the hunting." His voice was oddly distorted, as if the tongue he spoke was alien to him and he was using words for the first time.

Bohun glowered. "You speak in riddles. What is this place?"

"You don't know, I don't tell you," said Phirum, tugging at his short beard. He picked up an instrument that lay beside him, a battered old lute. As if the conversation was done, he ran his fingers over the strings. Suddenly he jerked his head up and jumped acrobatically to his feet on the plinth. He lowered the lute in his hand. "Do you hear?" he whispered.

"I hear only the prattling of a fool," retorted Bohun.

The misshapen giant raised a finger to his lips. Something in his manner impressed Bohun and he turned, his eyes raking the shadows.

"Listen!" the man said. "The whisper of wings! The night-feeders! The Elders must have their fun!"

"Elders? What is this place? Who are you?"

"Run, if you value your life! Run!"

For a moment Bohun opened his mouth to speak then closed it again. Evidently the man was quite mad. Then he heard it; the leathery rasp of something beating in the dark. He glanced sharply about, turning this way and that, glaring into shadows that now seemed to crouch menacingly over him. Slowly, he backed away and as he did *something*... a shadow deeper than the rest, fanned lazily over a nearby wall. He looked up and saw a strange shape lined against the stars. It was vaguely bat-like but huge and humanoid in appearance. It attached itself to a tower wall high up and for a moment was lost in darkness. Bohun stared there a moment as if in doubt of his senses. As he did, two red piercing eyes fixed him from the gloom. A high-pitched shrieking emanated from the thing and it sprang from its purchase, unfurling huge membranous wings. With a curse, he wheeled and fled back the way he had come, his sandalled feet slapping the marbled pave.

3 — City of the damned

The main gates should have been in front of him but there were only the crazy arched angles of the streets, the towers looming impossibly against the stars. Something passed overhead and he changed course, zigzagging down a narrow intersection. Bounding up a crooked stairway, he did not look round even when he heard a shriek of demonic rage from high up behind him. He ran on, his shoulders brushing the claustrophobic confines of the winding ways in which he found himself. He came up an arched ramp that reared between two towering citadels. It ended abruptly and without breaking stride, he leaped down into the street below. He landed on both feet then threw himself back into the shadows and stood frozen against the wall.

He faced a wide clearing. Somewhere, out beyond the tangle of twisted towers and high curving walls stood the obsidian gates and the way to freedom. He swept his gaze to and fro but could see nothing. A momentary panic gripped him. His initial instinct was to bolt across the square. But something held him in check, some primal instinct as when on the savannahs he felt the presence of the lion stalking in the grass or the crocodile waiting to drag the unwary into the murky depths of the river. That feeling was very much with him now as he gazed across the empty clearing. He saw the winged creature that was hunting him wheel against the stars a moment before settling on a ledge. Crouched there it seemed nigh invisible, even against the pale luminescence of the moon. He tensed in the shadows, clenching his fists. *Oh, but for a sword to cleave that dusky horror in two!* Narrowing his eyes, he stared out across the square.

There was danger. Danger he could not see.

Then he did.

There, among the citadels, he saw movement—men and women scuttling silently out of the gloom. Curious indigo coloured folk they were, naked as the day they were born. They moved in clustered groups of twos and threes. Never had he seen their like. Their movements reminded him of frightened deer as if they were somehow more animal than human.

A screech made him start and he looked up at the citadels with their yawning apertures. From them now poured a myriad of bat-like creatures, fractiously chittering, membranous wings beating horrifically against the stars. In frenzied swarms they came, spiralling down like hungry locusts. The weird shaped horrors descended on the naked indigo people, bringing them to the ground in shadowy waves. As he watched, the square was filled with screams and the sounds of tearing flesh. Wings folded over fleeing figures, smothering them in the leathery embrace of a dark and grisly death.

Bohun had seen death in many forms. But even he, a man hardened by a lifetime of war and rapine, stared aghast at the massacre being enacted in the silent streets of that phantasmagorical city. Blood showered in a crimson rain. Limbs were torn from struggling bodies and entrails were strewn across the age-old flags. In a scene ripped from nightmare, he saw those bat-like fiends tear in a ravening frenzy; talons and teeth ripping into flesh as they fought over the still twitching remains of the dying. Sickened, he turned into the shadows of a nearby building. He groped along a wall, his mind full of horror and repulsion.

It was the sound of a sobbing cry that made him freeze. He blinked, looking carefully around. To his left he saw the gloomy arch of a doorway. It was from here that the sound had come. He stepped inside, his eyes raking the gloom.

Nothing.

A soft light illumined a large square cut chamber. His first thought was to look for a weapon, anything that he could use to defend himself from those winged monstrosities. There was a static hum and in the far reaches of the chamber he saw a glass globe mounted on a trestle. It was like a gigantic pearl, perfectly opaque, with deep red burning fires. Stood on an ebon altar, it was wide around as both his arms could reach. He padded warily past. As he did a gigantic eye opened within, locking on his broad back. Hearing a soft footfall, he jerked his head to the right. A set of steps led up into gloom. Though he saw nothing, he heard naked feet pattering up them.

"Show yourself," he said, his voice reverberating deep and booming. There was no reply and so he came up those steps, taking them two at a time. At the top he found himself standing on the threshold of a wide chamber. He hesitated there a moment, taking in his surroundings.

The first thing he saw was a naked indigo child, totally devoid of hair. He could not determine its sex but, as it scampered across the room, it came to crouch at the feet of a woman reclining on a dais. At the sight of him, the woman raised herself up in surprise. She was pale as ivory with long slender limbs. Long waves of dark lustrous hair fell to the small of her back. Wearing naught but a wisp of gossamer and a brassiere of hammered gold, she regarded him with a mixture of fear and excitement. The child huddled on its knees, both arms locked around one of her shapely legs. It sat regarding him through strange golden eyes. Bohun stepped warily into the chamber. "I won't harm you," he said, approaching the couch. "I seek only refuge."

The woman stiffened. "You… you speak the tongue of Valentia. How do you come here? Who are you?"

"I am Bohun, a Damzullahan. Why should I not speak Valentian? Their empire rules half the world."

"Then you are from outside. This is not the city of any land that you know, stranger. This is a city that exists beyond time, beyond even death itself. Long have I yearned to hear the language of my people again. I had given up hope. Now you are here to remind me of what can never be."

A deep sadness overcame the woman and she hung her head. Then, composing herself, she lifted her eyes. "Tell me… who reigns in Valentia? King Oztridius?"

Bohun shook his head. "I know no such name. There have been no kings in Valentia for five hundred years. The senate answer only to the triumvirate, the representatives of the Sun-God. No man knows their identities, save the Oracles."

For a moment she let that information sink in. Then she nodded, staring blankly into the distance. "My time has gone. I am truly lost and this is the underworld to which I have been consigned." As she spoke, one hand absently stroked the head of the child pressed against her thigh. Beside her was a dish on a trestle that gave off a blue coiling smoke. Leaning across, she breathed deeply of it then sank back with a sigh onto the couch. Bohun wrinkled his nose at the sweet cloying smell.

"What are those winged things that prey on these people?"

"The Elders call them night-feeders. They breed them in the towers. They loose them to feed on the captured folk of lands they visit when the moon rises."

"Chaka's skull! What evil is this place?"

"All is evil in Nekharet."

"Nekharet." He turned the name over thoughtfully. "The wasteland folk whisper of such a place. I thought it a tale."

"As you can see, it is real. It lures in the lonely and the lost, the weak and the weary. It can only exist in one place between dusk and dawn before it vanishes again. It must continually keep moving, shifting from one plane to the next. It is a city cursed to forever, by gods that perhaps no longer even exist. Even the Elders themselves have forgotten the nature of the curse that imprisons them here. In their senility they have become debauched and sadistic... evil far beyond the sins that originally doomed them."

"Then how is it you survive?" he asked.

"Survive?" The woman's laughter was like poisoned honey. "I have given myself to blasphemous rites and worshipped at the feet of unholy evils. That is my curse and my punishment. If am allowed to survive it is because the Elders desire it for their next torment."

A chill went down the Damzullahan's spine. "If you cannot lead me out of here at least give me a weapon with which to fight those winged horrors."

"The only weapons here are those held by the keepers, the guardians of the Elders."

"How do I get to these 'keepers'?"

She lifted a pale hand and yawned. "You will run into them soon enough. There is no escaping here, Bohun of Damzullah—save in death."

Her almond shaped eyes lowered as the vapours of the drug she had inhaled began to take hold. She smiled lazily and her head began to droop. Angered, Bohun reached across and jerked her roughly to her to her feet. Gripping a hand in her hair, he yanked her head back so forcefully that she gasped in shock. He stared into her upturned face. "I have no reason to trust you, wench, but you're the first sane person I've met in this cursed city, so you're going to lead me out of here whether you like it or not."

For a moment the woman held his gaze. At her feet, the child whimpered and mewled as it sloped away.

"You— you dare lay hands on me?" She tried to pull away, but his grip was as iron. Under the weight of those bruising hands, a terrible truth dawned on her. For a moment she glared at him then, with a cry, she pushed herself up against his chest. She threw her arms over his shoulders. "Take me with you!" she whispered fiercely. "To exist here is worse than any death. By Zaes, I was a woman once. With you beside me I am not afraid to die."

Bohun stared into her eyes. For a moment it seemed as if he was looking into the naked truth of her soul.

"We'll see," he said. "Lead on."

4— *The servants of the Eye*

"Will the child be safe without you?"

The woman blinked. Seeing it had fled, no doubt to

another part of the building, she shrugged. "The Elders allow me pets. None last. Either they succumb to their pleasures or are devoured by the night-feeders." She spoke as if the child was no more than a toy to be picked up and discarded. Perturbed by her lack of empathy, Bohun made to lead her back down the chamber but she pulled back on his hand.

"There is another way," she said. She turned, leading him to the couch and the onyx wall behind. Brushing aside a velvet hanging, she indicated a short passageway. At the far end was an arched embrasure that opened onto a balcony. Outside they could see stars, fast fading before the onset of an approaching dawn.

Passing a curving stairway, Bohun stood beside her on the balcony, glaring uneasily at the labyrinthine streets and twisted towers. She pointed into the distance. "Look!"

Squinting, he saw something curving around the parameters of the city. It was hazy and indistinct, flowing and ebbing with a rippling motion.

"What is it?"

"A barrier to keep the captured folk inside the city. None has made it to freedom before the sun rises. It is only in that briefest of moments when the sun climbs over the rim of the world that the walls of Nekharet become substantial and solid. Any fortunate enough to have made it there must first survive the terrors of the night-feeders and the keepers before they can escape. And they must do so in that briefest of moments before Nekharet vanishes again to continue its eternal haunting of all the myriad planes of existence. Reach the walls before the sun comes up over the horizon and you shall know freedom."

Bohun glared like a trapped lion. "How many have made it?"

"None."

His lip curled ruthlessly. Pushing away from the balcony, he turned to the dark stairway inside the corridor. The woman came after him.

"You would try then?"

"All the devils in this realm and the next won't stop me."

He halted at the head of the stair, eyes narrowing as he glared down into darkness. He clamped a hand against the base of her slender neck. "If this is a trap, you'll die quick enough, I promise you that."

She laughed bitterly. "And what if I yearn for death? What then?"

Bohun frowned and, with a grunt, took his hand away. As he made to descend, she caught his arm. "In my other life I was known as Livina."

Bohun looked at her. "Then we'll leave this city together, Livina."

Clasping her wrist, they glided down the stair, emerging at length into a wide sweeping hall lit by a greenish glow. As they came through, they passed another huge globe resting on an ebon dais. Unbeknown to them, inside its cloudy depths a huge eye opened to watch their progress. They passed through a curiously angled arch and out into a thoroughfare where slanted buildings and bizarre towers reared.

Together they came down a street, their feet making little noise on the hexagonal cut slabs. It seemed as if they were alone on a deserted world. Livina's eyes shot fearfully down each intersection. Before them in the distance, the undulating wall struck like white fire against the night sky. Thrice the height of a tall man it was. Beyond it was nothing but a cold sucking void. They came to the overhang of a building and stood staring across a square. Livina placed a hand on his arm. "The night-feeders will be gorged from their feast on the indigo ones. They'll sleep in their roosts for days. If we can—"

Suddenly a gong sounded, shivering the night to pieces. They jerked their heads, seeing a black hooded figure atop a strange curving citadel. Framed behind him, a shimmering disc gleamed in the light of the waning moon. Livina stiffened, her nails digging deep into the Damzullahan's mailed shoulder. "The servant of the Eye! We are discovered!"

Bohun set his teeth. "How?"

"The Elders... they have ways. We must turn back!"

Bohun glared at the ominous black clad figure atop that citadel then at the undulating wave that marked the city boundary.

"Like hell," he growled. Snatching her wrist, he pulled her out into the open and began sprinting across the square. As they emerged from hiding, the figure that had struck the gong shrieked in a tongue that had nothing of the human in it. At once, from the shadowed structures, poured a wave of bizarre pattern robed figures. In their hands they bore saw toothed swords that gleamed in the starlight.

"The keepers!" gasped Livina. Bohun bent his head, drawing further away as the figures came swarming toward them. He knew that he could not long hope to evade that rushing wave. But he vowed not to be taken captive by those alien fiends. As they drew closer from both left and right he saw that their robes were patterned with sigils and runes. To his horror he saw that they bore no faces, just a blank white oval of a head. Whatever these things were they were not human. He cursed even as he wheeled, flinging the girl behind him. She staggered then froze, gazing on the giant ebon warrior as he stood with his iron knotted fists raised.

"Run, girl! I'll hold them off as long as I can."

Livina came up to him, her eyes glinting strangely as she laid a hand on his thickly muscled back. "My destiny does not lie out beyond these walls, Bohun of Damzullah."

"What are you talking about, woman? If this is some sort of trick—"

"Your world is not mine. Take the opportunity I am about to give you and use it to fight for freedom."

With that she moved past him and came up before the keepers, flinging her arms wide under the cold light of the waning moon. In that moment she was a fierce and elemental thing. Her bare legs were braced, her hair tumbling and floating about her on the wind.

"*Livina!*"

She turned at his cry. In that brief instant their eyes met and locked. He saw her face, proud and aloof; the sadness in her eyes. Converging upon her, the blank faces of the keepers split apart into yawning, jagged-teethed mouths. Huge snake-like tongues lashed wildly, inverted teeth gnashing with ravenous hunger. Then she was gone, buried under a wave of bizarre, robed figures. He did not watch her end. Instead, he leaped back from among the press that was closing rapidly in on him and fled as one gripped in nightmare. Hands slid from his naked shoulders and thighs as he catapulted away.

What time she had gained for him was all he needed for suddenly, a white light struck over the tops of the brooding spires of that evil city. The keepers hissed and fell to their knees, clutching the sides of their heads. From their wide slavering mouths emitted violent screams of agony. Bohun sprinted on, a lone figure racing through a city of the damned.

He saw the walls and the great obsidian gates— tantalizingly close now.

He saw that the sun was rising, a fiery glow turning the tops of the towers and the walls behind him black. Even so, the gates before him shimmered like mist, becoming insubstantial to his gaze. He leaned forward, driving his legs to ever greater speed. Behind, he still heard the unearthly screams of the keepers.

Suddenly something came in from his right, tackling his legs and driving him to the ground. Untangling himself, he rolled desperately to his feet.

"Phirum!"

The giant misshapen hairy man stared at him, hands flexed, eyes black and cold as ice.

"I can't let you go. You must... stay."

"Don't be a fool," Bohun snarled. "Come with me. We can both make it."

Phirum's face sloughed and elongated. He grinned and that smile melted into fleshy slag. His arms flowed into a dark oily sludge and his torso spread out like the branches of a shadowy flower; his body forming into a grotesque tree, towering and all devouring, flowing toward Bohun in a hungry massed secretion devoid of all form and shape.

This then was the true form of an Elder.

Bohun turned and fled.

The thing rushed after him, flowing like a deep spreading shadow over the flags.

"Ssstaaayyy..."

The word was a mocking echo that ended in evil laughter. Bohun ran on. As he did it seemed that the city shimmered and faded all around him, vanishing into ghostly translucence. He reached the gates just as a great dust storm roared deafeningly around him, choking him, stinging his eyes and flaying his flesh. Through it all he ran. At times it seemed as if he moved not at all. The roaring wind in his ears was a great and mocking laughter that screamed inside his mind until it would drive him insane—

"Ssstaaayyy..."

He could run no more and with a great racking sob he fell headlong through the driving winds and into the drifts. He lay there with his eyes screwed shut, fingers clawed deep into the grey ash. Then at last the howling ceased and he opened his eyes once more. The sun was rising, slipping over the horizon in a searing wave of heat. Before it the towers and walls of that ghostly city receded into nothingness. He shielded his gaze. The grit of dust against his face made him blink and then there was only the open plain, the barren vista stretching endlessly before him.

5—The coin

Between wind carved rocks that jumbled the broken strata of the Grey Land, Bohun staggered. He came down an incline, half sliding in the dust. The sun was a fiery furnace above him and it was with some relief that he finally saw the caravan. Trapped in the narrow gorge where he had last seen it, the men had made a protective circle of the wagons. All through the long night, they had managed to fend off the raiders. The dead of those raiders, along with some of their own, littered the slopes and rocks.

Bohun limped wearily into the gorge. Seeing him, archers raised themselves up from between the makeshift barricades and swordsmen stared out from between the spokes of carts. Shouts and exclamations greeted him and men came running to his aid. Shrugging them aside, he came up to the back of a wagon and sat heavily on a tail board where he rested his huge arms over dust caked knees.

"Gods of the underworld, we gave you up for dead!"

exclaimed a wiry sell-sword from Carcynia. "What happened?"

Bohun lifted his head wearily. "A camel kicked me senseless. When I awoke I found myself lost. I wandered the storm, thinking I was following the sounds of battle. Instead I found a city."

"A city? In this waste? Where?" said another.

"It was no ordinary city, by T'agulla! It was a city of the damned! A city of demons and other things... things I have no name for. Gone now like a mirage in the rising sun."

"A city of the djinn!" gasped a bowman. The others began murmuring. Hardened warriors from a dozen different lands, they yet warded themselves against the evil eye.

"There was a woman," Bohun continued. "Livina. She spoke of Valentia, but her words were strange. She talked of dead kings and ages long past."

"Ha! Where is she now?"

"Dead."

Marcius, a battle-scarred veteran who had fought campaigns for Valentia in the north, scratched his jaw. "Livina? That's an uncommon name. Long ago there was a queen in Valentia called that. It is said there was a strangeness on her. She disappeared into the wastes not far from Quarr. Legend has it she poisoned herself. Other tales say that she was devoured by demons for a sin of black lust. It's considered ill-luck to name a daughter after her."

"Pah! I never heard of such a queen," sneered the sell-sword from Carcynia. The Valentian's grey eyes flashed angrily and he leaned forward, one hand snatching for the hilt of his spatha. "And what would you know, heathen?"

Reaching across, Bohun's hand clamped down on the veteran's scabbard. "There'll be no squabbles among us, Marcius. We need to pull together if we're to reach Suumata."

Releasing his sword hilt with a frown, the Valentian mercenary shrugged and stepped back again. Lifting himself to his feet, Bohun surveyed the rest of the wagons and the dromedaries bunched together in a snaking line down the trail. "Someone bring me some water. I want to wash the damned taint of this land out of my mouth. And we'll need to dig those end wagons out if we're to move out before the sun reaches over those crags." He jerked a thumb to where twin turrets of rock twisted into the sky.

Sometime later, after those last two end wagons had been dug out of the dust, Bohun, now wearing a fresh mail-shirt, mounted Captain Jaliya's black stallion.

With much complaining, the camels rose to their feet. The men mounted, hands on their sword pommels as they looked around. Others fingered their short horn bows. At last the caravan got moving again, lurching and rumbling under the watchful eye of the distant sun. The fallen lay in the dust and, as they moved off, vultures came down on blackened wings.

When they were far enough away and the moods of the men lightened, Marcius reined his camel up to where Bohun rode at the head of the trail. He flipped something to him that the Damzullahan caught in his left hand. Opening his palm, he saw a small, dented coin.

"A Valentian copper piece," said Marcius. "See? It bears the head of Livinia, last queen to reign in Valentia before the Oracles appointed the first triumvirate. That gutter snipe Carcynian knows nothing."

The coin was well worn from countless hands, but Bohun could still make out the features of a beautiful woman etched there. The profile of that face was proud and aloof with just a hint of sadness. He ran a thumb slowly over the image before clenching it in his fist. He looked at Marcius.

"My thanks, Marcius. With this coin, when we reach Suumata, I'll lift a flagon in her honour."

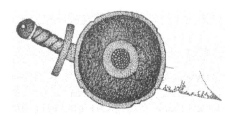

ALSO AVAILABLE *from* PARALLEL UNIVERSE PUBLICATIONS

Carl Barker: *Parlour Tricks*
Charles Black: *Black Ceremonies*
Benjamin Blake: *Standing on the Threshold of Madness*
Mike Chinn: *Radix Omnium Malum*
Ezeiyoke Chukwunonso: *The Haunted Grave & Other Stories*
Irvin S. Cobb: *Fishhead: The Darker Tales of Irvin S. Cobb*
Adrian Cole: *Tough Guys*
Adrian Cole: *Elak: Warrior of Atlantis*
Andrew Darlington: *A Saucerful of Secrets*
Kate Farrell: *And Nobody Lived Happily Ever After*
Craig Herbertson: *The Heaven Maker & Other Gruesome Tales*
Craig Herbertson: *Christmas in the Workhouse*
Erik Hofstatter: *The Crabian Heart*
Andrew Jennings: *Into the Dark*
Samantha Lee: *Childe Rolande*
David Ludford: *A Place of Skulls & Other Tales*
Samantha Lee: *Childe Rolande*
Jessica Palmer: *Other Visions of Heaven and Hell*
Jessica Palmer: *Fractious Fairy Tales*
Jim Pitts: *The Fantastical Art of Jim Pitts*
Jim Pitts: *The Ever More Fantastical Art of Jim Pitts*
David A. Riley: *Goblin Mire*
David A. Riley: *Their Cramped Dark World & Other Tales*
David A. Riley: *His Own Mad Demons*
David A. Riley: *Moloch's Children*
David A. Riley: *After Nightfall & Other Weird Tales*
David A. Riley: *A Grim God's Revenge: Dark Tales of Fantasy*
David A. Riley: *Lucilla – a novella*
Joseph Rubas: *Shades: Dark Tales of Supernatural Horror*
Eric Ian Steele: *Nightscape*
David Williamson: *The Chameleon Man & Other Terrors*

www.paralleluniversepublications.blogspot.com

Crimson Quill Quarterly

Volume 4

Featuring the Talents of :

Mike Adamson

Alexander J. Azwell

Shephard W. McIlveen

R. K. Olson

Carson Ray

Ethan Sabatella

Logan D. Whitney

October 2024

READ FREE

JANUARY 21

SAVAGE
REALMS
M O N T H L Y

TALES OF
SWORDS AND SORCERY

FEATURING THE TALENTS OF:

WILLARD BLACK   STEVE DILKS

DAVID SIMS   AND   KELL MYERS

https://bit.ly/SavageRealmsFreeMag

Elak was introduced to the world by Henry Kuttner in the legendary *Weird Tales* in 1938.

Now Elak returns in this first volume of a sword & sorcery trilogy that is a celebration of the classic genre and a homage to such grand pulp masters as Edgar Rice Burroughs and Robert E Howard.

In *Warrior of Atlantis*, Elak the young adventurer, a reluctant king of one of Atlantis' northern realms, sets out to begin his unification of he vast continent. He meets sorcerers, decadent gods, demonic armies and every kind of aquatic monster imaginable, fighting his way to glory with his companions, Lycon, and Dalan the Druid, in a blood & thunder feast loaded with battles and mayhem.

This thundering, no-holds-barred pulp saga is by the author of *The Dream Lords*, *The Omaran Saga* and *The Voidal Saga*, together with *Nick Nightmare Investigates*, winner of the British Fantasy Award in 2015 for Best Collection, as well as the epic historical fantasy, *War on Rome*.

With an introduction from celebrated Sword & Sorcery writer David C Smith.

"...Cole should be considered one of the best Sword & Sorcery writers around..." - *Black Gate*

Elak's fabulous adventures continue in the forthcoming
ELAK - KING OF ATLANTIS and ELAK - SEA HAWKS OF ATLANTIS
PARALLEL UNIVERSE PUBLICATIONS

Adrian Cole's

Elak of Atlantis Trilogy

Elak - Warrior of Atlantis
Elak - King of Atlantis
Elak - Sea Raiders of Atlantis

Three collections of tales
from the fabled
Atlantis of Elak - warrior and king

Illustrated by Jim Pitts

To be published by
Parallel Universe Publications in 2024

TuleFogPress.com

Swords & Heroes

Sword & Sorcery
from Tule Fog Press

Fragments of a Greater Darkness
by Michael T. Burke

Razored Land
by Charles Allen Gramlich

Welgar's Curse by David A. Riley

Pale Reflection by Gustavo Bondoni

Path of the Swordsman by Tim Hanlon

The Eternal Assassin Chronicles
by Andrew Darlington

www.TuleFogPress.com

Childe Rolande
The Myth and the Legend

Childe Rolande, Hermaphrodite and Freak, is born into the fiercely matriarchal society of Alba at a time when the fabric of the nation is crumbling.

Rolande fulfils all the technical requirements of an ancient Prophesy which promises that one day a 'Redeemer' will arise who will be 'the one and the both', and who will sweep away the age-old tyranny of Alba's female rulers to 'bind the nation together in peace'.

The hopes and dreams of Alba's downtrodden males are centred on this mystical being, whose eyes hold the wisdom of the ages and who can reputedly change into an eagle at will.

Can Rolande live up to their expectations, wrest the antlered throne from the Warlord of the Clans, drive the evil Sorceress, Fergael from her stronghold in the Dark Tower, and unite the polarised Kingdom?

A seething dark fantasy set in a dystopian Scotland in the far future, where myth and magic are alive once more, *Childe Rolande* is a gritty, no holds barred story of bloodshed and mayhem, of betrayal and brutality.

Optioned to be filmed as a TV mini-series, Samantha Lee is already at work on a sequel.

Available as a paperback and a kindle e-book.

PARALLEL UNIVERSE PUBLICATIONS

Printed in Great Britain
by Amazon

51206909R00137